McCurry's War

Chuck Thompson

McCurry's War

iUniverse, Inc.
Bloomington

McCurry's War

Copyright © 2012 by Chuck Thompson

Certain characters in this work are historical figures, and certain events portrayed did take place. However, this is a work of fiction. All of the other characters, names, and events as well as all places, incidents, organizations, and dialogue in this novel are either the products of the author's imagination or are used fictitiously.

iUniverse books may be ordered through booksellers or by contacting:

iUniverse
1663 Liberty Drive
Bloomington, IN 47403
www.iuniverse.com
1-800-Authors (1-800-288-4677)

ISBN: 978-1-4759-4949-0 (sc)
ISBN: 978-1-4759-4951-3 (e)
ISBN: 978-1-4759-4950-6 (dj)

Library of Congress Control Number: 2012916483

Printed in the United States of America

iUniverse rev. date: 10/3/2012

Cover design by George Rodemer of G. Rodemer Assoc. (www.grodemer.com)

For Christine
My best friend, my hero

The Coffee Cup

ike McCurry arrived at the Defense Language Institute in
Monterey in the summer of 1966, following basic training and
a thirty-day leave. Using the travel allowance he had received
from the Army, he flew into San Francisco. It was a hot, muggy
August afternoon, which was unusual for the City by the Bay.
Dressed in his Class A uniform and lugging a duffel bag with all
his clothing, McCurry was soaked in sweat as he walked out of
the airport building to find a cab. Somewhat fatigued from his
cross-country trip, he was buoyed by his excitement over entering
a new phase in his life's journey. Most of all, he looked forward to
the language training he would receive at the Defense Language
Institute in Monterey.

McCurry spent his teen years in a white, middle-class
neighborhood in Northeast Philadelphia. He was identified as
a gifted student in high school and admitted to the advanced
curriculum, which he often still felt was less than challenging.
Bored and more enthused with the new discoveries he was making
in his sexual education, he skated through high school with a low
B average.

After a couple years in college, McCurry found himself
fascinated with, but not yet understanding, the hippie counter-
culture and sexual revolution just beginning to take root in the
U.S. While he got caught up in the protests over Vietnam, his

understanding of the lifestyle of a typical so-called hippie was difficult to accept since it was anathema to the values he was taught all his life: respect your elders, work hard and you will get ahead, and abide by the law. His interest in the culture, however, led him to the decision that he needed to learn more about life, so he dropped out of school.

This made him a prime target of the draft and its need for more bodies to ship off to Vietnam. McCurry believed that learning more about life was one thing; dying in a war he had already decided was wrong was quite another. Those values of his youth precluded a flight to Canada, as a few acquaintances had done, so he joined the Army. It was the beginning of McCurry's real education.

Test results he took before actually enlisting qualified him for the elite Army Security Agency and indicated an aptitude for languages. Although he had to sign up for four years, he was told the first year and a half would be spent in schools.

He would have to qualify for top-secret clearance. This entailed an in-depth investigation by the FBI that could take six months or more to complete. Since McCurry had led a relatively uneventful life to date, he couldn't think of any activity that would prevent him from getting the clearance. So, he signed on the dotted line and became the property of the U.S. Army.

The recruiter told McCurry that once he had completed basic training he would move on to what the recruiter envisions as an enchanted existence in the Army Security Agency. Members of the ASA were under the jurisdiction of the National Security Agency rather than the Pentagon. Because of this, ASA personnel were selected to monitor the progress of new recruits during basic training. A few weeks into basic, McCurry and a few other ASA trainees were shepherded into a meeting with an agent overseeing their progress. The agent asked if there were any problems he could help with. When no one spoke up, the agent gave a short pep talk and said to "hang in there." Only a little more than a month remained before they would be finished with basic.

Now in San Francisco, McCurry took a cab to a rooming house where he was able to shower and change out of his sweaty clothes.

He decided he would do a little exploring in San Francisco. He'd catch a bus to Monterey in the morning.

He spent a few hours checking out the Haight-Ashbury district. He had read a news account about it recently that described the influx of so-called hippies to the district. According to the article, more than 15,000 members of this counter-cultural movement now called this area home.

The article didn't prepare McCurry for the environment he found himself in when he arrived on the corner of Haight and Ashbury streets. Although somewhat reminiscent of the twenty-four-hour party scenes at university frat houses since nearly everyone was college-aged and younger, here many were handing out flowers to passersby. Scantily clad girls were in abundance, too, free from any college-imposed behavior restrictions. He felt as if he had entered a new universe. As he casually strolled down the crowded streets, music became a common background regardless where he turned. The new psychedelic sounds of Iron Butterfly, the Byrds, Big Brother and the Holding Company, and Jefferson Airplane blared from speakers set up in the windows of apartment buildings. Small groups of musicians gathered throughout the area and were surrounded by people obviously high on marijuana or LSD. More than once McCurry was invited to share a toke but declined. He couldn't jeopardize his security clearance while still under investigation.

Dwellings in the area seemed to be overflowing with people in all sorts of clothing, much of it alien to McCurry. Women in everything from granny dresses to halter tops, hip-hugger and bell bottom jeans, micro skirts, Pocahontas headbands, beaded necklaces and flowers in their hair. Men wore fringed vests, tie-dyed t-shirts, combat jackets and fatigues and sported all manner of beards and mustaches. The peace symbol was in evidence throughout, either sewn onto clothing or worn on chains around the neck.

During his brief outing, McCurry met and spoke with people who were clearly dedicated pacifists with strong arguments about how war was an unnecessary means of settling differences between countries. He realized that there were also a significant number who were there simply to take advantage of the free sex and proliferation of mind-altering drugs. But, there was a small percentage of obviously violent people who equated their hatred of the war in Vietnam with the soldiers who fought and died in it. McCurry was vehemently against the war and would have filed as a conscientious objector had he needed to. Yet he couldn't understand denigrating the courageous men who were actually fighting the battles there.

In the morning, McCurry boarded a bus for Monterey. As he approached the Peninsula, he was captivated by the rocky shoreline and deep blue waters glimpsed from the bus. He was growing excited about the opportunity to learn German and then put it to use overseas. And most of all, he felt as if he were turning a page and opening a new chapter in his life story.

*   *   *

After several weeks of daily six-hour sessions in the classroom, McCurry was amazed at how quickly he was learning German. That all those who taught at the language institute were required to be native speakers of their respective language hastened his acquisition, as did a requirement he speak only German while in the classroom; he also was encouraged to speak German while in the barracks, which in fact were more like dorms than typical Army dwellings.

Once they became relatively fluent in the language, McCurry and his classmates were told they would move on to learn all the major dialects while always adding more words to their German vocabulary. They similarly would have to learn colloquialisms and usages peculiar to specific cultures.

Trainees were segregated by the languages they were learning – German, Russian, French and Vietnamese. There were two men to a room with a bed, dresser and desk for each. This was a luxury after basic training and helped create the laid-back atmosphere of a college dorm.

On many evenings, McCurry and his roommate, Hank Moreland, would haul beach chairs and beer they had smuggled into the barracks up to the roof to watch the sun set over the Pacific Ocean. The language institute was located in the Presidio of Monterey, high atop a hill overlooking Monterey Bay, Old Fisherman's Wharf and the ocean beyond. While the area was often cloaked in fog in the morning, in the evening the view was magnificent.

In time McCurry decided to do some exploring on land rather than from the rooftop.

Just before noon on a Saturday, McCurry, Hank Moreland and Rich Sezov, a Russian linguist, were at Old Fisherman's Wharf, seated in a restaurant's outdoor area enjoying coffee and pastries. The pier was already filling up with tourists. Farther down the wharf, a few fishing trawlers, back early with their day's catch, were unloading baskets of fish buried in shaved ice. The cries from hundreds of seagulls rose above the din of the crowd as the birds circled the boats, swooping down when they saw a chance to pluck an unguarded fish. Just off the pier, sea lions lounged near the shore and made swiftly through the shallows like underwater gulls in their own search for food. Their barks and roars were at times overwhelming.

Moreland said, "A friend of mine back in college would have thought this must be how the rich people live. Nothing to do but lounge around, drink a few beers and take in nature."

"Shit, yeah. And to think, we're getting paid to stay here along with free room and board," Sezov added.

"Yeah, if you can call a hundred bucks a month getting paid," McCurry said.

"C'mon Mike, you have to admit that living here is a luxury compared to basic training," Moreland countered.

"Maybe so, but another luxury I'd like to discover involves those California girls the Beach Boys sing about," McCurry said.

"Hey Mike, a friend of mine in the Russian group said the best way to find chicks is to stroll the grounds of Monterey Peninsula College," Sezov said. "Man, that's my idea of sightseeing."

"Yeah but we'll have to conquer that front on another day," McCurry said. "Today it's just around here. But who knows, maybe we'll meet some of those MPC co-eds anyway."

They didn't meet any women that day at Old Fisherman's Wharf, chatting only with some of the fishermen working their boats. Moreland and McCurry decided that on the next day, Sunday, they'd make that trip to Monterey Peninsula College.

* * *

"I think all we need to do is to head down Franklin to Pacific in downtown Monterey," McCurry said.

Moreland chuckled at that. "Yeah, downtown Monterey. D'ya think we'll recognize it? We might get lost, ya know."

"Shut up, wise ass. It's what you would call a quaint community and I kinda like it here."

"Is that really you, Mr. Philadelphia? Quaint? It might be nice for a visit, but you would go out of your mind if ya had to live here. I'll take the East Coast cities any day of the week."

"Well, this is where you are right now," McCurry said. "When we get to Pacific, we can ask directions to the college."

They arrived at the campus around noon. To McCurry, it looked like any other college campus, east or west coast. Kids were out on the lawns playing Frisbee. Couples were cuddled up on blankets under the trees. Here and there, groups of young men and women were sitting cross-legged in circles, oftentimes arguing over some concept they were studying, or trying to make sense of current events. Remembering his days in college, McCurry assumed that not a few of the conversations centered on the war in Vietnam.

"You don't think they're worried about where they will be heading after they graduate, do ya?" McCurry asked Moreland.

"What d'ya think? Unless, as the song goes, 'your daddy's rich and your mama's good looking,' it's probably all they fucking think about."

"No kidding, this war and draft shit really sucks. Must've been nice to be able to go to college with nothing to worry about but finding a job when ya graduated."

"All right, McCurry, time to find us a couple of girls who want the company of German-speaking spooks."

Eventually they found their way to the student activities center, a sort of cafeteria with a number of tables at one end and pool tables and pinball machines at the other.

"Look at that table over there," McCurry said, indicating a spot where two attractive young women were sipping Cokes and engrossed in an animated conversation. "Let's grab a couple of drinks and see if they'd like some company."

At the counter, McCurry ordered a Hires Root Beer and Moreland got a Coke. They made their way over to the table with the two women and, when the girls looked up, McCurry said, "Hey, would ya mind if we sat down here."

"Not at all," said the redhead. When McCurry and Moreland sat down, the redhead said her name was Trish Kelly. She was dressed in short shorts and a halter top, had flaming red hair, startling green eyes, a tiny nose and pert breasts that were clearly accentuated by the flimsy top.

Her friend introduced herself as Carmen Giordano. Somewhat taller than Trish, Carmen had jet black hair; an olive complexion with black eyes set in an angular face that, while not beautiful, was certainly seductive; and very long legs that were exquisitely set off by hot red shorts.

McCurry introduced himself and Moreland and took a seat next to Trish, leaving the chair next to Carmen open for Moreland. "So, where are you from?" McCurry asked as he pulled his chair up to the table.

Trish said she was from Bakersfield and Carmen lived in Santa Barbara.

"Are you guys in the Army?" Trish asked.

"Why, does it show?" Moreland remarked.

"The short haircuts kind of give you away," Trish said, smiling at McCurry in a way that made him feel she was interested and not put off by the Army connection.

"We're both in the German language program at the Defense Language Institute," McCurry said. "Becoming Army linguists seemed better than waiting to be drafted and sent to Vietnam. I'm told they don't have much of a need for German linguists in 'Nam."

"I'm glad you won't have to go over there," Trish said. "America shouldn't be there to begin with. The boys I've known who've gone there aren't the same when they get back."

"I'm glad we don't have to go too," McCurry said. "It's gotta really suck to have people shooting at you and not understanding why. Other than the fact that you're in their country shooting at them, of course."

"Enough about us, what are you two studying?" Moreland asked.

"We're both in the nursing program," Carmen said. "My goal is to get a job in a city hospital and then party all the time."

"That's cool. How much longer d'ya have?" McCurry asked.

"Two more years to get our bachelor's degree. Trish is thinking she may go on to get her master's, but I'm just anxious to get through this program, get to work and start having fun."

"I think you'd have to be somewhat of an idealist ta go into nursing, right?" McCurry suggested.

Trish said idealism may have played a small role in her decision. What really sold her on the program, she said, was the significant role she felt nurses play helping people heal. "Since we provide patients with the care they need day in and day out, we really get to know and understand their needs."

"Hmm, Mike," said Moreland, "looks like you've got some competition the next time you step up on your soap box."

"I guess I do get carried away," Trish said, visibly blushing,

"Okay, okay, enough with the serious talk," said Moreland. "Any recommendations on what we should see while we're in your fair state? Outside of Monterey, which we have pretty well covered already."

"Do you know the 17-Mile Drive?" Trish asked. "Spectacular views of the ocean and nature, not to mention some pretty spectacular mansions."

"Unless we can get a bus there, I don't think we'll be making that trip," Moreland said.

Trish turned to McCurry. "We have a car. We could take you there. I'd love to see it again."

"Seriously? That is cool. How about next Saturday? Will that work?"

"Sounds like a date," Trish said. She opened her purse, pulled out a small pad and pen. She wrote her number, tore the sheet out and handed it to McCurry. "If you need to call, just tell whoever answers to come and get me."

"Great," said McCurry. "In the meantime, feel like showing me around the campus."

As McCurry started to get up, Trish looked over to Carmen and asked, "You don't mind if we go off, do ya Carmen?"

"No, I'm fine," she said.

After a leisurely stroll through the campus in which Trish pointed out some of the significant structures, she explained to McCurry that she shared an apartment with Carmen and two other nursing students nearby off Fremont Street. "It's just a short walk if you want to see it," she said.

"Absolutely," he said, taking her hand as they turned to make their way off campus. After walking a couple of blocks, they came up to a non-descript two-story apartment building.

"Well, here it is," Trish said. She led McCurry to the front door. "Anyone who doesn't live here has to buzz our apartment to get in. My father particularly liked this, quote, security feature, but sometimes it can be a pain in the ass."

Trish said two of her roommates lived nearby and went home on weekends. "We're alone right now," she added, "but that doesn't mean Carmen won't show up with Hank any minute. She can be pretty wild at times, but I like her company."

"I guess we oughtta take advantage of the alone time," McCurry said, leading her toward the sofa. She willingly followed and soon they were involved in some heavy making out. McCurry was surprised that she didn't object as his hand made its way under her halter. He was just beginning to enjoy caressing her breasts when they heard the key turn in the front door. Both jumped up and straightened themselves out when Carmen and Hank came in the room.

"Oops, thought at least ya'd be back in your bedroom by now," Carmen casually remarked.

"Carmen!" Trish said, turning visibly red. "We were just taking some time to get to know one another better."

"Yeah, right."

"C'mon, McCurry, we'd better get back to the barracks," Moreland said.

"Yeah, okay." He turned to kiss Trish goodbye.

"Want to meet here about nine next Saturday morning?" she asked. "That should give us the whole day to explore the drive."

"Sounds good to me," McCurry said. "All right by you, Hank?"

He was a little let down when Moreland didn't beg off. "We'll be here," Moreland said, turning to kiss Carmen goodbye. She gleefully put her arms around his neck and pulled him close, giving McCurry the clue as to why Moreland would be accompanying them on their excursion.

"See you Saturday," McCurry said to Trish, grabbing Moreland by the back of the pants to pull him away from Carmen and then ushering him out the door.

*   *   *

On the following Saturday morning, McCurry and Moreland showed up early at Trish and Carmen's apartment. The girls came out within minutes of being buzzed. Trish got into the driver's side of her 1962 Nash Rambler and McCurry slid over the bench seat next to her. Carmen and Moreland piled into the back. McCurry was hoping they could keep their hands off one another for at least the beginning of the ride.

They drove over to Pacific Grove to enter 17-Mile Drive.

"Wow, Pacific Grove seems so much different than Monterey," McCurry said to Trish. "It's so peaceful and these homes're beautiful."

"One of our roommates lives here. The town and the people really are nice. I can't imagine why she doesn't live home and save on the rent for our apartment, although she *can* do a lot more at the apartment than she could at home," Trish added, giggling.

Once on the toll portion of the 17-Mile Drive, McCurry took hold of Trish's free hand and marveled at the beauty of their surroundings as they made their way inland and came up on Spanish Bay.

"Let's get out and take a walk," McCurry said.

McCurry was awestruck by the rocky shoreline being battered by a crashing surf. The undulating background noise of the waves washing up on the beach along with the unmistakable fragrance of the ocean and its environs was something that drew McCurry to the shore as a child and still held a grip on his soul. He hoped he could let Trish know how pleased he was to have someone to share it with.

When the foursome got closer to the surf line, McCurry noticed that large portions of sandy beach rose like the tide itself before once more yielding to the rocks that lined the shore. "What're those beautiful flowers?" McCurry asked, pointing to a proliferation of plants with flowers that had purple petals surrounded by a yellow center.

"It's known as ice plant. Surprisingly, it's actually a weed," Trish said. "I guess it does provide a spectacular ground cover though."

McCurry and Trish decided to sit down and relax on a large, flat rock near the surf line. Moreland and Carmen continued to explore. Lost in thought, McCurry wondered, as he often did, what role, if any, fate played in a person's life. His parents argued he had made a bad choice in dropping out of college. Yet to him it seemed as if it ended well with his acceptance into the Army Security Agency's language program. This was the beginning of the travel and adventure he hoped to experience during his stint in the military. He wondered what fate had in store for him in the days, weeks and months ahead.

"A penny for your thoughts," Trish said

"Oh, I don't know. I'm not sure they'd be worth a penny. Just thinking how lucky I am to be in such a beautiful place and enjoying my life. Six months ago I was totally adrift, not knowing what I wanted to do. And look how it turned out."

"Well, then, I'd say that was worth at least a nickel."

"C'mere," he said, pulling her close and putting his arm around her.

Just as McCurry thought he would have some quality alone time with Trish he heard Carmen calling, "Hey, cut it out you two. Get up and get moving. We've got lots more to see."

At Pescadero Point, McCurry squeezed Trish's hand and said how much he was enjoying this tour. "This was a great choice for our first trip. Being with you made it even more special."

"Jeez, I think I'm going to puke," Moreland said.

"Put a cork in it, Moreland, or we'll drop you off and let ya walk the rest of the way."

"Like hell," said Carmen, laughing, "I don't want him worn out when we get back to the apartment tonight."

"Well, then, let's finish our tour and find some place to eat in Carmel," McCurry suggested.

"Sounds good to me," Trish said.

After exiting the 17-Mile Drive in Carmel, it wasn't difficult to find a cozy restaurant in the town known for its idyllic eateries and rich artistic history.

"Well that really was an exciting day," McCurry said as they were driving back to Trish's apartment. "What d'ya think we should do now?"

"I have a good idea of what I want to do," Trish said as she slid her hand over and squeezed the inside of his thigh.

That night, McCurry made it back to Trish's bedroom, although he didn't get much sleep.

*　*　*

Over the next several weeks, McCurry and Trish continued their explorations of the area, including Cannery Row and the shops in downtown Monterey, relaxing on the beaches of Carmel and motoring along the drive hugging the coast of Big Sur. They continued other explorations as well, made love often, both knowing that no commitment was implied. McCurry would eventually be leaving and Trish was determined to finish her education. For the time being, they were just happy enjoying each other's company.

In fact, McCurry was so involved with his relationship with Trish, that he hadn't taken much time to get to know the other guys he was in school with, let alone the officers and non-commissioned officers who were in charge of the base. He heard the grumbling among his fellow students following hassles with those in charge. McCurry felt as long as the career guys – known as treads because of the hash marks on their uniforms for every four years of service – left him alone, he could tolerate a little of their bluster.

ASA students were pretty much allowed to come and go as they pleased. This really rankled the regular Army personnel who were more used to troops who required passes and regular inspections before leaving base.

McCurry was jolted back to the reality of life in the U.S. Army when a new base commander was installed at the facility.

During his first week at the institute, Major Barclay, the new commander, conducted a surprise inspection, an exercise foreign to language students. When Barclay – already referred to as Mad Dog because of his surly disposition – got to McCurry's room, he saw a coffee cup on McCurry's desk.

"What the fuck is that, soldier," the commander barked.

"A coffee cup, sir."

"I know it's a fuckin' coffee cup, you idiot. What the fuck is it doing there?"

"Ah, that's where I use it, sir."

"Are you just tryin' ta piss me off, trooper? If so, you're doing a good job and you'll regret it."

"No sir. I'm just answering your questions."

"Then I'll ask you again, what the fuck is a coffee cup doing in here?"

"I don't know what to say. It's how I get coffee from the mess hall to here so I can drink it while studying."

"Well, you moron, it doesn't belong here. It ain't standard issue. Having it in your room is gonna cost you. Maybe you won't be so flip the next time a superior officer asks you a question."

The Great Coffee Cup Caper, as Moreland called it, resulted in an Article 15 for McCurry. This instrument of military law was used by commanding officers to inflict pain on an errant enlisted person. In this case it cost McCurry $30 a month for three months and he was forced to serve KP for a week. So-called kitchen police was a particularly abhorrent duty in which soldiers helped prepare meals by peeling hundreds of potatoes, serving in the chow line and scrubbing an endless stream of dirty pots and pans for twelve to fourteen hours a day.

The theory behind an Article 15 is that if requirements of the penalty were met without further incident, it wouldn't become part of a soldier's permanent record. In reality, it was a way for officers to punish enlisted men and women who, without benefit of counsel, felt they had no choice but to accept it.

McCurry determined it would be the last Article 15 he would be handed without a fight. He obtained a set of basic regulations and began reading them. He discovered he didn't have to accept the Article 15. Instead, he could request to be tried in any one of the three types of courts martial – summary, special or general. A general court martial is typically for serious crimes, such as rape or murder.

I can imagine them giving me a general court martial for having a coffee cup in my room, he thought while scrubbing an endless train of pots on his last day of KP duty. From then on, he determined he would request a general court martial every time he was threatened with punishment. This would happen more often than he would have thought during a mostly pleasant year in Monterey.

*   *   *

After completing his training at the Defense Language Institute, McCurry was sent to Voice Intercept School in San Angelo, Texas. It was here that his impression that the military was controlled by lunatics began to take shape. He and his classmates were told when they completed this course that they could display their diploma, but they couldn't hang it on the same wall as their Defense Language Institute diploma. "Gee, I get it," McCurry told Hank Moreland. "As long as our language diploma is on one wall and our voice intercept diploma on another, no one will figure out that the Army taught us German so we could listen in on German conversations. That makes sense to me."

"Right on," Moreland agreed.

The Trolley Ride

McCurry's first stop in Germany was in Frankfurt for processing before heading on to Berlin. The day he checked in, he hooked up with a good friend from high school, Dave Weinstein. Weinstein worked in headquarters company and knew McCurry was arriving. He showed up in the barracks just as McCurry had found an empty bunk for his gear.

"Get some rest and be ready to go out on the town tonight," Weinstein said.

Weinstein, McCurry and a friend of Weinstein's, Gary Abrams, started out early in the evening on a walking tour of downtown Frankfurt. The processing center was located across from the I.G. Hochhaus, which housed various Army command centers. It was once the world headquarters for I.G. Farben, a munitions company that also produced the gas for Nazi Germany's death chambers. It was on the outskirts of downtown, within walking distance of the nightspots Weinstein had in mind.

McCurry had consumed his share of alcohol in college, so he didn't expect difficulty keeping up with his high school buddy. What he didn't know was how much more potent German beer was than that produced in the U.S. Three bars later and more than a dozen beers into the evening, McCurry found it hard to keep his friends in focus.

"You're not going to get sick on us are you?" Weinstein asked. "We Philadelphians have a reputation to uphold, don't we Gary?"

Although unsteady, McCurry assured Weinstein he was fine.

"Come on," Weinstein said to Abrams, laughing, "we'd better get him back to the barracks."

Since it was getting late and McCurry was walking unsteadily, Weinstein decided they should take a trolley back. Typically, the first car of the trolleys had a conductor while passengers with exact change had the option to board the second through a coin-operated turnstile. "A German wouldn't think of bypassing the turnstile, but then, we're not German," Weinstein explained, hoping McCurry could comprehend. "When the trolley pulls up, we'll take the second car and hop over the turnstile. D'ya think ya can make it?"

"Sure I can. Don't worry about me," McCurry said, although the world was still going in and out of focus.

When the trolley pulled up to the stop, much to McCurry's surprise he made it over the turnstile without falling on his face. After a few minutes though, Weinstein got upset. "Oh shit, city hall. We're on the wrong line. We've got to get off if we're gonna get back ta the barracks on time. Gotta jump, Mike. Think ya can do it?"

McCurry watched as first Weinstein jumped and Abrams followed. Oh well, McCurry thought, and leaped into space. He lost consciousness when he slammed into a telephone pole along the track. He woke up the next morning in the barracks, bruised and bloodied but alive. He found out later that Weinstein and Abrams had picked him up off the ground and he seemed okay. He even managed to walk with them back to the barracks. God takes care of fools and drunks, he thought. But he couldn't remember anything after hitting the pole.

* * *

The day before McCurry was scheduled to fly out of Frankfurt to Berlin, Weinstein came by his room to tell him he was expected to attend a meeting at ten that morning.

"Wassit about?" McCurry mumbled.

"I don't know," Weinstein responded. "Some business with the ASA. You know. Somethin' all secret and such."

When he arrived at the meeting room, there were a half-dozen guys seated in classroom chairs. At a desk at the front of the room, a sergeant with a string of hash marks on his sleeve was going through papers. McCurry saw Hank Moreland in a seat near the door, but didn't recognize any of the others. As McCurry came into the room, without looking up from his paperwork, the tread told him to close the door and find a seat. Before he could get to his seat, the tread stopped him in his tracks by nearly shouting, "Jesus Christ, soldier, what happened to your face."

"Uh, z'okay. Jew shoul' see z'other guy," McCurry said through swollen lips.

"Take a seat asshole," the sergeant said, rising from his seat and getting ready to address the group. "What's your name?" he asked McCurry.

"Mike McCurry."

"Well, *Specialist* McCurry, whatever it was, this is the kind of shit that won't be tolerated when you get to your unit in Berlin. Now sit down and pay attention.

"I'm Sergeant Gerald Gaffney," the tread said, addressing the full group. "My job's ta brief ya on what to expect when ya get t' your unit so none a ya end up in deep shit. Berlin's a hot spot in the cold war and c'n be a dangerous city, particularly for guys like y'all with top secret security clearances."

Gaffney went on to explain that Berlin had more spies from more countries than any other spot in the world. "You'll be livin' in Andrews Barracks," he said, "and it's no secret that it houses the Army Security Agency."

Gaffney said they all should assume when entering or leaving Andrews, they were being monitored by agents of either the Russian KGB or Stasi, the East German security agency. Therefore, any stranger who tried to strike up a conversation should be viewed with suspicion, he said.

They would all be flown into Tempelhof Airport, Gaffney said, where designated drivers would meet them and take them to Andrews.

"Before goin' anywhere with one of these drivers, ask ta see their orders. Y'all know what official orders look like, right. If they hesitate or try to give ya a load a bullshit, back off and find someone in the Military Police. If there aren't orders with your name on them, you don't go.

"Ya got that McCurry?"

McCurry nodded.

"All right. When ya get ta Andrews, you'll be assigned to a trick, or shift, and briefed on your duties. Pay attention, do your job and you'll be okay. Dismissed."

Great God Zulu

After an initial shock, McCurry knew he was in his element during his first day at work on Teufelsberg, or Devil's Hill, which was built from the rubble of war-ravaged Berlin. The listening post was commonly referred to simply as the Hill, or sometimes the Rubble Pile. In the midst of his first shift, McCurry was startled when, just as he was getting settled in, a half dozen guys left their positions, went to the front of the room and dropped to their knees in front of a large digital clock. When all the digits turned to 0, they bowed and cried "Zulu, god of time. We worship your majesty and ask for your blessing of peace."

"What the fuck was that all about?" McCurry asked Dwight Evans, the voice intercept operator in the position next to his.

"At the risk of being spurned for helping a newk," Evans said with a smile, "when the digital clock lines up with numerals such as all zeroes as it just did, you've got to get there in time to pay homage to the great god Zulu. It could also be zero, one, two, three, and so on."

"Hey, Evans, get the fuck over here."

"Oh fuck," Evans said quietly to McCurry. "I wonder what he wants."

Evans got up from his position and shuffled to the front of the room where Buck Landry, the sergeant in charge of the B-trick German linguists, waited impatiently.

"What's up Sarge?"

"It's just so nice to see you're so newk-friendly, Evans. And just when I was trying to figure out who I could assign to show McCurry the ropes. By this time next week, I expect you to have him up to speed on all his essential duties."

Evans realized that Landry was assigning him to train McCurry because Landry, like most of the treads on the Hill, really didn't understand the scope of duties of the personnel under his command.

"You want him to know everything in a week, Sarge? Like when it's Uncle Wally on the phone, is he talking to someone important or just one of his girlfriends? Or just the basics like how to thread a tape on a machine without fucking everything up?"

"Stop being a wiseass, Evans. You know what I mean. Just make sure he knows how ta do his job."

Evans wanted to really test Landry by asking him what job he was talking about, but he decided to let it slide.

"Sorry for the headache," McCurry said when Evans returned.

"Ah, it's not a problem. I just like to give Landry a hard time whenever he tries to push his weight around. Fuck doesn't have a clue about what we really do here. I could probably make something up and he'd fall for it."

"All right then, is Uncle Wally a real person, or were you just making him up?"

"Uncle Wally's Walter Ulbricht. He's the head of the Central Committee that rules the East German government. If you ever do get Uncle Wally on the line, grab an old-timer quick."

Evans told McCurry they were tied directly into the Central Committee phone system. And any upper echelon leader who came on the line almost always identified himself.

He then went on to explain the basics to McCurry. How to operate the ten voice-activated, reel-to-reel tape recorders at each position, how to set up the log sheets used to note the time and recorder count number of significant conversations and how to wrap up tapes that were complete.

"And like I said," Evans went on, "These treads don't have a clue about what you're doing. If Landry comes over to your position and you don't want to be bothered, just say 'Look Sarge, I've got four conversations going here, so get out of my face.' He'll bug out quick just to make sure he can't be charged with fucking something up."

"Speaking of treads," McCurry said to Evans, "how do these guys, who clearly don't have much going on upstairs, get ta be in charge?"

"Hey, if you hadn't been afraid of being drafted and sent to Vietnam, would you have voluntarily joined the Army?" Evans asked.

"Fuck no."

"That's the point. When we do our time and get out, who's left to be in charge?"

The room Evans and McCurry worked in was about thirty feet wide by sixty feet deep and packed with electronic equipment. Metal racks, set up with columns of audio tape recorders, lined both the side and the back walls of the room. Each column had four of the reel-to-reel machines. There were two columns on each side of a small metal desk, where the operator sat with two more recorders situated over the desk. The racks were set out from the walls about two feet to allow room for the miles of wires that ran out of them and into the walls.

There were nine voice intercept operators in the room, four on each side wall and one at the closed end of the room.

After McCurry had been on site for a while, he would learn there were various rumors about the purpose of a dome that sat atop the facility and concealed a giant microwave dish. The dome could be seen from points outside the Grunewald forest where the Hill was located. Some of the most ludicrous stories were circulated among non-ASA soldiers in Berlin, the "gators," whose lives overseas comprised a lot of nonsensical war games. The most prevalent rumor was that the bubble concealed a giant laser that could vaporize Russian reconnaissance planes. It wasn't difficult to find someone who had actually seen the dome open and the laser operating.

There were five voice intercept operator rooms, or wings, on the Hill, three for German language operators and two for Russian linguists. Russian operators listened in on Warsaw Pact maneuvers. The Warsaw Pact consisted of the eight communist states of Eastern Europe and its officials were well aware that their radio communications were being monitored. It was said that through the Russians' own intelligence activities they often even knew the identities of the personnel assigned to monitor their airwaves. Rich Sezov, the Russian linguist McCurry hung out with at the language institute in Monterey, was shocked into reality on his first day on the Hill. Shortly after picking up his headphones and getting settled in for the shift, he heard a Russian say, in plain English, "Good morning, Mr. Sezov. We hope you enjoy your stay in Berlin and will come back often." Sezov wasn't sure, however, whether the voice on the other end was really a Russian or if he had been set up by the guys who had been around for a while. Newks, or newcomers, were often the butt of jokes and pranks.

In addition to the voice intercept operators, there were analysts, specialists who monitored Morse communications and others who maintained the equipment and kept the operations up and running. In all, there were about 80 men in the American contingent on each eight-hour shift. Since the end of World War II, the joint control of the western sector of Berlin was shared by America, Great Britain and France. Great Britain also conducted its own covert activities in another facility on the Hill.

As they were filing out to the bus for the ride back to base, Evans asked McCury if he thought he would get the hang of it all.

"Fuck yeah. If not, I'll fake it."

"Now you got it," Evans said and slapped him on the back. "I dub thee newk fucking first class."

                               *   *   *

"Hey McCurry, wanna join us for a few beers at the Limp Dick?"

Evans and McCurry had just gotten back to the barracks after a swing shift. Although it was after midnight, most of the guys were usually too keyed up to sack out.

"The limp dick? What the fuck, Evans?"

"Just follow along, McCurry. This is part of the required training for all newks."

The Limp Dick was a dump of a bar located just outside Andrews' gates. Its real name was the Long Shot Saloon. It's said that it got its nickname from the fact that no matter how horny a soldier might be, when he saw the women at the Long Shot, he'd end up with nothing but a limp dick.

Lee Grimes, a B-trick old-timer, grabbed McCurry by one arm and, with Evans taking the other, they started escorting him toward the front gate. After less than a block walking on Finckensteinallee, they arrived at the Limp Dick.

As they passed through the front door, the smoke was so thick McCurry's eyes began watering almost immediately. His senses were also assailed by a cacophony of raucous laughter, high-decibel conversations, and whistles and catcalls as German women worked the tables for free drinks

"Y'd be surprised what these girls would do for a few free drinks," Evans shouted in McCurry's ear. "And they don't look too bad after a half dozen beers."

Before the threesome had gotten very far inside, an enormous German fräulein sidled up alongside Grimes, who was trying to clear a path through the mass of bodies in the room. She had to be over six feet tall with massive breasts to match her height.

Before she could say anything, Grimes grabbed her arm and turned her aside. "Not now, Bertha. I'm still sober." A number of guys at the table they were passing called out for Grimes to show a little kindness. One grabbed Bertha, pulled her on to his lap, saying, "C'mon Bertha, don't worry about him. I'll buy ya a drink."

At the next table they came to, Grimes leaned over, grabbed one of the guys by the shoulder and shouted "Got room for three more here?"

"For you Grimes, anything. Y'might have to grab a few chairs from another table. Just don't steal one from a gator," he said, generating a roar of laughter from the others around the table.

As the trio grabbed seats and pulled them up to the table, Grimes pointed to the guy next to him and shouted to McCurry to be heard above the din, "This monster here you should know is Hank Andrews, since he works with us, though he is easily missed in the crowd. Next to him is Stu Mason, a lucky fuck who works straight days packaging up items for our friends back in the states. Dave Blake I think you met during your first shift and that last ugly guy is Tom O'Connor, a German mary on A-trick.

"This newk here," Grimes shouted to the group, "is Mike McCurry, a fellow mary on B-trick. I figured he needed to start his formal education here at the Limp Dick."

McCurry had been told that using the slang "mary" was the safest way to refer to a fellow voice intercept operator outside of the confines of the Hill.

"I'll buy the next pitcher of beer if someone will fight his way to the bar to get it," Grimes said. "The newk here will help clear the path."

When Blake volunteered to go, he and McCurry got up and started wading their way through the crowd. On the way back with two pitchers, they had to use their hips to muscle their way through, leaving a few disgruntled soldiers in their path.

For the next hour, McCurry's table mates tried to top one another regaling him with ever escalating tales of the terror they caused unsuspecting treads. During this period, they also fought off the advances of a string of barflies, all scantily dressed and made up in a way that they looked not entirely unlike clowns.

"Hey Evans," McCurry shouted in his ear, "I thought you said these women wouldn't look too bad after a half dozen beers. I guess I haven't gotten there yet."

"It must depend on how horny you are," Evans shouted back. "But you know, give one of them like Big Bertha a 20-mark note and you can get a pretty good blow job. Top a her head ain't too ugly."

"Yeah right. Jesus Christ, what is that smell?"

"Look over at Andrews," Evans said, pointing to where he was slumped down with his head lying on the table. "He pulls this all the time. Drinks a shit load of beer, falls asleep and then lets out a locomotive train of farts that could clear a room. 'Round here we just put up with it."

"Whew. It smells like something crawled up inside him and died."

About that time, O'Connor was on his way back with another pitcher of beer when he bumped into a gator and spilled some on him.

"Hey, ya fuckin' ASA freak" the gator called as O'Connor skittered away. "Get back here ya mother fuckin' moron."

O'Connor, all five feet five of him, kept moving toward the table and what he hoped was the safety of his friends. Just when it seemed as if things would simmer down, Andrews rose from his slumber and stood up, all six foot four, 250 pounds of him and bellowed, "Who the fuck are ya calling an ASA freak, ya fucking scumbag?"

"Uh oh," Evans said to McCurry as he pushed his chair away from the table, "get ready to get the fuck out of here."

Andrews was on the gator before he could react, taking him down to the floor and overturning two tables in the process.

"Time to hat up," Evans said, racing for the door, with McCurry in hot pursuit.

When they got safely outside and managed to catch their breath, McCurry asked, "Shouldn't we have stayed there to help Andrews?"

"Did you see how many gators there were there?" Evans asked. "We would have gotten killed. The military police will be there soon enough to break it up and Andrews can take care of himself."

McCurry and the Flying
Green Weenie

After McCurry had been on the job for a week, he was getting bored with the bus ride to work. Three buses were needed for each trick change. Grimes told him men who got their licenses and were designated as trick drivers were relieved of any extra duty such as KP.

"They're exempt from all extra duties, including burn detail," Grimes told McCurry. This consisted of the boring and dirty work of reducing each day's sensitive documents into harmless ashes. Grimes had also told him one of the B-trick drivers would be heading back to the States to muster out in a couple weeks.

That's perfect, McCurry thought. Driving would relieve the tedium of the ride each day and also get him out of extra work.

"Is there any training involved?" he asked Grimes.

"Nah, ya either have the ability to drive 'em or you don't," Grimes said. "Have you ever driven bigger trucks or things like that?"

"Well, yeah. During high school I worked at a day camp and had to drive all kinds of trucks and tractors."

"Well, you won't have any problem, then," Grimes said. He warned McCurry that the test would be given by a German national who worked for the Army. The Germans took the authority given them seriously and could make life miserable for any supplicant who required their stamp of approval.

After signing up for the test with the company clerk, McCurry reported to the motor pool the following Monday morning to try his luck behind the wheel of the 37-passenger Mercedes bus. His instructor, Dieter Mueller, was waiting for him and he did not look pleasant or pleased.

"You were supposed to be here at nine o'clock, nein?" Mueller growled.

Evans had told McCurry before he left that morning he should be deferential if he wanted to pass this test. "German nationals who work for US forces don't often get much respect, so they eat it up if they think you are showing them the respect they think they deserve," Evans explained.

"Yes. It is nine, isn't it?" McCurry asked.

"Nein, it is three minutes after ze hour," Mueller barked.

"I apologize," McCurry said. "My watch must be slow."

"Okay, zen, let's get up in the bus and see how you do," Mueller said in a much more moderate tone. McCurry figured he must have passed his first test.

Mueller sat in the seat right behind McCurry, clipboard in hand.

"Now, zis is a diesel vehicle," Mueller explained. "Zat means you cannot just turn a switch and start it up. You see zat knob on ze dash? It operates a heater for ze fuel. Pull it out until the glaz on top of it glowz."

McCurry began to think Mueller's accent sounded almost like an affectation.

When the knob started glowing, Mueller said he could let it go and start the engine.

"All right, put it in first and start driving out of ze motor pool," Mueller instructed. "Go out ze main gate and turn right onto Finckensteinallee."

As McCurry was making his right out of the main gate, he drove up and over the curb.

"Nein, nein, nein, nein," yelled Mueller. "Pull over and stop." When McCurry had come to a complete stop, he turned and looked at Mueller. "Your vheels are almost directly under vhere you are sitting," Mueller said. "You cannot turn right like you vould a car. You must turn a little to the left as you get to ze intersection and zen turn right. All right, start out again. Up ahead you can make a right onto Theklastrasse."

As McCurry approached Theklastrasse, he pulled out to the left as told and then swung right. This time, he merely scraped the curb rather than riding up over it.

"Better, better," Mueller said. "Now go on to Altdorfer Strasse and make another right." Obviously McCurry's deferential attitude must be paying the dividends he had hoped for. He managed to make the turn smoothly at Altdorfer Strasse.

"Now go up to Baseler Strasse, make a right and head on back to Finckensteinallee, the base, and zen back to the motor pool," Mueller said.

When they had returned to the motor pool, Mueller signed the papers McCurry needed to get his heavy vehicle license and a week later he was assigned as a permanent driver for B-trick.

On his first day as a driver, McCurry picked up his bus at the motor pool and pulled it in behind the other two in front of the barracks. At the end of the shift, the other two drivers had already gotten into the first two buses, so once again he took the third in line. Evans got on to lend him moral support and, as they wended their way down the hill and out through the Grunewald, McCurry brought up the topic of how long it took to get back to base, considering it was only about 22 miles.

"Some of these guys drive more slowly than my grandmother," McCurry said. "What do you think? They're afraid of having an accident?"

"Got me," Evans answered. "Maybe they never had anyone challenge them."

"Well, maybe it's time to change that."

When they got out of the Grunewald and onto the autobahn, McCurry pressed the pedal to the floor and pulled up alongside the other two. Within minutes, he was well ahead of them. The second bus came in almost 10 minutes after McCurry reached Andrews.

After McCurry closed the door and was preparing to take the bus back to the motor pool, Jim Crocker, the driver of the second bus in, came running up and started pounding on the bus door.

"What the fuck is the matter with you?" Crocker said when McCurry opened the door. "Are you just a stupid fucking newk, or are you just plain stupid?"

"What's your problem, Crocker?"

"My problem is that you were driving like a fucking maniac. You wanna be an asshole in your own car, that's your affair. But when you're responsible for a bunch of other guys, then it becomes my problem."

"What're you, Crocker, the fucking bus monitor or something?"

"You fucking newk. Give me any more shit and I'll make life here miserable for you."

"Yeah, yeah. Get the fuck off my bus, Crocker, and then go fuck yourself."

*   *   *

As McCurry was walking back from the motor pool, Evans caught up with him and asked if he wanted to join him for a few beers at the Stork Club. Located inside the Andrews compound, the Stork Club sold beer cheap and was a popular gathering point for tricks coming off shift.

After McCurry and Evans grabbed a couple beers and found a table to sit at, Evans said, "I heard that asshole Crocker flaming all over you. Don't worry about it, most guys on this trick can't stand him. He's nothing but a wannabe tread."

"He is one flaming asshole. Shame you weren't able to see his face when I told him to go fuck himself. He turned beet red, but when he opened his mouth to respond, nothing came out except a little bit of spittle that slowly rolled down his chin as he backed out of the bus."

"That about sums up our friend Crocker," McCurry heard over his shoulder.

When he turned to see who was speaking, Claude Simmons, another B-trick linguist, said, "Mind if I pull up a chair."

"Help yourself," McCurry responded.

"I heard you guys talking, and Evans is absolutely right," Simmons said. "Besides, I was on your bus and I like getting back sooner, so keep it up."

"Ya know, we could use this little incident to get something started, something that will make the Crockers on our shift shit their pants," Evans said.

"What d'ya mean?" McCurry asked.

"Well fuck, McCurry, no one likes to sit on those buses any longer than they have to. Why don't we get a race started among the drivers? Add a little excitement to the trip home?"

"I'll vote for that," said Robert Davies, who had been listening in on the conversation from the table next to McCurry's. Sliding his chair over to join the group, Davies said, "I even think we should create a trophy for the ultimate winner."

"Yeah right. How're you gonna get the other guys to join in. I can't see Crocker racing for some damn trophy," McCurry said.

"He might, if his manhood is challenged," Davies said.

Davies suggested they put conspirators on the other two buses to push the drivers to keep up the next time McCurry passed them on the autobahn. "After all, you're not only a newk at work, but a newk driver too. Who's going to let a newk show them up?" Davies asked. "I'll make sure any driver who refuses to put the pedal to the metal gets heckled unmercifully."

"I can see it now," Evans said. "Fearless newk Mike McCurry wins the Flying Green Weenie award in the first annual trick bus race series."

"Cool fucking idea," Simmons said. "Trust me, I can create a trophy that will be the envy of the trick."

They decided they would use the remaining days of the current shift to push the other two drivers into trying to keep up with McCurry. Davies said he would get a group of guys together to jump all over Crocker if he tried to give McCurry a hard time again or if he didn't take up the race challenge.

"I don't think there's anyone on this trick who doubts I can cause him so many problems he will either fall in line or give up driving altogether," Davies said.

In the end, Crocker not only quit driving, but requested a transfer to another trick.

*   *   *

The initial practice races were a lot closer than McCurry thought they would be.

After leaving the autobahn, the route they took to work wended its way through small, two-lane city streets on the perimeter of downtown before merging onto the four-lane Kurfürstendamm, where it remained on the Ku'damm for about four miles before returning to two-lane streets for the remainder of the trip to Andrews.

If either Frank Garner, the other regular B-trick driver or Eric Weiss, who replaced Crocker, were in the lead when they exited the autobahn, the only opportunity McCurry had to pass them was on the four-mile stretch of the Kurfürstendamm. So far, McCurry had managed to take the lead here if he needed to, but it had required some close encounters with other vehicles that got in his way. In one instance, as he shot toward a gap between a large truck on his right and oncoming traffic on his left, a concerned passenger shouted for him to slow down. He pressed on and, just as he was passing the truck, there was a large explosion. When he turned to look in his right-hand outside mirror to see what happened, he discovered the mirror and its attaching arm were gone. Apparently the explosion was the result of his mirror connecting with the mirror on the truck at high speed. He had to use his powers of imagination to explain that one to the motor pool sergeant.

After a couple weeks of practice, Simmons called a meeting of the three bus drivers as the mids shift neared its end. As they gathered around a table in the break room, he said, "I think it's time to get this thing officially under way. And I think the prize is something the winner will cherish for the rest of his life."

Simmons took hold of a cloth that was covering an object on the table and, with a great flourish, pulled it off and announced, "Behold the Flying Green Weenie."

Using a toy bus he must have picked up in the Post Exchange, Simmons had attached a large sausage to the top and stylized wings to the side. He spray-painted his creation in Army green and mounted it on a polished wooden base.

It was decided that the races would begin with the first day of the next days shift, continue through the swing and end on the last day of the following mids shift. Simmons offered to set up a board to keep tally of who won each day.

"Sounds like we're ready to roll," Evans said.

"What about the rules." Garner asked.

"What rules?" Evans responded. "There are no rules. This is ASA racing, not gator racing."

*   *   *

Over the break before the days shift began, two of McCurry's Monterey classmates, Rich Sezov and Hank Moreland, Dave Alexander, a fellow B-trick mary, Evans and McCurry were invited to an impromptu beer blast at Lee Grimes' off-base apartment. This wasn't unusual, but the fact Grimes said not to mention it to anyone else was.

After making sure everyone had a beer, Grimes said "Look, you guys, we gotta plan a strategy to make sure McCurry wins this fucking race series."

"What do you mean by a strategy?" Sezov asked. "All he's gotta do is ram the gas pedal to the floor and keep taking the crazy fucking chances and he'll be a shoe-in to take the trophy."

"I wouldn't be so cock sure, Rich. Granted the most fearless driver probably will win most of the time, but that's still only probably. I kinda went out on a limb for this newk and want our chances to be better than probably."

"Lee's right," McCurry said. "If we're all using the same route to get back to base, the winner at the end of each shift will be pretty much a crap shoot. Which means we've gotta look at alternative routes."

"The only problem with that is, the one we use is mandated by company regs," Grimes said.

"I've been wondering about that, Lee. If you look at the map, we're kind of going out of our way, taking the autobahn all the way up to the Ku'damm and then coming back down through the center of the city. What the fuck's up with that?" McCurry asked.

Grimes explained that the ASA brass recognized that the buses going up and back to the Hill carried passengers who had top secret clearances and worked in a facility whose mission was a highly guarded secret. The buses traveled unguarded through a city that contained more spooks on more cloak and dagger missions than any other in the world.

The route the buses took, which was also supposed to be a secret, was chosen because it was considered the safest way to get from the Hill, high up in the British zone, to Andrews Barracks down in the American zone. Buses identical to those used for trick changes were used as loop buses to take Army personnel to the shopping districts downtown. This made it difficult for an enemy to determine which buses were transporting ASA personnel and which were loop buses

Leaving work, the buses traveled through the wooded portion of the Grunewald, which was always teeming with gators on maneuvers. This provided cover until they reached the autobahn. When they left the autobahn, they were close to center city and on well-lighted streets. Then they traveled down the Ku'damm, one of the busiest sections of the city before exiting onto more well lighted streets taking them back to Andrews.

"Bottom line, we're supposed to stick to this route," Grimes said.

"The operative word there is 'supposed'," McCurry said.

The final strategy adopted was to find a shorter alternative route that could be used and making this an even more closely guarded secret among the guys who rode on McCurry's bus.

A couple of days later, McCurry and Grimes launched their exploration for shorter, alternative routes to the Hill. The first route they chose had too many very narrow streets with practically no lighting. After making a few adjustments on the way down, however, they came up with one that McCurry believed would work and was about five miles shorter than the prescribed route.

"I hope you've got this all down, Grimes, because I'll be counting on you to be my navigator. I'd hate to get lost and come in twenty or thirty minutes late. They'd send out the fucking MPs to find us."

"Don't worry, McCurry, I'll get you home safe," Grimes assured him.

*   *   *

At the end of the first day of the days shift, Garner, Weiss and McCurry waited until all three buses were loaded before starting the trip back to the barracks. A couple of the treads grumbled that the buses should be leaving as they filled up, but they had learned not to push the drivers. It could be a long, slow trip back at twenty kilometers per hour. McCurry and Grimes decided that while on days, they would use the prescribed route. Since the shifts were seven days long, with three days off between each, they figured they could easily win the series without exposing their strategy during daylight hours.

After six days, Weiss had won one, McCurry had taken two, and Garner was in the lead with three wins. McCurry was determined to be tied with Garner at the conclusion of days shift, but he had gotten held up on the Ku'damm and Garner slipped past him onto the two-lane streets. The remainder of the streets leading to Andrews were too narrow to attempt to pass. McCurry did, however, envision one possible way he could still win this run.

The last leg ran down Paulinenstrasse to Finckensteinallee and then straight across into the entrance to Andrews Barracks. As Garner approached Finckensteinallee and slowed for the stop sign,

McCurry pulled up alongside him in the oncoming traffic lane. Garner saw what McCurry was planning and hit the gas just as McCurry edged past him heading toward the gate. There was no way McCurry could push over to the entrance ramp, so he shot through the exit a half bus ahead of Garner.

The pair of MPs who guarded the gate were half asleep when the two buses startled them awake as they flew past the guard shack. "Fucking ASA assholes," one said before settling back on his chair.

When the two buses pulled up in front of the barracks, Garner jumped out of his and ran forward to McCurry's bus where his passengers were still on board celebrating the win and shouting "losers" to the guys filing off Garner's bus.

"What the fuck, McCurry. That doesn't count. You can't come flying through the exit lane to win the race."

"Sure I can. I just did," McCurry said. "Don't be a sore loser, Garner. We've still got fourteen more runs. Maybe you should check a bus out and practice during the break."

"Fuck you, McCurry," Garner said and stomped back to his bus.

*   *   *

A little after midnight three days later, the guys from B-trick started shuffling out to the buses after their first day on the swing shift. McCurry was surprised to see how many more were getting on his bus. They'll get a little surprise tonight, he thought.

When all three buses had gotten on the autobahn, McCurry started dropping back to let the other two leave him behind.

"Okay," McCurry said to Grimes, who was seated right behind him, "we pull off at the next exit, right?"

"Right. It should be coming up in about two miles."

McCurry found the exit and moved over onto the exit ramp. He knew that Evans was letting the rest of the guys know that this was a planned exit to a route that would get them back to base more quickly than usual.

As McCurry made a right off the exit ramp, he was enveloped by near total darkness. "Jesus Christ, Grimes, did you think these streets would be this dark when we planned the route?"

"Don't sweat it McCurry. That's what you've got headlights for. Take it a little easy tonight and by tomorrow night it'll become second nature. 'Sides, we can't win every race or the other guys would know there was something fishy going on. Take a right at the next intersection."

"It's just a good thing these Herms hit the sack so early," McCurry said as he maneuvered the bus onto a street that seemed even narrower and darker than the one he was leaving. "I'd hate to run into any traffic on these streets."

McCurry maneuvered carefully along the narrow, dark streets for the next fifteen minutes until they came out into an area that actually had street lamps. "Shit, I'm going to need shades to handle all this light," he said to Grimes.

"Well then, step on it. I don't think we can ever beat the other guys now, but I don't want to be too far behind."

When McCurry reached Finckensteinallee, he made a left and then drove about a half mile before reaching the point where Paulinenstrasse crossed over to the gate at the Andrews compound. After turning right and passing through the gate, he saw the other two buses were in front of the barracks and still unloading passengers.

"At least we're not too late," he said to Grimes.

When McCurry pulled up behind the other two buses and opened the door, Garner was waiting for him.

"Hey, what happened to you, McCurry? Guess you can't drive as fast after dark, huh asshole."

"That must be it, Garner. Who knows? Maybe you'll win this thing after all."

"Hey listen you guys, this is just a friendly competition," Grimes said. "How 'bout we all meet for a few beers at the Stork Club after you get rid of the buses."

"Fine with me. How about you, Garner?"

"Sure, no problem," Garner replied, turning to go back to his bus.

*   *   *

The next night, McCurry was flying through the darkened and deserted streets leading away from the autobahn. He knew he only had to speed it up a little to get in ahead of Garner and Weiss, who was really out of the running after losing three to McCurry and four to Garner. McCurry's tactic, though, was to make sure he had made the right into Andrews before either of the other two buses could make it down Paulinenstrasse and see that he was coming from another direction. Ultimately, McCurry had made it all the way to the barracks before Garner's bus came through the gate followed a few minutes later by Weiss.

After they had turned in their buses, McCurry, Garner, and Weiss walked back to the barracks together. McCurry said he was going to stop off at the Stork Club to have a beer with Grimes and Evans and asked if the other two wanted to join him. Weiss declined but Garner, who at least was beginning to warm up to McCurry, said he would join them.

After the two picked up a pitcher of beer at the bar and joined Grimes and Evans, Garner asked, "How the fuck did you get past me McCurry?"

"I managed to catch up to you on the Ku'damm and I slipped by before we pulled off."

"Fuck all. I didn't see you."

"Well, I saw you. Better luck tomorrow night. I've been meaning to ask you," McCurry said, changing the subject, "have you had any complaints from the treads on your bus? I haven't really had any on mine."

"Nah. They're fucking clueless. All they care about is getting back to the barracks and away from us."

Finishing his glass of beer, McCurry said, "Well, I don't know about you guys, but I'm bushed. Time to head back and sack out."

*   *   *

McCurry came in well ahead of Weiss and Garner on the next three nights. Garner didn't say anything when he, McCurry, Evans and Grimes met for beers after the shift, but McCurry got the feeling Garner was beginning to suspect something was amiss.

On the sixth night of the shift, Garner maneuvered his bus in behind McCurry's. When McCurry eased back on the throttle hoping Garner would pull out and pass, Garner slowed his bus to keep pace with McCurry's.

"Fuck, Grimes, I think Garner's caught on."

"What d'ya mean?"

"He's staying right behind me. Won't pass even when I slow down."

"Well, then, fuck him. You'll lose him in a hurry on those back streets."

"Yeah, but if I lose 'em, he's liable to get totally lost since he doesn't know the route we're taking."

"So," said Grimes, ending the discussion since their exit was coming up.

＊　＊　＊

McCurry was able to leave Garner behind once they hit the dark, back-street section of the alternate route back to the barracks. And, as a result, Garner got totally lost and was more than an hour late getting back to the barracks. This led to the filing of an incident report.

During his investigation, company commander Capt. James Hanover questioned one of the treads on Garner's bus who happily recounted the races that were being held by the B-trick bus drivers, and how Garner got lost after following McCurry off the autobahn on an unauthorized route.

After the last day of the swing shift, during which Grimes and McCurry drove at normal speeds over the authorized route, the two were told by the company clerk to report to Hanover's office the following morning. Apparently none of the treads had caught on to the fact that Weiss was part of the races. McCurry wasn't too worried because Hanover was known to be one of the very few treads who understood that ASA troops serving in Berlin were a breed apart and needed to be treated differently to insure their mission wasn't compromised.

"What am I going to do with you guys?" Hanover asked the next morning as McCurry and Garner stood at attention in front of his desk.

"Do you want me to answer that Captain?" McCurry asked innocently.

"Shut up, McCurry, and both of you listen up. You're fucking lucky that we don't have enough bus drivers as it is or I'd throw you both off and give you two weeks of KP to boot. But, I need you to continue driving and I need you at your posts on the Hill. So, if I let this one go, can I count on you to cut out the shit and do your jobs?"

"Yes sir," McCurry and Garner said in unison.

"All right then, get the fuck out of here."

*   *   *

When McCurry and Garner met up with Grimes, Evans, Simmons and Davies for drinks later in the day, McCurry said drily, "I guess the races are over."

"We still have to crown a winner," said Simmons, "and according to my tally, Weiss won one, Garner four and McCurry took seven. So my friend," he said turning to McCurry, "you get the Flying Green Weenie award. Make sure you display it with pride."

"Thanks. And that means you can stop calling me a newk."

Grimes, who was leaning back in his chair, blew beer out his nose laughing and fell over, cracking his head on the concrete floor. Luckily he was drunk enough to prevent any real harm.

A Propitious Meeting

McCurry's first winter in Berlin was nearly over. He was getting more familiar with the city and found he enjoyed discovering new, local pubs away from the traditional hangouts of the Americans stationed in the city.

On a day that had the hint of spring in the air, McCurry decided to board a bus and head uptown to explore some sections of the Ku'damm he hadn't seen yet. As he waited for the bus, he brooded over how the country he had left behind less than a year ago was rapidly changing.

Richard Nixon, for god's sake, would probably become the next president in this fall's election. And Spiro Agnew vice president. These two amounted to nothing more than a couple of thugs who frightened America's voters into believing the answer to everything was the blind enforcement of law and order.

One of the guys returning from leave in the States recently related how scary things had become. "You wouldn't believe you were in the good ole U S of A," he said. "Everywhere you go you see signs proclaiming 'America, love it or leave it.' I don't even know if I wanna go back."

McCurry agreed with that sentiment. With Nixon and Agnew in charge, things could only get worse. They represented everything that was wrong with America. Everything McCurry and his fellow protesters had been revolting against in college.

41

But, there was little he could do about it here in Berlin. For that matter, he realized, there was probably little he could do about it even if he were back in America. The best bet, he thought as he boarded the bus, is to let it go and focus on the life he was building here in Berlin. American voters, as always, would get what they deserved.

He decided to get off the bus at the Kaiser Wilhelm Memorial Church and stroll along that section of the Ku'damm. The church was a good representation of what Berlin looked like following World War II. It was badly damaged in the bombing raids and only one section with the spire was left standing. Only a few years before McCurry arrived in Berlin, a new building was built alongside the bomb-damaged structure, which had been retained and turned into a memorial.

McCurry took some time to explore the church's memorial hall, marveling at what the cathedral looked like before and after the bombing raids. He couldn't imagine what it was like for the civilians who lived through that period. Of course, he realized, it was no worse than what residents of London suffered during the blitz of 1940 and '41 in which the Germans bombed the city and its surroundings for seventy-six nights straight.

As he emerged from the memorial into the sunlight, McCurry continued to stroll along the Ku'damm until he found a small pub that didn't look terribly crowded, even though it was nearly noon. As his eyes became adjusted to the dimly lit facility, he made his way to a table near the back of the room. When the waitress came over, he asked for a bratwurst and a bottle of Bock beer.

Scanning the room, McCurry caught the eye of one of the occupants who was also sitting alone. The stranger picked up his beer, walked over and asked if would be okay if he joined McCurry.

"Sure," McCurry said. "Funny, when I first saw you, I thought you were a German. I haven't met many Americans in these small, neighborhood pubs."

"My name's Wachter, Horst Wachter, and I am a Berliner, not an American" he said, reaching his hand over to shake McCurry's.

McCurry was startled. Wachter not only spoke perfect English, but had a distinct American accent. At just under six foot tall, with a slightly rotund build and dirty blonde hair, he didn't even look like a typical German national.

"I'm McCurry, Mike McCurry. Pleased to meet you."

"Pleased to meet you as well, Mike. And, like you, I haven't met many Americans in these types of establishments. When I do, I like to strike up a conversation to help improve my English."

"Doesn't sound as if it needs much improvement. You could have told me you were American and I would never have caught on."

"I practice a lot. I've got a kiosk up the street on the Ku'damm where I meet a lot of American tourists. I'm trying to get my wife to speak English around the house too 'cause I would love to be able to move to America some day."

When the waitress arrived with McCurry's order, he asked Wachter if he could buy him a beer. "Yeah, thanks. Ich werde einen Entwurf Pils, bitte," Wachter said to the waitress.

"So, what're you doing in a place like this rather than one of the typical GI hangouts?" Wachter asked.

"Well, I hope I am not now nor ever will be a typical GI. Those places are just a lot of noise and filled with too many drunken idiots. Besides, I often get a chance to improve my German and meet new friends in these pubs."

"So, you're a German linguist," Wachter said. Seeing McCurry's look of consternation, he added, "Don't get paranoid. This is a small town and many of us know that the Army houses a bunch of linguists over at Andrews. I'm not looking to uncover any secrets or compromise your work. I have my own reasons to want to see the Americans succeed and defeat the Communists. And bring down that fucking wall."

Wachter explained that he had escaped from East Berlin when he was just a teenager. He negotiated the treacherous no-man's land that separated the Democratic German Republic from West Berlin because he was running from police. On a dare from fellow students, he had climbed an administration building on campus and cut down an East German state flag. He left his homeland and a number of family members after hearing from friends that he was wanted for questioning as an enemy of the state.

"Right now, I can't even go back to visit my mother," Wachter explained.

After chatting for an hour or so, Wachter said he had to get back to his kiosk. "It's only about a block from here. Want to walk along?" he asked.

"Sure," McCurry said. He called the waitress over to pay his bill. Then he followed Wachter out the door, not realizing then that the German would become one of his best friends in Berlin.

The Clueless Treads

everal months after the infamous bus races, McCurry couldn't remember any other time when he had to deal with so much traffic. All 12 recorders were running and he was switching back and forth among them, frantically making notes on his log about what was being discussed and how much time each discussion lasted.

"Hey man, slow down a bit. You'll live longer," said Grimes.

Grimes, who had been on the Hill nearly a year longer than McCurry, had noticed how stressed McCurry appeared trying to keep up with the voices streaming out of the Deutsche Demokratische Republik Central Committee headquarters.

"Man, this is insane," McCurry replied, pushing one side of his headset back so he could hear Grimes and listen in on the conversations being recorded at the same time.

"You're taking it too seriously, Mike. When it gets this busy, just let the recorders run and use your imagination to fill in the log. Just get the gist and pull any number out of the air for the duration of the calls. If there is really something important going on, you'll see recorders start popping all around the room. Till then, figure it's bullshit."

"What about when the logs go back for analysis?"

"With all the shit that flows through here, do you think the analysts have time to sort through anything other than stuff marked 'high priority'? They get enough of that from the newks and other guys who think everything's important."

Grimes explained that the analysts spent most of their time sorting the daily logs into color-coded folders indicating the day of the week and then using the duration numbers for a daily report on activity. Tapes had color codes to match them up with the logs in the folders.

He explained that at the end of the week, analysts package up the color-coded folders and tapes and put them in a color-coded box. When a month is complete, the color-coded boxes are sent back to NSA where other analysts unpack them, combine them with daily logs and tapes from other voice intercept sites and store them away on shelves, all marked "top secret."

"They will probably still be packed away in a top secret storage facility when you're telling your grandkids about the great years you spent as a spook in the Army Security Agency."

Grimes told McCurry that if he had trouble filling up his log at the end of the day, he had several samples McCurry could copy from.

"Hell, one week I submitted the same info for every day I worked. Like most everything else in the Army, it's all bullshit anyway."

*   *   *

A couple of days later, McCurry was taking a coffee break when he saw Grimes and Evans engaged in animated conversation, Grimes gesticulating wildly and Evans laughing uproariously.

"What the fuck's going on?" McCurry asked as he pulled up a chair and set his coffee cup on the table next to Evans.

"Our clueless G2 back in headquarters decided he wanted to impress some Red Chinese visitors by suggesting they be given a tour of the Hill," Grimes said. "He actually called Captain Hanover into his office and in front of this Chinese delegation suggested Hanover personally escort them to the Hill."

The G2 in Berlin, Col. Eric Anderson, worked out of the Berlin Brigade headquarters in McNair Barracks and was in charge of all intelligence activities in Berlin. Much to Hanover's consternation, Anderson refused to recognize that Army Security Agency personnel and the Teufelsberg installation were outside his jurisdiction. This was precisely why regular Army units were stationed in McNair and the ASA units sequestered in Andrews. Nevertheless, it galled Anderson that he wasn't even permitted to go near the Hill.

"I'm the goddamned fucking G2 in Berlin," Anderson would bellow at Hanover. "How can I be in charge of all intelligence activities if I'm not allowed to know what is going on at the most important intelligence facility in this city?"

Hanover wanted to tell him that he shouldn't even be aware that Teufelsberg was an official Army facility, but he would inevitably patiently explain to this clueless moron the difference between the mission of Army intelligence and the top-secret activities that fell under the jurisdiction of the National Security Agency.

"Hanover nearly shit his pants when he answered the summons to Anderson's office and found him openly talking about T'berg in front of these Chinese officials," Grimes went on.

"Not having a clue about what goes on here, he probably figured this was a way for him to slip in through the back door," Evans said. "Anderson may be in charge of intelligence activities but no one said he had to be intelligent. He rose from the ranks of gators after all."

"Instead," said Grimes, "he'll be lucky if he isn't subject to a court martial."

"How did Hanover back out of that one?" McCurry asked.

"He told Anderson the Hill was shut down for the week for annual maintenance," Grimes said. "It's an indication of the breadth of his *intelligence* that he fell for that one."

Apparently Hanover made a report of the incident because within a few days Anderson was relieved of his command.

*   *   *

A few weeks later, McCurry was sitting at his position during a much quieter period of the day when his trick sergeant, Buck

Landry, came into the room, picked up McCurry's boots and started to walk out with them.

"Hey Sarge, what're you doing with my boots?" McCurry asked.

"Don't sweat it, McCurry. I've found a volunteer to polish them and when I bring 'em back I want 'em on your feet."

"What the fuck? Why would you get someone to shine my boots?"

"Because trying to get you to do it wouldn't be worth the hassle," Landry said. "The new sergeant major of the Army is in Berlin and he's coming through here on a tour. And I mean it, McCurry, I don't want any shit out of you when he arrives. I'd send you back to base if I didn't need you here doing your job."

It wasn't uncommon for VIPs to be given a tour of Teufelsberg as long as they had the proper security clearance. McCurry had read in *Stars and Stripes* that a new sergeant major of the army had been sworn in earlier in the fall. George W. Dunaway was only the second person to hold this position, and he decided he wanted to tour European bases and meet the enlisted personnel he purportedly represented.

"Hey, this is the guy who is supposed to help enlisted personnel with any problems they might have, right," Evans said. "Maybe we should start making up a list before he comes here, see if he can give us a hand."

"Yeah, right. If you believe that I've got a bridge in Brooklyn I'll sell ya," McCurry retorted.

A while later, Landry returned with McCurry's shined boots. "Put these on and clean up your position," he said. Turning to the rest of the room, Landry said, "Sergeant Major of the Army Dunaway'll arrive here shortly. When we bring him through here, I want you all to keep your traps shut unless Dunaway addresses you directly. Anybody gives him or me any shit'll have their asses kicked all the way back to Andrews when he leaves. Understand?"

When Landry left, McCurry turned to Evans and said, "Jesus Christ, that was quite a speech for Landry. Do you think the lieutenant wrote it out for him?"

Surprisingly, Dunaway actually did wander into McCurry's section with Landry and Lt. Vincent in tow. Probably trying to show off for the new sergeant major – or perhaps steer him away from McCurry – Landry went over to Alexander and asked him for his headset. After putting the headset on and listening for a few seconds, Landry asked Alexander, "What's this guy saying?"

With a perfectly straight face, Alexander said, "That's kind of hard for me to decipher since you have the headset on."

Quickly turning to Dunaway, Landry handed the headset to the sergeant major and said, "Here, you wanna hear an East German commie talking?"

Just as Landry, Vincent and Dunaway were about to make what Landry hoped would be a graceful retreat from the room, the GMT clock turned to 12:12:12 and everyone instinctively rushed to the front of the room, dropped to their knees and cried as one, "Zulu, god of time. We worship your majesty and ask for your blessing of peace."

Father's Day — German Style

Horst Wachter and McCurry were quickly becoming fast friends. Over the next few shift breaks, McCurry had met Wachter at his kiosk and chatted for a while as he was closing up. More than once, they had spent the night on the town, where Horst introduced McCurry to some of Berlin's exciting party spots. One that was quickly becoming McCurry's favorite was the Back Stage Club, which Wachter described as one of Berlin's hottest new night spots. Every night Wachter and McCurry visited the club, it was packed with young Berliners whose primary aim was to drink, party and, more often than not, hook up for a night of sex. Fortunately, Wachter didn't object to those times when some winsome young girl convinced McCurry he should leave his friend and come home with her.

As winter waned, McCurry had to admit he wasn't sorry to see it go. McCurry felt this first winter in Berlin would never end. He was surprised how bleak and bitter it was. There were less than seven hours of daylight during December and January. It seemed like darkness pervaded every aspect of life. The cold penetrated layers of clothing and went right to the bone. Despite gloves, McCurry's hands seemed to freeze as soon as he went out and ached all winter long. Feet would get so cold that local cobblers did a big business in attaching an extra layer to the soles of boots. The humidity was so bad there were days when Dwight Evans would stand next to

McCurry on the trip to the Hill and continuously scrape the ice off the *inside* of the windshield.

But it did end. One bright, balmy day in May, McCurry decided to take advantage of the break in the weather to go for a walk in the city.

Daydreaming, McCurry was startled when he nearly tripped over a man passed out on the sidewalk. He came up short and was surprised to see people just walking around the prone figure – or, in many cases, McCurry observed, stumbling around him. When he reached the man, he started to kneel down to see if he could be of help. The overpowering smell of beer, however, made him realize the only thing this fellow needed was a strong pot of coffee.

"Don't worry about him," a passerby said to McCurry, "he's just enjoying his Vatertag."

Vatertag, McCurry knew, translated literally to father day, or, he assumed, Father's Day. He hadn't thought much about how other cultures celebrated dates like Mother's Day or Father's Day … if indeed they did at all. He was about to be introduced to a bad case of culture shock. Vatertag, he would learn, was one cultural phenomenon his instructors in Monterey had failed to mention.

As he headed up Brandenburgische Strasse approaching the Ku'damm, the number of local bars and pubs increased as did the incidences of public drunkenness. Had all of Berlin gone mad? he wondered.

Groups of older men with what were probably their sons came lumbering out of the bars, arms linked and loudly singing drinking songs. Often one or more stumbled to his knees, with the others dragging them back to their feet. They were going back and forth from bar to bar. At one point, McCurry watched as one group, with a member too drunk to make it any further, laid their nearly comatose comrade out on a roadside bench.

The words of the famous German drinking song floated on the gentle spring air: "Ein Prosit, Ein Prosit der Gemütlichkeit." Gemütlichkeit was one of the few German words that McCurry wished had an English equivalent. It is a state of mind more than a word. Good company enjoyed in the confines of a warm, cozy atmosphere probably best described how McCurry would explain it. Others might have similar but different descriptions of the word. Thus "Ein Prosit der Gemütlichkeit" means, basically, a toast to good company and good cheer. And there was a *lot* of that going around.

One group tried to drag him into their traveling party. After sharing one of the beers being passed around and singing a verse of "Ein Prosit der Gemütlichkeit" with them, McCurry bowed out as graciously as he could.

He decided to catch a bus and visit Horst Wachter. Wachter lived in the Charlottenburg section of the city. While he worried about what he might encounter on a bus, the short trip was relatively peaceful. Apparently all the revelry was confined to the streets.

Wachter was outside his flat and saw McCurry approaching on foot. "What the hell you doing out here?" he asked.

"Nice greeting. What was I supposed to do, call ahead and ask permission to visit?

"What the fuck's going on, Horst?" McCurry asked as they started entering his apartment. "I thought it would be a nice day for a walk, but it appears that all of Berlin has gone totally nuts."

Wachter laughed and said, "You mean Vatertag? This is one day where, unless you are part of the drunken mobs going from bar to bar, it's best to stay inside."

"You mean Father's Day here is just an excuse to go out and get drunk?" McCurry asked.

Wachter explained that, at one time, Father's Day was set aside to honor God, the father of everyone. It was marked with parades and other public celebrations. Over time, it transformed into a version of that celebrated in America, a day to honor a person's father.

"Eventually, however, Germans being German, it was changed into what could best be described as a 'booze day.' It's basically a boys' night out, although the 'night' starts quite early, as you have seen."

In the city, Wachter explained, fathers and sons band together, make a lot of noise and travel from bar to bar. Many will also travel to a rural or scenic area, such as the Grunewald, where large groups gather around kegs of beer and attempt to sing all the old German drinking songs.

"So in essence, it is group insanity," McCurry said.

"I guess so," Wachter answered, "but if you want to join in, it actually is quite a blast."

The two jumped into Wachter's car and headed out to the Grunewald to a spot Wachter knew people from his neighborhood congregated on Vatertag, careful not to run over men passed out in the streets. As they pulled up into a clearing in the Grunewald, there were a couple dozen men gathered around a bon fire singing at the top of their lungs and mostly out of tune.

"Jesus Christ," McCurry observed as they got out of the car, "how do they avoid falling into the fire."

"Luck," Wachter shot back, "pure luck."

Large galvanized wash tubs were scattered at various spots around the group, all filled with bottles of beer. Some, surprisingly, even had ice. One of the party goers had apparently brought along a table and it was weighed down with pounds of bratwurst, currywurst and all sorts of cheeses and breads.

One of the revelers grabbed McCurry by the arm and dragged him into the group. "Essen, trinken und fröhlich sein, mein freund," he said and another thrust a bottle of beer into his hand.

"Danke, danke," McCurry said. Hoisting his bottle in tribute, he proclaimed, "der Gemütlichkeit."

When he managed to break away and find Wachter, he said, "Jesus Christ, I hope some idiot from military intelligence didn't follow us out here. My neck would be in a noose for sure."

"Cool it, McCurry. Lose the paranoia and just have fun."

"Good advice, Horst." He did, and the next day he couldn't even remember how he got back to Andrews.

The Making of an Expert Marksman

Once a year, as the guys in McCurry's unit put it, they had to go out and do "Army stuff." Re-qualifying with the M-14 rifle was one of those obligatory duties, although it didn't necessarily occur on the yearly schedule as required. Rumor had it that the treads were frightened to give loaded weapons to a large group of ASA personnel.

But, as autumn approached in 1968, members of the ASA's Field Station Berlin were ordered to re-qualify on their M-14s. McCurry was one of three bus drivers assigned to transport the men to the firing range. When he joined the others to check out his weapon, his trick sergeant, Buck Landry, said he didn't need one. As a bus driver he would remain with the bus and not go to the range with the others. He could fill out his own score card and turn it in afterwards, Landry said.

"I wonder if that's really true," said Evans, "or if Landry's just afraid to give you a loaded weapon."

"After that incident with the Herm worker, I guess you've got a point," McCurry said. "I guess being a fuck-off has its privileges."

Germans were often referred to by American soldiers as "Herms" as in "Herman the German." Surprisingly, they were frequently employed to work on facility maintenance at the Hill, such as the air-conditioning and ventilation equipment. Whenever a German national was brought inside the compound, he was assigned a guard who carried an M-14 rifle.

If a worker had to go inside the building, a paper bag was put over his head and he was guided to the work area, which had a shroud erected around it to maintain security. When finished, his head was bagged again and he was led out.

McCurry recognized this works fine to keep the Herms from seeing any sensitive equipment or information. However, the first time he saw one brought in this way, he wondered aloud about how the worker was kept from overhearing mission-related conversations.

"After all, we're not the quietest people in the world," he said to Evans.

"Supposedly the help they choose don't understand English," Evans said.

To be safe, though, he said, when the worker is turned over to the trick sergeant to be bagged and led in, the guard at the gate says, "When he's finished, just take him out back and shoot him."

"When the guy doesn't bolt," Evans said, "he is considered a safe bet."

Knowing the breadth of Evans' imagination, McCurry wasn't sure about the veracity of this account, but had to admit it made for a good story.

Outside the main building, German nationals working on equipment were just assigned an armed guard to stay with them while they were in the compound. Recently, McCurry was tapped for this duty.

"What the fuck, if he runs am I supposed to shoot him?" McCurry asked Landry as he was issued his weapon.

"Don't worry about it, he won't run. It's more for show than anything else."

"Oh, okay. Then the gun isn't loaded, right," McCurry said.

"Of course it's loaded, you ass. And it isn't a gun, it's your weapon."

"Okay, I know where my gun is. And it's a hell of a lot more useful than a *weapon* that's just for show."

"Just shut up, McCurry, and get out there and do your job," said the exasperated sergeant.

McCurry sat on a rock smoking a cigarette while the German worked on an air-conditioning unit. It was early in the evening on a swing shift. Rather than keeping his eye on the Herm, McCurry was thinking how much more he would rather be hitting the night spots with Wachter than babysitting this guy.

McCurry started looking over the M-14 in his lap, trying to determine if he remembered anything about it from basic training – the last time he had seen one had been more than two years ago. In basic, he had had to take it apart and put it back together again. Now, he wasn't even sure he would know how to shoot it.

What the hell, McCurry thought, it's a nice night for fireworks. He picked up the weapon, aimed it high over the fence toward the wide expanse of the Grunewald and fired off two rounds.

The German dived under an overhang near the air-conditioning unit he was working on. Before McCurry could move, his trick sergeant came running. Damn, McCurry thought, I never realized Landry could move his fat ass that quickly.

"What the fuck's going on, McCurry?"

"I don't know, Sarge, I just thought if this German knew my gun was loaded, he wouldn't try anything funny."

"Are you fucking kidding me? Give me that thing," he said, grabbing the weapon out of McCurry's hands. "Get the fuck out of my sight."

McCurry figured Landry wouldn't do anything about it. It wouldn't look good on his record if something like this were reported. And, more than likely, McCurry wasn't qualified to carry the M-14 since so much time had lapsed since he had last fired one.

He was right. Less than three weeks later, the qualification session was set. Not a few of the guys blamed it on McCurry, so he hoped they all had their weapons on safety.

"I think I can say with some surety that I will have a higher qualification score than you, Dwight," McCurry said to Evans as they were pulling up to the range.

"Yeah, I don't doubt that. What are you going to do, fill it out as if you got an almost perfect score?"

"Almost? Fuck that. I'm getting a perfect score. I can't wait to get my expert marksman badge."

When the trick returned to the buses, Evans informed McCurry that he had qualified as an expert as well. "It didn't hurt that they let your partner do your scoring."

That's how McCurry became an expert marksman. He would learn as time went on that this wasn't far off from how treads get most of their badges. Army brass cared more about paper work than reality.

The Tread and McCurry's Hat

As the days and months wore on, McCurry's confrontations with treads in supervisory positions at the Hill increased in frequency. With the improvement in his ability to sort out significant conversations from the meaningless chatter among East German officials he was monitoring, he began to realize how important the mission on Teufelsberg was. What he couldn't tolerate was treads who worried more about meaningless regulations than the real intelligence work being done by those they supervised.

So, when a newk tread showed up on his bus, he was in no mood to be hassled. "You'd think we could take turns breaking in these assholes," he had once complained to Evans, "I get tired of having to do it myself all the time."

A few of the career guys in supervisory positions had actually requested the assignment with an Army Security Agency unit because it sounded exciting. McCurry could imagine them telling their girlfriends, or more likely their mistresses, that they were going to be "spooks." These were the ones who came in with a load of bluster and went out with a lot of whimpering after suffering the punishment McCurry and others could mete out.

Recently one of these newcomers, in his heavily starched fatigues and highly polished boots, boarded McCurry's bus for the trip to work and made the mistake of trying to assert his authority.

"Where's your hat, troop?"

McCurry pointed to the floor next to him.

"Well, put it on," he ordered.

"I don't have to wear a hat if I feel it interferes with my driving."

"You're not driving now. Put it on."

McCurry leaned over, picked up his cap up and put it on. About two minutes later, McCurry started the bus and closed the door. He threw his hat back on the floor near the feet of the sergeant who had taken a seat at the front of the bus. McCurry could practically feel the rage building in this guy. Just as they were reaching the downtown area, the tread's cork blew.

"Goddamn it, trooper, I'm not going to tell you again. Put your hat on!"

McCurry slowly pulled the bus over to the curb. When he had come to a complete stop, he turned around to face the sergeant, amused at how red his face was. "I thought I had explained that since it interferes with my driving I don't have to wear it."

"And I'm saying you're full of shit. Now put the fucking hat on!"

"Have it your way," McCurry said. He picked up his hat, put it on, opened the doors to the bus, descended the steps and started walking back toward the barracks.

"Soldier, you get your fuckin' ass back here," the tread shouted. McCurry kept walking. He knew the guy's pride would keep him from trying to chase him down and drag him back. He had seen so many of these guys tongue-tied and totally bewildered when someone ignored their orders. There weren't any guidelines about what to do in those cases since, in the units they came from, direct orders were rarely disobeyed.

McCurry walked back to the barracks and sacked out, waiting for the next move by the career team. When the guys on the shift returned from work that evening, Evans told him it was more than a half hour before an MP happened to drive by and see them parked there. And it was another hour or so before someone could be found to drive the bus up to the Hill.

"You would have loved it," Evans told McCurry. "That fuckin' tread thought he was going to have you drawn and quartered. He was even talking about having you kicked out of the military on a bad conduct discharge."

Apparently it wasn't hard to hear the dressing down the new sergeant got from the trick commander, Evans continued. Something to the effect that he should learn more about the people he was working with before giving needless orders. That these guys were different than the gators in the field the sergeant was used to working with. That he had better think hard before he caused another disruption in the sensitive operations on the Hill.

Nothing more was said of the incident. The guy never got on McCurry's bus again. Two months later his request for a transfer to another trick was approved.

Inflexible Wonders

When McCurry was walking back to the barracks following a day shift, he heard someone beeping a car's horn at him. He turned just in time to see Wachter pull up alongside him in his new Austin Healey 3000.

"Jesus Christ Horst, how did you get past the MPs at the gate?" McCurry asked.

"I just told them I was your cousin from Jersey and I wanted to surprise you."

"And they fucking believed you? They didn't ask for any identification?"

"I'm here, aren't I? When I told them you were the crazy mother fucker bus driver, they knew who you were. I said I was just transferred from Frankfurt to McNair and wanted to see you before we went out on maneuvers. So, they just waved me through."

"Unfuckin' real. And the fate of the free world rests on the shoulders of goof balls like that."

"Got any plans for tonight?" Wachter asked.

"Yeah. I told a couple of the guys I would meet them at the Grossen Apfel. You can tag along if you fucking behave."

"Hey, you're the crazy mother fucker, remember? I'm just your gator cousin from Jersey."

"Yeah, right. Give me a ride over to the barracks so I can change and then we'll head out."

The Grossen Apfel was another GI bar near the Andrews gate, although much more sedate than the Limp Dick. It was run by a former cab driver from New York, hence the name he adopted, Big Apple. It was purported to be less boisterous than other American hangouts because the owner kept a baseball bat behind the bar and didn't hesitate to use it.

As McCurry and Wachter entered the bar, Grimes signaled to them from a table near the back of the room. McCurry saw Grimes was with the usual cast of characters, Hank Andrews, Stu Mason, Dave Blake and Evans. Dylan's "Like a Rolling Stone" was playing on the juke box, which was dominated by an eclectic collection of counter-culture performers selected by the owner, Jim Jenkins. If asked, Jenkins would say that he had emigrated from the U.S. for two reasons. He was married to a German woman and he was fed up with the way violence of the hard-hat construction workers against anti-war protestors was overlooked by New York City police.

"Hey, make some room," McCurry said as he and Wachter grabbed a couple of chairs from another table. After they were seated, McCurry introduced Wachter to the other men. "He promises not to pass on any secrets you guys may be discussing."

"You know, McCurry, bullshit comments like that are going to get you in hot water one of these days," said Blake, one of the more serious members of B-trick. "You never know when some CID agent might be nearby."

The CID, or Criminal Investigation Division, was a specialized unit in the Army tasked with investigating breaches in security. While there were supposedly quite a few CID agents in Berlin, it wasn't difficult to pick them out in a crowd.

"Relax Dave. If there were a CID agent nearby, we'd know it."

"Even so, it isn't funny."

"Okay, buddy, I'll behave and so will Horst. Drink up. The next round is on me."

The six work mates and Wachter spent the next hour discussing American politics. McCurry and his friends had all joined the Army Security Agency to avoid going to Vietnam, so politics normally played a major role whenever they got together after work. This was particularly so since the recent assassination of Martin Luther King followed just two months later when Bobby Kennedy's presidential bid ended in his assassination.

"There was still a chance to turn things around, change attitudes and end this fucking war if Bobby hadn't been killed," McCurry said. "Fuck, now we've got Tricky Dick back and he could actually win this time."

"Give it a rest, Mike," said Grimes. "It is what it is back in the States. There are enough voters in the center to keep the pendulum from swinging too far to the left or to the right."

McCurry felt that Nixon used fear to rouse up a base of voters that would give him the victory in November. It was surprising to see how people could so easily be frightened about the anti-war protestors and the violence that erupted in the wake of King's assassination that they were ready to give up some of their rights to feel safe.

Overcoming his fear of being viewed suspiciously as an outsider, Wachter pointed out that Germans have long felt personal freedoms should be subjugated to long-standing but often out-dated standards.

"Germans have elevated group think over common sense and that can be frightening," Wachter said.

"I don't think that's fair," said Dave Blake. "I know a lot of Germans who don't seem to feel they can't pretty much do or say whatever they want."

McCurry knew Blake was engaged to a German girl and admired the culture. He even felt he could understand this from Blake. The 23-year-old had spent years in foster homes in Detroit at a time when the city tried to burn itself down every Mischief Night. The neighborhoods he knew were littered with broken bottles and stripped-down automobiles. He saw kids beaten up or even shot in gang wars, and crime was part of his daily life. He was fortunate when a high school counselor took an interest in him and helped him get a full scholarship to college. Not surprisingly, he got his degree in criminology.

What Blake saw in Germany impressed him. Clean streets and neighborhoods where you could walk at any time of the day or night without fear of being accosted. He didn't recognize that many of the people encountered on the streets or in pubs were people who, just a little more than two decades ago, would turn in their own mothers during the Nazi years if it would enhance their position or keep them safe. McCurry believed that culture existed before Hitler came to power and continues to exist. Both Wachter and McCurry firmly believed that even today Germans as a society felt personal freedoms should be subjugated to the will of the majority.

"Oh fuck it," said McCurry. "Let's change the subject. Who thinks the Packers will win a third Super Bowl victory this season?"

*   *   *

McCurry had no difficulty keeping the treads he worked with on the Hill in line. Generally speaking, they didn't fully understand the mission. They particularly couldn't understand the conversations linguists were monitoring. What they did understand was that the work being performed on the Hill was critical to national security. As a result, they were easily intimidated by the very people they were supposed to be supervising.

The same couldn't be said about the motor pool sergeant who issued McCurry and the other drivers their vehicles. He was a huge, crude tread who looked and smelled as if he had just crawled out of an oil pit. Always with a wad of tobacco in his mouth, he was full of bluster, his tirades only interrupted when he spat a stream of tobacco juice into puddles on the floor. McCurry decided from the start that he wasn't going to let this moron intimidate him. As a result, they often butt heads when McCurry showed up to get his bus.

Recently, McCurry tried to explain that one of the buses issued to him had loose steering he felt was unsafe. He tried to make the sergeant understand that it was so loose it seemed to take a fraction of a second before responding to his turns.

"It's been inspected and found t'be safe," the sergeant had said. "That's good 'nough for me."

"That inspection was months ago. I'm telling you that now, today, it's not safe to drive and I want ya to check it out."

"Fuck you McCurry. That's the bus I'm givin' you and it's the bus you'll drive."

"Okay, Sarge. Have it your way."

The Mercedes buses used by the military were powered by low-compression diesel engines. When McCurry took his driving test, the instructor told him the motors couldn't withstand high RPMs and shouldn't be downshifted until they were within the proper range for that gear. McCurry remembered that advice as he approached 80 kph on the Autobahn. Without a second thought, he put the transmission in first gear and popped the clutch. The bus skidded and screeched along the road until he could get it under control and pull over on the shoulder. When he got out, he looked back to see a trail of oil and little pieces of metal. Afterward he explained that he didn't really know what happened. "Seemed like the motor seized up and then died," he told the motor pool sergeant. He later learned from one of the guys who worked in the motor pool that when he got ready to pull the engine, he discovered the steering box was so loose it was ready to fall off.

*   *   *

When McCurry showed up at the motor pool to pick up his bus following the demise of the Mercedes, the motor pool sergeant had smug grin on his face. "There's your new ride, McCurry," he said, pointing to a big, boxy Chevrolet bus, apparently the only one of its kind in the motor pool.

"What the fuck is that?" McCurry asked.

"Well, since you seem to have difficulty with diesel engines, I thought you'd be more at home with a good ole internal combustion gasoline engine. Unfortunately, this is the only one I got."

"All right, I'll bite, what's unfortunate about it?"

"Well, ya see, you know how the Army insists that all their vehicles come equipped with manual transmissions? Well some fool ordered this bus with an automatic transmission. When it came into Frankfurt, someone said we can't have that. So they yanked the automatic and jury-rigged a manual. Once they'd finished their handiwork, they discovered very few people could actually drive it. Some bastard then shipped it on to us."

"So why would it be so difficult to drive?" McCurry asked.

"Well, let's take a look and see," the sergeant said, spitting tobacco juice on the pavement while opening the door on the bus. "Oh my, would ya look at that. The gear shift is practically behind the driver's seat. When I saw this, I said to myself, 'A smartass like McCurry shouldn't have any problem handling this.' I's right, wasn't I?"

"Fuck you. Just give me the keys."

When the sergeant walked away, McCurry looked the gear shift over to determine where reverse was and then the three forward speeds. He started it up and, with his right hand, reached behind his back and was able to get it in reverse with his first try. After backing it out of its spot, he managed to find first and then slowly started to head for the exit to the motor pool. Before he got there, the sergeant came lumbering up.

"By the way, I forgot to tell you. This is basically your own personal ride now. It'll be assigned to you for every shift."

"Well guess what, you numb nut, you'd better hope there are others who can drive it down from the Hill or you could be seen as interfering with very sensitive, top-secret operations."

With that, McCurry popped the clutch and bounced his way out of the motor pool with as much dignity as he could muster, trying to find the gears behind his back without running the bus off the road.

He drove the bus around the barracks a couple times to build his confidence in behind-the-back shifting. He even took a break behind the barracks to smoke a bowl of hash to mellow out and then pulled back out front to load up.

"What the fuck is this piece of shit?" Evans asked as he boarded and took a seat right behind McCurry.

"It's your basic bus, green, fucked up beyond belief by Army ingenuity," McCurry said, really beginning to feel the effects of that last bowl. "And it's all mine. At least until I hand it off to some other poor, unsuspecting sucker when we reach the Hill."

"You can actually shift this?" Evans asked while playing with the floor-mounted stick shift. "Seems to have an awful lot of play in it."

"Well, we'll see," McCurry said, feeling more mellow by the minute.

When the bus was full, McCurry pulled the lever to close the door and began to ease away from the barracks. He felt he was doing okay as they maneuvered through the city portion of the trip, although at one point he almost panicked when Evans had pulled the gear lever back a little beyond his reach.

"Cute, Dwight, cute," was all he could say when Evans pushed it back into his open hand.

By the time they reached the autobahn, McCurry's confidence was back and he wound it up to almost a 100 kph. When he reached the exit, however, he couldn't gear down quickly enough to slow the bus sufficiently. He realized too late he was taking the curve too fast and actually thought he felt the bus tip slightly when he heard what sounded like a loud explosion. The bus started to skid out of control, but he managed to hold on to it and maneuver it to the side of the road. When he got out to inspect what had gone wrong, he discovered that he had actually rolled both left rear tires completely off their rims.

McCurry looked from the mangled rims to Evans, who was at least as high on hash as he was. All they could do was look at each other and laugh.

They had to hang around there until one of the other trick buses got to the Hill and someone could call the motor pool to send out another bus for them to use. In the end, they were over an hour late arriving for their shift. It would be a long time before McCurry saw or heard anything about what they fondly referred to as the green beast again.

A Trip to the Dark Side

I t was a warm, early summer morning. With a full day ahead of him and nothing to do, McCurry decided to head up to the Ku'damm and visit Wachter at his kiosk. He got off the bus at the Kaiser Wilhelm Memorial Church and walked the block and a half to the kiosk. He was surprised to find the normally jovial Wachter in a foul mood. Sitting on a chair inside the small, wooden structure, Wachter was in the process of sorting out older magazines to return to the distributor. "Give me a second," he said in response to McCurry's greeting, and went on counting the magazines in his lap. When finished, he slammed the stack into a box next to his chair and wrote a number on another box that had been set on end under the kiosk's counter.

"What's got you in such a surly mood?" McCurry asked.

"Aw, mother fucking, piece of shit wall!" Wachter exclaimed, tears welling up in his eyes.

"Hey, man, what the fuck's going on?"

"Today's my mother's birthday. I've been sending her stuff, but I haven't heard from her in several weeks."

"Oh man, that's rough. Didn't you say Monica's gone over there a few times? Couldn't she go over and see what's up?"

Wachter's wife, Monica, was a native of West Berlin. When the wall first went up, no residents of West Berlin were permitted to visit the East. Little by little, those restrictions were loosened so that now it wasn't too difficult for West Berliner's to obtain a visa to visit the Soviet sector of the city.

"The last time she went, she was really hassled. She had to say where she was going at the check point. They must have realized the family she was visiting was related to 'an enemy of the state.' They take that stuff seriously. She's just scared of going over again."

"Well fuck, man, why don't I go over for you?"

"Are you out of your fucking mind? You're not allowed to go over there."

"The Army Security Agency says I'm not allowed because of my security clearance. But shit, man, my identity card doesn't say I have a clearance and I *know* they don't have a list of personnel with clearances at Checkpoint Charlie. I'd just be a normal GI tourist checking out what's on the other side of the wall."

"Aren't you afraid of getting caught?"

"How? Only you and I will know, and I'm sure as hell not going to tell anyone."

"Oh man, that would be great!"

Travelers to East Berlin had to go through Checkpoint Charlie. The other checkpoint in Berlin was for those crossing the border between West Berlin and East Germany. While Monica was processed by East German officials when she crossed, American military personnel going into East Berlin are checked on the West side by military police. Neither the West German nor the East German authorities has permission to check members of the American Armed Forces.

"If you've got a gift or something for your mother," McCurry said, "I could take it over with me."

The two decided that Wachter would pick McCurry up the next morning at ten and take him to the Checkpoint Charlie crossing. Wachter's family lived on John-Schehr-Strasse in the Prenzlauer Berg section, a trip of a little more than five miles from the checkpoint.

"I'll just be a typical tourist and ask how to get there when I'm on the other side," McCurry said. "A dumb GI who doesn't speak

German." He said he would try to get back to the checkpoint by five.

*   *   *

Wachter picked up McCurry outside the gates to Andrews right at ten the next morning. Arriving on time was very unusual for Wachter, so McCurry got a quick indication of how important this was to his German friend. It was a little more than ten miles to Checkpoint Charlie, so they had some time to talk on the way.

"In the bag in the back, I have a box of chocolates for my mother and several pairs of jeans for my sisters and brother. Do you think you'll have any problem with the MPs over this?"

"Nah. I'll just tell them I met a girl on my last visit over there and wanted to impress her. They'll get it."

After they found a parking spot, they walked up to the guardhouse together.

"Well, guy, good luck," Wachter said, reaching out to shake McCurry's hand.

"Don't worry, Horst. It's not like you. Just be sure you're here to pick me up at five."

When McCurry, entered the guard shack, the MP asked to see his ID card and asked where he was going. Handing the card over to the guard, McCurry said he had met a girl on his last trip and was going back to see her.

"What's in the bag?" the guard asked. "I'm hoping when I give her these, she'll take the stuff she has on off, you know what I mean."

"Yeah, yeah Casanova. Okay, get the hell out of here."

McCurry realized he was shaking as he traversed the walk through the fenced-in area over to the Soviet sector. He had to stop on the East German side to exchange twenty-five dollars for East German currency. As he proceeded to the exit, the Volkspolizei eyed him warily, but when he flashed his Armed Forces ID card, they waved him through.

As McCurry emerged onto the street, he felt as if he had traveled back in time. Instead of Hitler's feared GeheimeStaatspolizei, or Gestapo, there was a proliferation of Volkspolizei, all armed with rifles slung over their shoulders. With their high boots, dour demeanor and absolute power over the people they were supposed to protect, the Volkspolitizei were no less fearful than the Gestapo two decades earlier. McCurry figured they were stationed here to keep an eye out for anyone looking suspicious after exiting the checkpoint. They certainly didn't look approachable, so he decided to stroll on, looking for a civilian who might be able to help with directions.

Dismal wasn't a strong enough adjective to describe this world he encountered. A grayness seemed to pervade everything, from the uniforms of the Volkspolizei to the combat vehicles stationed along the streets, even to the buildings themselves. McCurry felt the gray environment on the ground literally sucked the color out of the sky. I don't know if I could last a day here, he thought.

He continued to walk up the eastern portion of Fredrichstrasse, surprised that he didn't see any civilians. The street seemed deserted. As he got farther away from the checkpoint, however, he did see lights on in some of the apartments. Unlike West Berlin, however, there was no bustling traffic, no street-corner kiosks, and the few storefront businesses that did exist, appeared closed up tight. He couldn't remember the last time he felt so alone.

McCurry had a pretty good idea of the route to take to get to the Wachter family home. If he had to, he could walk the five miles. He continued up Fredrichstrasse and finally came across a small food market that was open with customers inside.

He entered the store and realized how much he stood out when the three customers turned from the counter to stare at him.

"Does anyone speak English?" he asked.

"I speak a little," said a young woman.

"Oh good. I am trying to get to John-Schehr-Strasse 22. Is there a bus I can catch?"

"Come. I show you, okay?"

She picked up her small satchel of groceries and headed outside with McCurry following.

After leaving the store, she turned right, walked a few paces and then stopped. "Go that way," she said, pointing down the street. "On Leipzigerstrasse, wait for bus. It will take you to John-Schehr-Strasse."

"Danke schoen," McCurry said.

"Bitte," she answered. She turned and immediately headed in the opposite direction.

As he continued on, the street was still nearly deserted. When he got closer to Leipzigerstrasse, however, he began to see signs of life. A couple of women walking toward him moved to the right to allow him to pass by. He smiled and said "Guten morgen," but they kept their eyes down and continued walking without a reply. After turning on to Leipzigerstrasse, he finally saw some older cars parked along the road, but was unsettled to see that the only vehicular traffic was a couple of armored personnel carriers. The people he approached on the sidewalk moved slightly to allow him by, but their eyes remained focused on the pavement in front of them.

When he got closer to the bus stop, he saw three Soviet soldiers standing next to one of the shops, talking and smoking cigarettes, their weapons leaned casually against the wall. One of them caught McCurry's eye and said, "Hey GI, you got cigaretten in that bag?"

"No, just some gifts for my girlfriend," McCurry said, edging toward the street to stay as far away from them as possible.

"Let me see," another one said, sticking his leg out to keep McCurry from passing.

"Listen, I am an American Soldier," McCurry said, pulling out his identification card and flashing it at them. "Now move your leg and let me by."

McCurry was surprised by his own vehemence and even more so when the Soviet trooper pulled his leg away and backed off. It reminded him of the behavior of sergeants on his shift when he or others stood up to their bluster. I guess treads are no different in the Soviet army than they are in ours, McCurry thought. Nevertheless, the confrontation had shaken him and he quickened his pace to get to what he hoped would be the safety of the bus stop.

When he arrived at the stop, he was relieved to see there was a small bench where he could sit and await the arrival of the next bus. He was still shaking a little over his confrontation with the Soviet soldier and hoped the rest would help settle his nerves. He was also fighting paranoia over what he felt were the stares of people who passed by. Get a grip McCurry, he told himself. They're just people going about their business and maybe a little curious over the obvious stranger in their midst.

After about a quarter of an hour, another man joined McCurry on the bench. Dressed in what appeared to be bib overalls and a light flannel, long-sleeved shirt, the man smiled at McCurry as he sat down and put a satchel he was carrying on the ground between his feet. McCurry assumed the satchel contained the man's lunch and he was on his way to work.

"Excuse me, but do you speak any English," McCurry said to the man after he was settled.

"A little," he replied.

"Do you by any chance know when the next bus will be arriving?"

The man looked at McCurry, and then rocked back on the bench laughing. "This is East Berlin, my friend. Buses come when they come. No schedule. You sit, you wait. If lucky, you wait thirty minutes, maybe less. If bus on this route breaks down, who knows how long." He reached into his satchel, pulled out a bottle of beer. Wedging the top of the bottle against the wooden bench seat, he smacked down on it with the palm of his hand. The top flew into the air and landed in McCurry's lap.

"Here, drink," he said. "It make wait seem less long."

"Danke," McCurry said, taking a long swig of the warm beer and then handing it back. "My name's McCurry, Mike McCurry," he added, feeling a little safer in the company of this friendly stranger.

"Schmidt, Gunther," the man said, extending his hand. Shaking it, McCurry said, "It's nice to meet a friendly person who speaks English. So far, it seems as if everyone moves to the other side of the walk when they see me coming."

"Don't blame them," Schmidt said. "East Berlin not a friendly place. Always, the Stasi, they be someplace around. Better, be quiet. Keep to yourself."

The Stasi were the secret police in charge of state security. McCurry knew from his indoctrination that it was common practice for them to imprison people just for telling a political joke. It was also rumored that many dissidents were executed in Stasi prisons.

McCurry learned that Schmidt worked in a textile factory in Weissensee, a sector in northeast East Berlin. Although his place of work was less than 20 minutes away, he left each day at least an hour early because of the unpredictability of the buses. Which is why he brought along his satchel with an ample supply of beer, cheese and bread. Schmidt said that getting paid was about as unpredictable as the buses he used to get to work.

"But I make enough to keep bread on table for my wife and me," he said. He leaned in close to McCurry and said, "Truth, we just get by, wait for that wall to come down. It not long, no?"

McCurry just shrugged his shoulders, knowing Berliners, both East and West, pinned many of their hopes and dreams on the day when the wall would be dismantled. He felt that day probably wouldn't come in his or Schmidt's lifetime.

By the time McCurry and Schmidt were finishing their second beer, an ancient bus spewing a trail of black smoke pulled up to the stop, Schmidt and McCurry got on. McCurry looked at the driver and said, "John-Schehr-Strasse" to let him know where he was going. The driver just said, "Zwei Mark." After paying the driver two East German marks, McCurry followed Schmidt to the back of the bus.

About ten minutes later, Schmidt got up, grabbed his satchel and turned to shake hands with McCurry again. "Next stop mine," he said. "Hope your trip here is good." Turning, he walked to the front of the bus. It was then that McCurry realized Schmidt had never asked what he was doing or where he was going in East Berlin.

* * *

When the bus started moving again, McCurry looked up and saw a strange character sitting a couple rows up and across from him. He was dressed in a long, black coat, which seemed to McCurry a bit much for the mild weather. His face was shielded by the brim of a large black hat and, as he crossed his legs, McCurry got a glance of tall, black leather boots. His outfit probably cost more than most East Berliners made in a week, McCurry thought.

McCurry hadn't seen this stranger board the bus and was starting to feel paranoid again. When this trip is over, Wachter is going to owe me one big night on the town, he mumbled to himself. He got up and moved to the front of the bus where he could exit quickly when it got to his stop. If that guy gets up and moves up too, I'll freak, he thought.

Another ten minutes went by before the bus pulled up to the curb and stopped. The driver turned, looked at McCurry and said, "John-Schehr-Strasse."

After exiting the bus, McCurry went right on John-Schehr-Strasse in search of 22. After passing several homes without numbers, two of which still showed damage from the World War II bombing raids, he found a home with the number 138. When he came across 126, he realized the numbers were going down, so he knew he was going in the right direction. He had the odd sensation he was being followed, but was sure he hadn't seen the man in black exit the bus behind him. At the end of the block there was a traffic signal. Before crossing, McCurry knelt on one knee and started fiddling with the string on one of his shoes. As he did so, he looked back and immediately caught a glimpse of the man in black, who had stopped and appeared to be studying buildings on the opposite side of the street.

McCurry got up and, rather than head on down John-Schehr-Strasse to 22, he turned left, waited for the light to change to green, then crossed over and headed up Werner-Kube-Strasse. After about a hundred yards, he came to an alley on his left and darted into it, stopped short and stood with his back against the wall. His fear had turned to rage and he was ready for a confrontation.

Sure enough, the man in black came darting around the corner, obviously afraid of losing his quarry. McCurry grabbed him by the lapels of his black leather coat and slammed him against the brick building on the opposite side of the alley.

"What the fuck is your problem, asshole," McCurry shouted after letting go of the man's coat and stepping back a pace.

As he straightened out his trench coat and flexed his back to recover from the shock of the confrontation, he said nothing. Standing close to him, McCurry recognized that for the first time in his life he was staring at a being who was truly evil.

"Okay mother fucker. I asked you a question."

Apparently recovered, the man sneered at McCurry and said in perfect English, "If there is any questioning to do here, it is I who will be questioning you. What is your business here in East Berlin."

Taken aback but still in a state of rage, McCurry slowly moved toward the man, who backed up against the wall again. When the two were nose to nose, McCurry said, "You fucking little cowardly prick. I know who you are and I know your kind. You may be able to throw your weight around and lord it over East Berlin citizens, but you have no authority over me. None, mother-fucker. I'm an American soldier and can come and go as I please."

Crowding him even closer and finally recognizing fear in the man's eyes, McCurry said, "Now get the fuck out of here and head back the way you came. If I see you one more time during my visit, I'll be back another day with friends. We will hunt you down and when we are done with you, you won't be able to bully anyone again. Got it?"

McCurry grabbed him by the lapels once more and threw him out of the alley. The man in black went flying back up Werner-Kube-Strasse, turned right on John-Schehr-Strasse and was out of sight.

McCurry picked up his package and strolled back to John-Schehr-Strasse. As he was crossing back over the intersection, he thought he could just catch sight of the man in black, his ridiculous black trench coat flying back behind him like Batman's cape.

* * *

As he turned to walk the next half block to the Wachter home, McCurry realized he was shaking all over. The confrontation over, the adrenaline in his system waned. McCurry sat down on a curb to collect himself. Mother fucker, where did *that* come from? He asked himself. Maybe I'm not as much of a pacifist as I thought.

McCurry recognized in that moment that he had never really felt threatened before. Schmidt's warning about the Stasi lurking around every corner made him think about how vulnerable he was. When he realized he was being followed, his initial fear turned to rage. He wondered now whether he had only succeeded in putting a target on his back.

Oh well, he thought, all I can do now is get this visit over and then get the hell back to the western sector.

A car driving slowly by was all the encouragement McCurry needed to get up and moving. He grabbed his package and began walking, hoping he hadn't drawn too much attention to himself.

* * *

McCurry couldn't miss the resemblance between Wachter and the middle-aged woman who answered his knock on the door. "Frau Wachter?" he asked. He knew now he was in a safe haven and could use German for the remainder of his visit.

When he introduced himself and said Horst was a close friend, tears came to her eyes, but she recovered quickly and asked him to please come in. He couldn't help but notice how she looked all around outside before closing the front door. She got him settled and insisted he allow her to put on some coffee, which McCurry knew was a commodity in very short supply in East Berlin. He would have liked to decline, but understood it could be taken as an insult.

As McCurry listened to her moving around in the kitchen, he looked around the sitting room. It was spare but almost clinically clean. Wachter had told him that his mother took care of the home while his brother and two sisters worked to support the family. East Berlin's chronic shortages of the basic necessities of life limited the amount of entertaining families did for friends and neighbors. He felt Wachter's mother was as excited about having someone visit as she was anxious to learn how her son was doing.

On the tray she brought in were two cups of coffee, a small container of milk, a small bowl of sugar, and a platter with several Apfelstrudel and Topfenstrudel. As McCurry started to drink his coffee, she immediately asked about the health of her son, saying she had been worried because she hadn't heard from him in some time.

McCurry explained that Horst was doing fine and that the reason he had made this trip today was that Wachter was concerned about her health.

"He sent you a number of letters and hadn't had a response. He was frightened and upset, especially yesterday on your birthday."

"Ach so, I should have known. Those verdammte Stasi. Ever since Horst fled to the west, they have made life difficult for his brother, sisters and me. I told Monica on her last visit, but asked her not to tell Horst too much because I didn't want him to worry. They must be confiscating his letters. I think they enjoy finding ways to harass us."

"I am so sorry," McCurry said. "I think I got a taste the treatment the Stasi accords visitors today."

"Oh no. What happened?"

"Just some evil-looking guy in a long trench coat was following me. But don't worry, he didn't follow me all the way here. I managed to convince him he had better, perhaps safer, things to do elsewhere."

"Mein Gott! They are relentless."

McCurry spent the next half hour telling Frau Wachter about Horst's business, how well he and Monica were doing, and about how he had become close friends with her son. He was enjoying the strudel she had brought out and listening to her tales about Horst as a young boy when all of a sudden he remembered the gifts he had brought.

Putting the plate with his second helping of Apfelstrudel down, McCurry pulled the bag out from where he had placed it next to his chair.

"I almost forgot. Horst sent some gifts for everyone." He pulled out a half dozen pairs of jeans and put them on the couch. "These are for Manfred, Magda and Brigitta. And this," he said as he lifted out the large box of chocolates, "is for you for your birthday."

He realized it was starting to get late and he had to be back by five to meet Wachter. "Frau Wachter, I really wish I could wait around to meet Manfred, Magda and Brigitta, but I told Horst I would meet him at Checkpoint Charley at five. He will be anxious to hear that you are doing well."

She told him that she had just finished writing a letter to Horst and asked if he would mind taking it with him. While carrying a letter to a person accused of sedition and crimes against the state could cause him real problems if he were caught, McCurry knew he couldn't say no. He explained that because of where he worked, he wouldn't be able to come back again, but said he was sure he and Horst could find someone else to visit later.

Thanking her for her hospitality, he stuffed the letter she gave him inside his shirt, said his goodbyes and left.

After leaving the Wachter home, McCurry decided to walk back to Checkpoint Charlie. He didn't like the idea of being trapped within the confines of a bus with the letter he had hidden under his shirt. He also felt with the uncertainties of the bus schedule, it probably wouldn't take any longer.

This far from the Wall, life seemed almost normal. It had turned into a warm, sunny day and a number of people were out for a walk or running errands. Here, if he said "Guten Tag" to passersby, his greeting was acknowledged. Even so, the demeanor of most remained taciturn.

After a few blocks, McCurry started keeping an eye out for his Stasi friend. It wasn't difficult to pick out the Soviet troops who were often gathered at street corners, smoking and talking among themselves. Their cocky attitude indicated they still held the German people in contempt. They didn't give McCurry a second glance as he passed by. I'm not as interesting without a bag that might contain American cigarettes, McCurry thought.

As he got closer to the wall, the hated Volkspolizei began to outnumber the strollers. Once again, passersby kept their eyes focused on the ground and gave him a wide berth. After his skirmish with the Stasi thug, he was better able to understand their fear.

He couldn't be sure, but had the distinct feeling that he was being followed once more. This may be why people are avoiding me, he thought. Quickening his pace, he scanned every alley he passed. He stopped to tie his shoe, looking around as he did. He couldn't make out any obvious tail, but still had the feeling he was under close scrutiny.

Continuing along the last few blocks before Checkpoint Charlie, his imagination started to kick into high gear. What if some Volkspolizei decided, fuck, I'm going to have some fun with this arrogant American, Armed Forces I.D. card be damned. I couldn't do anything about it, McCurry realized. If they had him strip-searched and found the letter, he could disappear into a Stasi prison.

Before he tumbled into a total panic, Checkpoint Charlie came into view. He was sweating profusely and feeling slightly ill as he flashed his I.D. card at the Volkspolizei and entered the wire-enclosed passageway across no-man's land to the safety of the American checkpoint.

*   *   *

It was about five fifteen when McCurry exited Checkpoint Charlie. He immediately saw Wachter sitting across the street in his Austin Healey. He resisted what he knew to be an irrational urge to run too quickly to put distance between the checkpoint and himself. Instead he walked at what he felt was a casual pace until he reached the car. He jumped in and said, "Get me to a bar quick. I need something to drink."

"Jesus Christ, what's the matter? You're as white as a ghost. Did something go wrong?"

"Everything's fine," McCurry said. "Just get the hell out of here. I'll tell you all about it when we get to the pub."

* * *

During the drive to the pub near Wachter's kiosk, McCurry worked to get his breathing under control. He rolled the window down and lit up a cigarette. Soon his trembling started to dissipate and he was feeling nearly normal as they pulled up in front of the pub.

As they were walking in, McCurry pulled the letter out from under his shirt. "I'll get a couple of beers and give you time to read the letter," he said. When he got to the table with the beers, he saw that tears were running down his German friend's cheeks.

"God, I miss them," Wachter said, folding the letter back up and putting it in the envelope.

"Yeah, I know what you mean," McCurry said. "But they are all fine and miss you as well. I didn't have time to wait around for your brother and sisters to get home from work, but your mother said they will love the jeans. And, of course, she was thrilled with the box of chocolates."

"I wonder why they haven't been getting my letters," Wachter mused.

"Who knows," McCurry replied, not wanting to alarm him over his mother's speculation. "Nothing gets done right over there. They might just have gotten lost in the system."

"Yeah, I suppose," Wachter said, finally starting to work on his beer. "So, how was it? Why did you look so shook up when you got out of the checkpoint?"

McCurry told him about his confrontation with the man in black and the threat he had made, even though he knew the guy probably worked for the Stasi.

"I know it was a dumb thing to do, but the guy was so arrogant it really pissed me off."

"Obviously," Wachter said, finishing off his beer. "My turn to buy. I'll be right back."

When he returned with the beers, McCurry continued his story, telling him about his visit with Wachter's mother and how pleased she was that he was doing so well.

"I decided to walk back. Public transportation over there isn't very reliable and it was a beautiful day. As I got nearer to the Wall, I got the feeling I was being watched. Then I let my imagination get the better of me, wondering what would happen if that guy I roughed up got some of his buddies and decided to pull me in for questioning. I know that is far-fetched, but that place is really scary."

"Well, I owe you big time, buddy."

"That's okay, Horst. But I can't go over again. Rational or not, I feel like I am a marked man over there. If you don't get some letters soon, I have a couple of friends without security clearances who visit there pretty regularly, although I can't imagine why. At any rate, I might be able to get them to carry messages to your family."

"Well, we'll see. Now, drink up. It was a great mission and I owe you a great meal."

The Great Burn Shack Incident

When McCurry arrived on the Hill to begin his midnight shift, he was in no mood to deal with any more treads. That afternoon, he had pulled into the Andrews parking lot to visit the PX for some personal items he needed. It was a beautiful day. McCurry, in a good mood, thought he might take a stroll through the neighborhood surrounding the Andrews compound after his visit to the PX. He missed the long walks he had often taken before recently purchasing his Volkswagen microbus with the brightly colored flowers he had added to cover the rust spots.

As he was about to head over to the PX, he noticed a second lieutenant from the military police approaching him. Uh oh, he thought, this doesn't look good.

"What's your name, soldier?" the lieutenant asked.

"Mike McCurry," McCurry responded.

"Mike McCurry, sir," the military policeman barked.

"Mike McCurry, sir," McCurry said, thinking, Okay, I'll play your game.

"Is that your vehicle?" he asked, pointing at the VW.

"Yes sir."

"What the fuck is wrong with you? Don't you have any respect for the military, driving something like that?"

"I'm trying to get by on an enlisted man's salary, sir. What kind of car would you expect me to have?" McCurry responded.

"I'm not talking about what kind of vehicle it is, moron. I'm talking about those flowers painted all over it. It's an affront to the military."

"Flowers. An affront to the military?"

"Fucking A. Nothing but some goddamned hippie would do something like that to their automobile and we don't need no hippies in the Army. If you were in my unit, I'd have you busted for something like that."

"Well, sir, I guess it's a good thing I'm not in your unit."

"What unit are you in, soldier? I think I need to speak with your commander."

"I'm not permitted to say what unit I'm in," McCurry said. "All I can tell you is my name and rank."

"Are you trying to piss me off? You realize, if I want, I can arrest you right now for being out of uniform."

"How am I out of uniform?" McCurry asked.

"You don't have any unit patch, for one thing."

"Now, sir, I know the Army can get a little twisted in its reasoning sometimes. But, if I'm not permitted to say what unit I'm in, why in the world would I be permitted to wear a patch that identified that unit?"

McCurry could feel that the lieutenant was beginning to realize he should never have initiated this confrontation. Although sometimes it seemed too easy, he enjoyed tying these treads up in knots. Often they couldn't even remember what had started the encounter. It wasn't difficult to undermine their self-confidence by raising the specter of stepping on the wrong toes. McCurry decided that this skirmish had already lasted too long.

"Sir, if you will just write down your name, rank and how you can be reached, I will be happy to have my commanding officer contact you," McCurry said.

"That won't be necessary soldier. Carry on then." The lieutenant turned and beat a quick retreat.

Now, with eight slow hours on the midnight shift ahead of him, McCurry pulled off his boots, pulled his headset down around his neck, propped his stockinged feet up on the console and laid back with his hands clasped behind his head.

McCurry hoped the treads he worked with here on the Hill would have the sense to leave him alone. He was pretty sure that those who had been around long enough knew the dangers of starting a battle with him. He was having enough problems with the Germans he had to deal with in businesses he and Wachter operated. During the development of their friendship, the pair discovered they had a lot in common. Both were apolitical, though they were vehemently opposed to war for any reason. Both snubbed their noses at senseless regulations, whether they were part of the American military or the German's dedication to dogma. Wachter had been repulsed by the rigidity of his countrymen in the East and surprised to find them no less committed to authority in the West.

"I'll tell you, Horst, I think these guys need instructions on how to take a leak," McCurry remarked during one of their many nights on the town.

"Tell me about it. You wouldn't believe all the complaints I get when you visit my flat and park your car on the wrong side of the street. 'What kind of people do you associate with?' they ask."

McCurry knew the East German refugee hoped one day to emigrate to America. Wachter felt the more Americanized he became the better his chances would be. McCurry was often amazed at the grasp Wachter had on the language, including idioms and slang. He knew Military Intelligence often kept ASA personnel under surveillance and wondered what they thought of his friendship with Wachter.

"That's why I make it a rule to park there. I love to see them give you a hard time. Notice how they never say anything to me? They can't stand it when I act as if I can't understand German."

The two of them had developed a number of acts they employed when out drinking. One was to pretend they didn't understand German so they could frustrate the help at the mostly German establishments they frequented. They both got a kick out of listening to the disparaging remarks made by those who assumed the pair couldn't understand the language. Another was to tell any barmaid that approached one of them for a drink that the other had the money and she would have to convince him to cough it up. They knew the "buy me a drink" approach in some of the raunchier places they visited was usually a scam. If the charge a patron paid for a beer was, say, 2 marks 50, he might feel the cost of a drink for one of the girls who approached him was a small price to pay for the company. Later, when he received his bill, he would discover that the charge for the mixed drinks for the barmaid was 50 marks or more. Usually there were huge bouncers around to make sure a disgruntled drinker paid his bill in full.

Wachter and McCurry figured they would rather be the hustlers than the hustlees. One evening one of the girls came over and sat on McCurry's lap. She promised to stay there and keep him company if he would buy her a drink. He told her his friend, Horst, who was on the other side of the table, had all the money. When she turned to face Wachter and negotiate with him for a drink, she was straddling McCurry with her rear to him. While talking to Wachter, she reached her hand behind her, unzipped McCurry's pants and reached her hand inside. Once she had him erect and was stroking him, she squeezed tight and told him he should *really* convince his friend to buy her a drink. The cajoling and squeezing went on for a few minutes more before, without warning, she stood up and walked away. She apparently realized that her mission with Wachter and McCurry would be fruitless.

"All you had to do was keep her going for another half minute," McCurry said while trying to get his zipper up.

"I did my best, buddy. You just need to exercise a little *less* self-control."

*   *   *

McCurry was dead tired and nearly nodding off when Donny Myers, a new sergeant on the Hill, began to give him a hard time.

"I've about had it with you, McCurry. Ya look like a slob. Your boots are a disgrace and ya oughta fuckin' know better than to put your feet up on the console, not to mention keeping your fuckin' boots *on* your feet."

"Hey Sarge, give me a break. I can concentrate better with my boots off."

"I'll give ya something to concentrate on. Get your boots on and come with me. You're on burn detail for the rest of this shift."

"You've got the wrong guy for this, Sarge. Since you're new, you probably don't know that I'm a bus driver and exempt from burn details."

The newk tread turned on McCurry with a vengeance. "You listen to me, you smart-mouthed motherfucker. I'm your fuckin' superior and if I fuckin' say you're on burn detail, ya'd better fuckin' believe that you're on fuckin' burn detail. Now get your fuckin' boots on and follow me."

Treads have such a limited vocabulary, McCurry thought.

"Have it your way, Sarge," McCurry said calmly as he started to put on his boots.

McCurry relieved the burn-shack guard and started loading up the burner with the bags of shredded material. The prick tread didn't even give me someone to help out, he thought.

The burn shack was located within the gated area of the compound but set a ways off from the main buildings. Each night, at the end of the four o'clock to midnight swing shift, a detail carried the day's accumulated bags of discarded documents to the shack. The bags were piled just inside the building. One person was left to guard them as they were being brought out until the burn detail, selected from the midnight to eight o'clock shift, relieved him. Since the hut couldn't be left untended until all the material was burned, the detail usually consisted of two people so each could take a break from time to time. The fact that McCurry was alone wasn't the worst of it. The burner, as with most military devices, didn't function properly. A blower, which helped incinerate the material more quickly and completely, hadn't worked for some time. This meant fewer bags could be put in at a time and it took longer for them to burn. Additionally, the door to the incinerator had to be left open a little to allow air in. This created a potential fire hazard that also needed to be closely guarded.

Fuck this shit, McCurry thought, stuffing the burner with as many bags as he could get in. He ignited them and, leaving the door open, went outside for a smoke. It didn't take long for sparks to ignite the other bags in the room, which in turn ignited the wooden structure. The main buildings in the compound were windowless, so some time passed before the MP guarding the main gate saw the flames. He wasn't permitted in the compound, so he called in to sound the fire alert. By the time the trick commander, Lt. Vincent, and Sgt. Myers got out to investigate, the shack was nearly burned to the ground. Ashes and partially burned material were floating in the breeze creating a scene not unlike early-winter snow flurries. McCurry was sitting nearby smoking a cigarette.

"What the fuck? Get off your ass, McCurry."

"Take it easy, Sergeant," Vincent, said. "Let's just find out what happened."

Junior officers were somewhat like the specialists on the Hill. Most were products of ROTC in college and just biding their time until they could get out.

McCurry had been offered Officer Candidate School while in Monterey. He was taken aback by the absurdity of the offer. He had joined the Army Security Agency as a way to avoid serving in Vietnam. Once he was safely on his way to Germany, why would he want to go to OCS, which was nothing but a factory to maintain the supply of officers for Vietnam. A second lieutenant fresh out of OCS on his first trip to the bush had a life expectancy of about twenty minutes. McCurry didn't like the odds. Those who accepted the offer were seen as treads at heart.

"All right, McCurry, what happened?" Vincent asked as Myers slowly boiled next to him.

"The shack burned down," McCurry replied nonchalantly.

"No shit. How did it happen?"

"I don't know. The damn burner didn't work for shit. At least I didn't know how to make it work. Maybe some bags caught fire and I didn't notice them. It started up while I was taking a smoke break."

"Well, when you saw it was on fire, why didn't you come and get help?"

"Because I was alone. I'm not supposed to leave the site untended."

"All right, get back inside. There's nothing we can do now. We'll talk about what we're going to do later."

While there was nothing that could be done about the burn shack, Vincent realized something had to be done about the partially burned top-secret and secret documents that had blown all over the site and the hill around it. The hard-nosed Myers got a new lesson in discipline after spending the rest of the night with a half dozen non-essential personnel scouring the area with flashlights, collecting all the shreds of paper.

The company commander called McCurry into his office the next day and informed him he would be issued an Article 15. McCurry informed him that he would exercise his right to request a general court martial.

"You know, McCurry, you're on really thin ice this time," Capt. Hanover lectured him. "For Christ's sake, man, you burned down the fuckin' burn shack. Do you really want to request a general court martial? This time your request might be granted."

"I'll just have to take my chances, Captain."

Two days later, Hanover called McCurry to his office once again to inform him that it had been decided that the incident was the result of an accident and didn't merit punishment. "But just keep it up," Hanover warned, "and you might not be as lucky next time."

The Entrepreneurs

McCurry and Wachter sat on a couple boxes in the kiosk going over the week's earnings. After they had known one another for a few months, McCurry wondered how difficult it would be for Wachter to develop a trade in liquor out of the kiosk. Using his Class VI card, which entitled McCurry to deep discounts on a wide variety of alcoholic beverages at the Post Exchange, and the cards of a number of friends, McCurry felt he could develop a steady supply for resale at the kiosk at greatly inflated prices. It turned out it wasn't difficult at all. Soon they were making a couple hundred dollars a week off the booze sales. At first, Wachter wanted the split to be sixty-forty since they used his kiosk for the sales and the clientele were people Wachter knew could be trusted. McCurry argued, however, that he was taking a larger risk since reselling the alcohol to German nationals was a violation of the Military Code of Justice. So, they decided on a straight fifty-fifty split.

"Ready for my next big idea?" McCurry asked when they had finished counting their proceeds.

"Ah oh. I'm afraid to say yes."

"Yeah right, asshole, like ya don't enjoy the couple hundred a week the last idea is bringing in."

"Okay, okay. Don't go start taking me seriously or we'll both be in trouble."

"All right, then listen. The idea came to me when you introduced me to your mechanic friend."

"You mean Carl Eller?" Wachter asked.

"Yeah, that's the guy. Anyway, there are always a lot of guys on base looking for a good deal on a car. How 'bout we work with Eller to scout out some cars we can pick up on the cheap, have Eller make sure they are running well and then sell them to the GIs for a hefty profit?"

"Why would they want to buy from you if they can get something cheaper on their own?"

"Because you know, and they know even better, how difficult it is to get those asshole Germans at the inspection station on base to pass a vehicle through. They love to put it to the Americans they work for."

"So?"

"We guarantee the cars we sell will go through the first time. Same way we got my bus through. The carton of cigarettes on the front seat bribe."

When McCurry told Wachter he was considering buying a vehicle from one of the guys on base who was rotating back to the states, he said his only concern was getting it through the German-run inspection station. Wachter told him to go ahead and get the microbus and he would show him the trick for getting it approved.

The day after he purchased his VW and picked up the license plates issued to U.S. servicemen, Wachter told him to go to the PX and purchase a carton of cigarettes.

"When you get to the station, make sure you leave the carton on the driver's seat when you get out of the bus," Wachter instructed.

After getting the cigarettes, McCurry headed over to the inspection station and got in line. When it was his turn to go through, he got out of the microbus, leaving the carton on the driver's seat.

"Papiere," the inspector demanded.

"Here's my title and registration," McCurry said as he handed the papers over.

"Out of ze vay, den," the German said as he elbowed McCurry aside and opened the door to the vehicle.

"Vas is dis?" the inspector said, picking up the carton of cigarettes and turning back to face McCurry. "You zink you can bribe a German official? You can go to brig for zat."

Oh fuck, McCurry thought. What has that crazy Wachter gotten me into.

"No. No bribe," McCurry said. "That's a gift for you. A gift to say thank you for the work you do for the U.S."

"A gift? For me?"

"Yes. Yes, a gift."

"Oh, okay," he said, tossing the carton over onto the passenger's seat. He got in and drove into the inspection garage. About 20 minutes later, he drove out the other side and brought the vehicle back out to the front. McCurry smiled when he saw the inspection sticker. The German just got out, handed McCurry his papers and walked over to the next person in line.

"What the fuck?" McCurry said when he got back to the kiosk. He told Wachter that for a brief moment he thought the German was going to turn him in for offering a bribe.

"You were never in any danger," Wachter assured him. "You have to understand the mentality of the German with a title. He expects his authority to be respected and his palm to be greased."

*   *   *

Wachter contacted Eller and the next day he met with McCurry and Wachter in his garage.

"What d'ya think, Carl? You have quite a few regular customers. Are there times where you could make a deal to take their cars off their hands?" Wachter asked.

"Sure, I do, and I could put the word out that I'm open to making an offer for anyone who wants to get rid of their car."

"I'd like to keep the cost between $300 and $500," McCurry said. "We could pay you a five percent commission plus whatever it costs to get the car running right. Does that sound about right to you, Horst?"

"Fine by me," Wachter said.

"Sounds good to me too," Eller said.

The three shook hands. In less than a month they had sold their first Volkswagen Beetle for $900. Eller had picked it up for $425. Adding in his $45 commission and $30 in parts, the profit realized by Wachter and McCurry was $400. This time, Wachter didn't argue about the fifty-fifty split.

Who Won the War, Anyway?

t didn't take long before McCurry found living on base seemed too restrictive, despite the little time he spent there. After a short search, he and Wachter found an inexpensive apartment for him in Berlin's Zehlendorf borough. It was against regulations for unmarried soldiers to live in off-base housing, but since ASA soldiers were free to leave base at any time when not working, it was another of those rules easily overlooked.

McCurry was surprised Wachter was able to help him find a low-cost apartment in Zehlendorf since it was in the American sector. Married men whose wives joined them in Berlin were required to find their dwellings in the American sector. As a result, German landlords knew the number of apartments were limited and often charged Americans nearly double what a similar rental unit would go for in the British or French sectors.

To make sure McCurry didn't get gouged, Wachter went in as if he were the one interested in renting the flat. Once he had negotiated the deal, he brought McCurry in to sign the rental agreement. The landlord, Adolph Rauschenberg, wasn't happy about this, but was led to believe McCurry could cause him problems if he tried to back out of the agreement.

The apartment wasn't in one of the areas favored by the Americans anyway. It was in an old mansion that had been converted into two rental units on the first floor with a much larger unit on the second floor for the landlord.

"Horst, this is cool," McCurry said as he made his way through the living room, bedroom, kitchenette and bathroom.

"Hey now, that's something ya don't see often," he said as he entered the bathroom and saw a shower head and controls had been installed in the wall across from the toilet. "I can save time by combining the 'shit and shower' part of the wake-up regimen."

As a rule, most German apartments had only a sink and a toilet in the bathroom. When German nationals washed, which was not very often, they sponged themselves off over the sink. The old man who owned the building smelled so bad that his odor lingered long after he passed by McCurry's front door.

McCurry's apartment was only about three miles from Andrews Barracks. One day while on mids, he decided to walk to the compound. He was often surprised by how many buildings were still bombed-out shells this many years after the end of the war. Here and there a *hausfrau*, or house wife, was out with a bucket of soapy water scrubbing down the stoop. It was this devotion to clean, neat neighborhoods that so impressed McCurry's friend Dave Blake. McCurry, on the other hand, thought it more a neurotic concern about appearances than anything else. During his short jaunt, he concluded that Berlin was indeed rising from the ashes, but its transformation was far from complete.

Part of the problem was that West Berlin was an island in the middle of Communist East Germany. Supplies, food and construction material had to be brought in by trucks, rail or planes. In June 1948, the first crisis of the cold war was precipitated when the Soviet Union, which was in control of the eastern half of Germany, cut off all road and railway access to Berlin. As McCurry recollected from college history courses, the Soviets hoped to strangle the city and basically have control ceded to them.

During the next 12 months, the Royal Air Force and U.S. Air Force flew over 200,000 flights with food, fuel and other necessities in what became famously known as the Berlin Airlift. The blockade was lifted in May of 1949.

I guess that proves that the military can do something right, McCurry thought. It was probably the competence and hard work of the men and women on the ground that made it work and not the normally clueless leadership back in Washington.

By the time McCurry made it to Andrews and went to the motor pool to pick up a bus, he was pretty depressed. Back in the States, he often found that he could clear his mind and lift his spirits by taking a long ride in the country. He enjoyed city life, but from time to time he needed some open space to roam. It was surprising how restricted life within the confines of the Berlin wall could make a person feel. One couldn't drive in any direction for very long without running into the wall separating East Berlin from West Berlin or the fence separating the city from East Germany.

He had asked Wachter to pick him up at the base after his shift ended at midnight. While the two were having some beers at a pub near his apartment, McCurry said, "We need to have a party Horst. A big blowout whose reputation will last long after I am gone. Something of monumental proportions."

"How about we lower the bar a little," Wachter said to his friend who had become not a little sloshed, "and just have a get-together with friends."

"Yeah, that'll work," McCurry said.

*   *   *

The two planned the party for the second day after McCurry's mids shift ended, and by the day of the event had lost track of how many of their friends they had invited. McCurry had a pretty good stereo system, a popular purchase for soldiers stationed in Europe because of the huge discount over stateside prices. Wachter had several hundred 45 RPM records, nearly all reflecting the popular Motown sound. While the pair had attended concerts by and had become enamored with many of the new groups, such as Cream, The Jimi Hendrix Experience and most recently Led Zeppelin, they were still locked in to Motown for party sounds.

They brought in several bottles of liquor they had stashed at Wachter's kiosk on the Ku'damm for their business. They also picked up several cases of Beck's beer for the party, which cost about $3 a case at the Class VI store, a fraction of what they would have paid for an American brand such as Budweiser.

Already into his third beer as well as a few hits on the hash pipe Horst had lit up, McCurry said "I think we're ready" as the first gang of friends came in through the front door.

*   *   *

About an hour into the party – and at a point where McCurry was feeling no pain after several more hits on the hash pipe – there was a loud banging at the front door. McCurry opened it to the sight of his landlord, Rauschenberg, whose face was so red McCurry was sure he was about to have a stroke.

"You must turn that music down immediately," Rauschenberg shouted without any preamble, spraying McCurry with a liberal amount of spittle.

"Hey Rauschenberg, can't you see we're having a party. Just settle down. You're welcome to join in, if ya wanna."

"No, I do not wish. I demand you turn that music down immediately."

"Go fuck yourself," McCurry, who hadn't really liked the guy anyway, replied. "We'll turn the music down when the party is over."

At that point, the old Herm started screaming in German, the words coming so fast and so full of colloquialisms that McCurry couldn't keep up, although he didn't miss a reference to Hitler. Before McCurry could respond, the landlord turned on his heel and marched away, leaving only his foul odor behind.

"What the fuck was that all about?" McCurry asked Wachter.

"Basically he said, 'You godforsaken, foul dog Americans think you're so high and mighty. Well, you're lucky Hitler went mad or we'd be ruling you right now.' He just misses that feeling that he is part of a superior race of human beings."

"Well, he is superior in one way … that smell. Close the door before it permeates the whole room."

This was McCurry's first exposure to a phenomenon that was not uncommon in Germany – people like his landlord who refused to believe the war was really over. They and many of their countrymen still fervently believed that a significant number of the Nazi hierarchy had fled to remote areas of South America and would someday return to restore the Third Reich to its former glory.

"Hey Horst," McCurry said after the party got back in full swing, "don't they know who won the war?"

*   *   *

"What's the story with guys like Rauschenberg?" McCurry asked Wachter the next morning as they were cleaning up. "Don't they get it that the war's over and has been for more than twenty years."

"It's still hard for them to accept the loss," Wachter said, "particularly when you realize how godlike Hitler was to people like Rauschenberg. He's not alone, there are a shitload more just like him."

Wachter explained that despite strict laws prohibiting Nazi sympathizers from publicly expressing their beliefs and barring them from the political process, the movement still persists.

"Hitler may be gone, but remember, his ideas and practices were embraced by the entire German nation and will be hard to root out," Wachter said.

"Listen," Wachter said, "I know some people that are part of a group that masquerades as a social club but is really designed to keep Hitler's principles and teachings alive. There's a meeting tonight. Wanna go and see for yourself?"

"Why not," said McCurry, who felt curious but repulsed at the same time.

*   *   *

After taking some time to rest up in the afternoon, McCurry arrived at Wachter's flat a little before eight that evening. The meeting they were attending was in a private home not far from Wachter's apartment in Charlottenburg.

"We'll walk there," Wachter said, grabbing his keys and turning off lights on their way out. "Don't wanna give 'em any way of finding out who we really are."

As they walked along, they passed more homes that remained bombed-out shells, something McCurry still found astounding. He pulled out a cigarette to settle his nerves. Knowing Wachter didn't smoke, he didn't offer any.

"You would think," McCurry said after taking a few puffs on his cigarette, "that the number of bombed-out buildings that still exist would serve as a reminder of the pain and suffering that resulted from Hitler's leadership."

"They don't look at it that way," Wachter said.

Today's adults are the children of Nazis, Wachter explained, whose parents have passed on to them a system of beliefs spawned by Hitler. They believe the only reason Germany lost the war was a worldwide Jewish conspiracy perverted their beliefs and turned other countries against them.

"They also believe they will regain support for the movement, and I'm not always so sure they're wrong."

The pair soon arrived at the home where the meeting was being held. It was clearly an old mansion that had at one time probably housed leading citizens of pre-war Berlin. Even in the dark, though, it was apparent it had fallen on bad times. Some of the window shutters were askew while others were missing entirely. In places the cast iron gutters had broken their restraining straps and hung at an angle, producing an odd slash across the face of the building. Magnificent windows facing the street appeared to be shrouded in wartime blackout curtains, making it nearly impossible to determine if anyone occupied the building while adding to its sinister appearance.

The property, surrounded by a decorative iron fence, was completely overgrown with weeds and vines, some of which had started to creep up the outside walls of the structure. As they approached the front gate, McCurry detected a somewhat repugnant smell. He guessed this was the result of frequent outside drinking parties and the detritus left behind. To the casual observer, the building had the appearance of just another gutted home left to crumble following the war, which is probably precisely how its occupants wanted it to be perceived.

Opening the gate, Wachter said, "When we get to the door, just stand behind me and let me do the talking. These are dangerous people. So just keep cool and keep quiet."

Walking up the pathway leading to the front door of the main house, McCurry was surprised at how the dark seemed to envelop them. The building's silhouette against the night sky was an ominous sign to McCurry, leaving him unsure about whether he should go forward or turn back. Before he could make up his mind, Wachter knocked on the front door. It was opened by a giant of a man who was the stereotypical version of Hitler's Aryan race. At least six-foot-six, he had blonde hair, blue eyes and muscles that strained against his black tee-shirt.

"Yah?" the monster inquired.

Speaking in German, Wachter introduced himself and McCurry as Reinhard Nicklaus and Karl Schulz. He said that Hans Dorfman had told him of the meeting and suggested he stop in to see what heroic Germans were doing to reclaim their homeland. The monster, who introduced himself as Adolph Zimmermann, told them to follow him. After traversing a hallway that seemed to stretch on forever, they turned right into a huge room that must have been a formal ballroom in the old mansion.

Holy shit, McCurry thought. This is surreal. On the wall facing them was a large Nazi flag. By McCurry's estimation, it had to be at least forty feet across the top by twenty-five feet down. Since the ceiling must have been at least forty feet high, the bottom on the flag was nearly fifteen feet off the floor. In front of the flag was a long table where apparently the leaders were going to sit, providing a dramatic stage designed to inspire awe. On the wall to the right was a gigantic photograph of Hitler. Under it was a flag holder with several parade flags. There were at least one hundred fifty men in the room, most in groups of ten or twelve. Chairs that had been set up facing the Nazi flag.

"You, sit here," said Zimmermann, pointing to two chairs in the last row. He then strode off toward the front of the room.

McCurry leaned over toward Wachter and asked, "Who the fuck is Dorfman?"

"Auf deutsch," Wachman whispered back, reminding McCurry that the men in this room wouldn't take kindly to a person speaking English. "He's a regular customer at the kiosk. Shows up on schedule weekly for the latest porn. It's kind of a mutual trust relationship," Wachter said with a wry grin.

Before they could say any more, everyone started taking their seats in the rows in front of McCurry and Wachter. When the leaders entered the room, distinguished by being the only ones in uniform, they filed behind the table and turned to the audience. Everyone rose and gave the Nazi salute, exclaiming as one "Seig Heil," or "Hail Victory."

"You may be seated," said the leader at the center of the table. "I am informed we have two guests with us this evening. Would you please stand."

McCurry and Wachter realized he was referring to them, since they were in the back row by themselves, and stood up.

"Herr Schulz and Herr Nicklaus, you are welcome to our gathering. As fellow Aryans, we hope you will join us as soldiers in the new army that will one day rise up and rid our country of these occupying foreigners and the vermin Jews who still remain within our midst. By joining us tonight, you are sworn to secrecy. The penalty for violating our trust is death. Do you understand?"

"We do," McCurry and Wachter immediately responded.

"Sehr Gut. Seig Heil!"

The two returned the salute and were told they could be seated. McCurry realized his hands were sweating. He took a furtive glance toward Wachter, who looked a bit more pale than usual. To those who didn't know him like McCurry, he would probably look normal.

The rest of the meeting was conducted pretty much like a Rotary Club might operate back in the States, McCurry thought. The only difference was that reports and other business weren't put to a vote for approval. The minutes from the last meeting were read. The leader called on the club's treasurer for a report, which indicated there was nearly ten thousand deutsche marks in their account.

Shit, thought McCurry, that's more than twenty-five hundred dollars. These guys must have some influential backers.

The final report of the evening dealt with plans to build a secure armory. The leader said arrangements for a large shipment of weapons and ammunition had been made through another of their organizations based in West Germany.

"We are getting stronger by the day and in the end we will prevail," he proclaimed. Extending his arm in the Nazi salute, he shouted "Sieg Heil."

Everyone rose and the building boomed with their enthusiastic "Sieg Heil" response.

As members started filing out of the seating section and moving toward tables along the sides of the room filled with food, McCurry and Wachter thought it would be a good time to make a quick retreat. As they started down the hallway to the front door, a booming voice rang out, bringing them to a halt: "Herr Schulz. Herr Nicklaus. You're not going to leave us so soon, are you? Come. Eat. Drink. Meet some of the other members."

Wachter turned and said, "That is very kind of you, mein Leiter. We were very much inspired and look forward to coming again, but we both work the night shift and need to get back to our homes."

"Well then, at least let me walk you to the door. We meet the first Wednesday of each month. That means I can expect to see you again next month, yes?"

"By all means, Wachter said.

"Just remember my warning about what we do to traitors. But I am sure neither of you would fall into that category."

As they reached the door, the leader pulled it open for them and then gave them the Nazi salute, which McCurry and Wachter returned.

"Stay safe," he said, as he closed the door behind him.

Once the door was closed, Wachter said, "Walk quickly, but don't run. I hope my referring to him as 'my leader' threw him off guard, but I still don't trust those fuckers not to put a tail on us."

After ducking behind a tree and then, farther on, down an alley and seeing no one behind them, they felt safe enough to casually stroll back to Wachter's flat.

"Now do you think you understand where Rauschenberg is coming from?"

*   *   *

The next day, McCurry hurried out to Wachter's kiosk as soon as he got up and dressed.

"I could hardly sleep last night," he said. "I don't think we're done with those Nazis, Horst."

"What d'ya mean, we're not done with them?"

"What the fuck's going to happen next month when we don't show up? Or if they decide to do some investigation even before then. Their leader pointed out what they do to traitors too many times for my comfort."

"Well, we were careful. We covered our tracks. I don't think we have anything to worry about."

"Are you totally nuts? You told them Dorfman told you about the meeting. That puts him on the spot if they come looking for us."

"Relax. If they come looking for us, they'll wish they hadn't."

He turned, reached up under his counter and pulled out a handgun that looked to McCurry as if it were a small cannon.

"This is a Browning .45 automatic," Wachter said. "If they come anywhere near us, it will blow a hole in them big enough to kick a soccer ball through."

"Where the fuck did ya get that? It's not legal for you to own something like that, is it?"

"One of my customers got it for me a while back for protection. And no, it's not legal, but do you really fucking care?"

Wachter said he hadn't thought about how Dorfman could point the finger at McCurry and him if asked who he told about the meetings.

"And he is one weak mother fucker," Wachter added. "I think we'd better set up a meeting with Herr Dorfman to let him know we are a lot scarier than those fucking Nazis."

Wachter told McCurry that Dorfman was due to come by the kiosk in two days to see if any new porn had arrived. "He'll show up around ten and we'll make sure he's no longer a threat."

"What d'ya mean by that?" McCurry asked.

"Just be here. You'll see."

*   *   *

McCurry arrived at nine to find out what Wachter had in mind. By way of greeting, Wachter shoved a gun into McCurry's hand, telling him to make sure he kept it in view when Dorfman came by. "Just shove it in your waistband," Wachter said.

"What, are you nuts?" McCurry said. "I don't want anything to do with guns. I'd probably end up shooting myself in the leg."

"What d'ya mean, you don't want anything to do with guns? You're a spy, aren't you?"

"Not that kind of a spy. And anyway, as far as you're concerned, I drive a bus for the Army. Shit man, I swear you're gonna get me arrested one of these days."

"Relax man. Lots of Germans know the people at Andrews aren't what they seem. Anybody ever asks, I guessed you were a spy. What do I know?

"If it makes you feel any better, just leave the gun on the shelf where Dorfman can see it. It isn't loaded anyway."

Wachter shoved his gun in his waistband and waited for Dorman to arrive. As expected, he showed up at ten exactly, anxious to see what Wachter had for him. Wachter introduced him to McCurry and then told him to take a seat inside the kiosk.

"Listen, Hans, I don't have any porn for you today," Wachter said after Dorfman was seated. "But I do have some advice."

Wachter explained that Dorfman might get a visit from his Nazi friends asking if he knew a Reinhard Nicklaus and Karl Schulz.

"You will tell them that you don't really know them. They were a couple of guys you met while waiting for a bus one day. They were grumbling about how bad things were with the Americans here and you thought they would be good recruits for the Nazi cause. Got it?"

Dorfman asked who Nicklaus and Schulz were. Wachter told him that they were a couple of guys who attended the social club Dorfman had told him about, and the two wouldn't be attending again. He said they looked very much like himself and McCurry. And, that he was quite sure the leader of the group suspected these two guys weren't legitimate.

"Jesus Christ," Dorfman said, realizing who Wachter was talking about. "Do you know how dangerous these people are? I don't know if can really tell them this lie. I'm not good that way."

"Well, you better practice," Wachter said, standing up in front of him so he could see the gun he was carrying, "'cause you'll discover you've got a lot more to fear from us if we find out you gave them any information about us."

Wachter told him he could go. As he was leaving the kiosk, Wachter said, "Remember, Herr Dorfman, practice makes perfect. Be believable and you'll be okay."

"What d'ya think?" McCurry asked after Dorfman disappeared down the street.

"He'll do okay. They may rough him up a bit, but I think he believes we will do a lot more than rough him up if he gives them any information about us."

Road Trip

"C'mon, get a couple of weeks off and we'll go on a road trip that'll spice up your otherwise drab and meaningless life."

Wachter had been trying to get McCurry to travel with him to England for quite a while. McCurry wasn't against the trip, but he knew Wachter was really hoping to scout out an older English sports car to buy for the used-car business. The older roadsters – particularly the MGs and Austin Healeys – were hot commodities among GIs. Fixing them up for transport back to the States had become a major pastime. McCurry, though, wanted to see Europe, not spend time haunting used-car and body shops.

Working out of Wachter's newspaper and magazine kiosk on the Ku'damm, the pair was making a good living selling alcoholic beverages on the black market. The used car business was just beginning to expand.

"I'll make you a deal," Wachter pleaded. "I already have a contact in London who's looking over possible cars for us. We'll go to London, pick up a car if any are worthwhile, spend some time exploring and then go back to Hamburg for a really great blowout weekend. What d'ya say?"

"All right, I'll set it up for next week. But goddammit, Horst, you've gotta promise that if we don't like the cars this guy shows us, we give up and concentrate on having a good time. Okay?"

"Deal," Horst said, poking him on the shoulder and giving him that mischievous grin that more often than not spelled trouble. The two comrades didn't foresee the kind of trouble they would find on the road.

* * *

Neither Wachter nor McCurry could travel through East Germany. McCurry was prohibited because of his security clearance and Wachter was justifiably concerned about being picked up and held in his native country.

A couple days later, Wachter and McCurry met at the kiosk to start planning their upcoming sojourn. Their most immediate need was to find someone to drive the VW they would be using for the trip to Frankfurt. McCurry said *Stars and Stripes'* classified section always had listings for GIs willing to drive cars out for the price of the gas and a few bucks spending money. Gators had no restrictions on where they drove and would buddy up for the drive and a cheap vacation. ASA members who used their services made the excuse that they were frightened of driving through East Germany, rather than citing the restrictions that came with their security clearances. This reputation for timidity was one the T-berg dwellers wore with pride. "If we take the ferry out of Calais," McCurry said, following a line on the map, "we could spend a little time in Paris before crossing the Channel."

"I don't think that's such a good idea right now," Wachter countered. "Haven't you been reading about the student riots? We don't need to be in the middle of that shit.

"Let's just go on up to Ostend in Belgium. We can cross the channel there to Ramsgate. If we work it out right, we can get some sleep on the way over."

"All right, sounds good to me," McCurry conceded.

* * *

On the first day of McCurry's leave, he and Wachter were set to catch a flight out of Templehof Airport to Frankfurt. Before the plane could take off, the two encountered a snag that McCurry felt was a bad omen for this excursion. All passengers on their plane were asked to exit. As they descended the stairs, they were herded to a line some distance from the plane.

"What the fuck's going on?" McCurry asked Wachter.

"I'm not sure, but I heard one of the passengers say the airline got a report that an explosive had been smuggled aboard in someone's luggage."

As McCurry and Wachter looked on, airline officials started off-loading all the baggage and laying it out in a line on the tarmac. Then a German police officer led a bomb-sniffing dog along the line, giving it time to examine each piece of luggage to determine if it could detect the presence of any explosive material.

The German cop apparently gave the airline officials the all-clear because the baggage handlers started loading the plane back up and passengers were told they could re-board.

"That's certainly an exciting way to start a trip," McCurry said as he and Wachter settled in their seats for take-off. "I wonder what it would be like if a bomb went off. One minute you and I would be talking and the next blackness, like a film being shut off in the middle of a dark theater."

"Relax, no bomb is going to go off," Wachter said. "I got that on good authority from a German police dog."

McCurry, who had never feared air travel, couldn't shake the queasiness he felt over the possibility of being blown out of the sky. He was glad it was a short trip into Frankfurt.

Their driver and his buddy were waiting for them when they came off the plane. After picking up their luggage and car, they headed to Ostend to catch the ferry to England.

When they arrived at the ferry terminal, McCurry eased the car into line with the others waiting for the ship, which was just making its way into the dock. He stood outside the car and lit up a cigarette while Wachter went into the terminal building to book their passage. He had noticed the driver of one of the cars in front of them looking him over, and wasn't surprised when the guy came over offering his hand as he approached.

"M'name's Colin Whitehead, mate."

"Mike McCurry. Nice to meet ya."

"You're a Yank, aren't ya?"

"Sure am," said McCurry, wondering what the stranger was getting at.

"In the Army?"

McCurry nodded his assent.

"So where ya stationed at?"

"Berlin."

McCurry finished his cigarette and crushed it out on the ground. Something about this guy was getting to him, but he figured it was just the distrust of strangers instilled in all ASA personnel.

"So, whatcha' do there anyway?" Whitehead pressed.

"A little bit of everything," McCurry evaded. "Work with a bunch of guys at McNair taking care of equipment, cleaning vehicles, that kind of thing. Not exciting work, but at least I'm here and not in 'Nam, if ya know what I mean."

"I got dat, fer sure."

"So what's your game?" McCurry asked, trying to steer Whitehad away from his probing questions. "You in the British Army?"

"Nah. I was jist over 'ere on 'oliday. On my way back 'ome to the East End in London."

Now McCurry was getting some real bad vibes. It was as if Whitehead's accent were feigned. Nothing about the guy seemed genuine. Just then, Wachter showed up with their boarding passes. McCurry introduced the two and hoped Whitehead would take the hint and get back to his car.

"So, you speak pretty good English for a Kraut."

Uh oh, McCurry thought, don't lose it Horst.

"Well, thank you mate, you speak pretty good English yourself, for a Brit that is."

"Ouch. touché," Whitehead retorted. "So tell me," he went on, "I bet you guys see a lot of spies in Berlin."

"Now, why the fuck would we see a lot of spies?" McCurry responded, starting to lose it himself. "I mean, they wouldn't be very good spies if we saw them, would they now."

"True, but I hear the city is loaded with them?"

"I think you've been reading too many dime novels. Hey, look, they're starting to board. Better get back to your car." Turning to get into the VW, McCurry shot over his shoulder, "Nice meeting you."

They got into the car and McCurry started it up, getting ready to move forward. "What the fuck was that guy's story?" Wachter asked.

"Damned if I know. Whatever it was, I wasn't buying it. His Cockney accent is clearly fake and I'm not even sure he is a Brit. Plus, how did he know you were a 'Kraut'?"

"Well, what then?"

"I don't know," McCurry mused. "A couple of the guys said to me some CID assholes have been asking questions about my relationship with you. If they got wind of our road trip, I wouldn't put it past them to try to set me up."

"What's the CID?"

"Army's Criminal Investigation Division. I guess it handles a lot of different kinds of investigations, but in Berlin its main mission is to snatch up anyone suspected of selling secret information to the enemy. That guy 'Whitehead' was such a bad actor. He could clearly be one of them.

"Let's just get on board, get some fish 'n chips and find a bunk to get some sleep. If he comes up to talk to us, tell him you don't feel well and might be coming down with something. Make sure you cough on him when you do."

"Right on, man. That sounds like a plan."

Ultimately, they did manage to elude Whitehead and get some sleep. They headed out for London on a beautiful late-summer morning. McCurry found he had no difficulty driving on the left side of the road, although he continued to have the feeling they were being followed. The only real mishap occurred at the first circle they came to when McCurry, out of habit, swung right. Fortunately traffic was light and he got off before getting hit.

"Nice maneuver," was all Horst had to say in his matter-of-fact way. They were headed for a bed and breakfast on Bond Street.

The pension was located only a short drive from the shop where Wachter's automobile contact worked. Better yet, it was within walking distance of the exciting – and sometimes sleazy – nightlife in the Soho district.

"Let's get unpacked and then get some rest before dinner," Wachter said as they arrived at their lodgings. "We'll meet up with Richard tonight."

Over dinner that evening, their contact, Richard, described a Jaguar he had found that sounded as if it would meet their needs, although it wasn't a roadster. "It's a 1953 model, built in limited quantities as a touring automobile," Richard explained. "It's got a huge rear compartment, loads of luggage room in the bonnet and two fuel tanks, each capable of holding sixty-eight liters of petrol. It's a real classic and there're very few left. Best of all, the owner's willing to let it go for about four hundred quid."

Currently the pound was worth about $2.40, but it had dropped significantly in recent months from a high of $2.80. Even if they couldn't bargain with the owner – which would be unusual – $960 would be a steal if it were in decent shape. Wachter told McCurry later they could probably turn it over for at least double that amount. The three agreed to meet at the owner's home the next day at two o'clock.

* * *

After dinner, Wachter and McCurry headed off to Soho, a small district just north of Leicester Square. McCurry still couldn't shake the feeling that he was being followed. The fact he and Wachter were strolling through an area known for its illicit attractions made it difficult to discern if someone were following them or merely being carried along by the mobs of gawkers.

The two settled on a pub that featured topless dancers. They found a quiet spot in the back and ordered up a couple of glasses of Guinness Draught. When the topless waitress returned with the two glasses of beer, she put them on the table in front of them and leaned over to whisper in Wachter's ear, managing to rub her bare breast across his face at the same time. Being careful where he put his hands, Wachter gently pushed her up and away from him, and said, "No thanks."

"What the fuck was that all about?" McCurry asked.

"She wanted to know if I wanted to join her in her room for a private drink. As you see, I politely declined."

"So, why you and not me?"

"I don't know. Probably because I'm better looking than you. Want me to go ask her for you?"

"Fuck you. She'll probably hit on me on the next round. Saving the best for last."

"Yeah right."

"So, what's on tap for tomorrow night?"

Wachter said that after they met with their contact Richard and checked out the car he had lined up for them, he wanted to visit the Hippodrome before heading back. Converted into a cabaret called "Talk of the Town" in 1958, the Hippodrome was used principally for circus acts following its construction in 1900. The Talk of the Town became a popular spot for dancing and live performances.

"We might get lucky there and meet some girls worth having a private drink with."

"I'll drink to that," said McCurry, who drained his glass and signaled to the waitress to bring another round.

When the waitress came back, she was all prim and proper, probably angry about being rebuffed by Wachter. After McCurry ordered two more beers, she suggested they might want to order more than one each.

"Last call's comin' up shortly 'n I won't be able ta serve ya after that."

"No, just the two will be fine," McCurry said. Turning to Wachter, he asked, "Last call? What the fuck's a last call?"

"Pubs in London have to stop serving at ten," Wachter explained. "I've been told the real action here takes place at the after-hours clubs. All we need is to find a taxi driver who can take us to one."

Even with a couple beers in him and plenty of topless waitresses to attract his attention, McCurry still couldn't relax. He had the distinct feeling he was being watched, and it certainly wasn't by any of the women in the room. The pub wasn't particularly large, but it was crowded enough that someone could be looking right at them and McCurry wouldn't necessarily notice. He scanned the bar, looking for someone who seemed out place, someone who was alone and not paying any attention to the topless entertainment. His attention was diverted when the bar tender shouted "Last call" loud enough to be heard over the din.

Wachter wacked him on the shoulder and told him to drink up. "Now the fun really begins," he said.

Around ten thirty, they had both drained their glasses. As they got up to leave, McCurry noticed two things. Many of the tables around them had a dozen or more glasses, an indication of how patrons loaded up in preparation for last call. The second thing he noticed was that these very same patrons were having more than a little difficulty making their way to the door.

As the two squeezed through the doorway, they were greeted by a street filled nearly beyond capacity with drunken, rowdy men piling out of the pubs that lined the thoroughfare. There was a cacophony of accents and languages, much of it consisting of loud curses for people who got in the way of an inebriated reveler. As they tried to make their way to the end of the street where the crowd seemed to be thinning out, a fight broke out on McCurry's right, and he felt himself pulled, as if to be drawn into it. Wachter grabbed his arm and yanked him free and the two started to push their way to the relative safety of the next block.

"Don't be courteous about it, just shove any way you can to get through," Wachter said. "Guess we should have left a little earlier."

At the end of the block, people were dispersing in several directions. Turning right, McCurry saw there were some cabs parked near the end of the next block.

"Maybe one of them will be able to take us to an after-hours club and get us out of this craziness," Wachter said.

Before they got to the end of the block where the cabs were parked, a taxi pulled up alongside them. Rolling down his window, the cabbie asked, "Lookin' for a liddle bit of excitement, gents? If so, hop in."

"Sounds good to me," Wachter said, opening the door to let McCurry in. McCurry jumped in and slid across to make room for Wachter. As Wachter was getting situated and ready to close the door, another man came up and asked if he could join them, suggesting they could save some money by splitting the fee three ways.

"Sure, hop in," Wachter said as he slid over closer to McCurry.

"So, are you guys lookin' for clubs with the real hard-core kind of entertainment, if ya know what I mean?" the cab driver asked.

"That's what we're looking for," Wachter said. "Sounds good to me," said the new passenger on his right.

"Well, sit back and relax. It'll take a bit to get there, but it's worth the trip."

McCurry tried to relax, but the nagging thought that something was wrong here wouldn't leave him alone. I mean, the worst that can happen is we don't like the place and leave, he thought. He was concerned about this stranger who hopped in the cab with them. Something about him looked vaguely familiar. But he and Wachter would have no problem beating the shit out of him if he caused any problems.

His concerns weren't helped by the fact that they were just leaving the relative safety of the crowds in Soho. After crossing Regent Street they were heading toward a darker, non-commercial part of town. Of course, you wouldn't expect the kind of place we're going to to be located in a neighborhood, he thought. Precisely. We should stop the cab and get out right now.

Before McCurry could whip himself into full panic mode, the cab pulled over in front a large building with darkened windows and no surrounding lights or signage.

"Let me take care of the cab fare," said the stranger, reaching into the pocket of his overcoat. When Wachter turned to look at him, he was staring down the barrel of gun.

"Whoa man, listen, we don't have much money, but you can have it all."

"Shut the fuck up Kraut. You listen to me. We don't want your fuckin' money. Just stay calm and follow orders and nobody'll get hurt. Understand?"

Wachter just nodded. "Hey you, moron, you understand?" the man shouted over at McCurry.

"Yeah. Yeah, I get it," McCurry responded.

"My friend up front is going to get out and open the door for you," the stranger said. "He's armed as well, so don't try to be a hero. Both of you stay cool and follow us inside and no one will get hurt. We just want a little bit of information."

After the "cabbie" opened the door, McCurry got out and was followed by Wachter. They were told to turn around and start walking toward the front door of the building. The stranger came around the front of the car to help cover them. Wachter opened the door and McCurry followed him in. Temporary work lights had been set up allowing them to see their way around. Their two captors were whispering to each other just inside the door. As McCurry awaited further instructions, it hit him. Kraut? How'd this guy know Wachter was a German? No wonder that asshole looked familiar. It was the guy from the ferry landing.

"Hey Whitehead, or whatever the fuck your name is, what the fuck's the deal here?"

"Shut up McCurry, you dumb fuck. I was wondering when you would recognize me."

"Your Kraut hint was your way of just rubbing in about how smart you are, huh."

"Something like that. Now shut up and start moving down that hall there."

As they entered the hallway, the cab driver shoved Wachter through the doorway of the first room on the right, pulled the door shut, produced a set of keys and locked it.

"Keep movin'," Whitehead growled, shoving McCurry in the back with the butt of his gun.

The next doorway was on the left. When they reached it, the cabbie shoved McCurry through so hard that he lost his balance and crashed to the floor.

"Get the fuck up and sit on that chair there," Whitehead said, kicking him on the sole of one of his feet to get him moving.

Once McCurry was settled on the chair, the cabbie went over and switched on another light they had set up on a tripod. It wasn't exactly intense, but it was certainly uncomfortable under the circumstances, McCurry thought.

"Now listen here, you fuck," Whitehead said. "We're with the CID and we've been following you and that Kraut for quite some time. So don't think we're not on to you."

As they paused to let that sink in, McCurry said to himself, All right, time to keep calm. Think before you speak. Look for their weaknesses. This is the CID. It isn't exactly the CIA. McCurry didn't know if Whitehead expected him to say something, but knew the only way to take control of the situation was to hold back until they revealed what they were looking for.

After a brief silence, the cabbie said, "We know you're here to turn over information to the enemy. We want to know who your contact is, what kind of information they expect and how you're supposed set up the meeting. Come clean now and we can help you out. Otherwise, you may be spending a lot of winters in Leavenworth."

Are you kidding me, McCurry thought. These guys are not only terrible actors but whoever provided their dialogue must have been reading too many cheap spy novels. Time to go on the offensive.

"Let me see your identification," McCurry snapped.

Waving the gun in McCurry's face, Whitehead said, "This is the only identification we need. Now start talking."

"You're even dumber than you look, Whitehead," McCurry said. Standing up and rolling his shoulders to get loose, he moved slowly toward the agent. "Now what moron ..."

"Sit the fuck back down, McCurry, before anyone gets hurt."

"You can't be that stupid Whitehead," McCurry said, continuing to move slowly forward. "Do you really think I'd believe you'd shoot a member of the Army Security Agency in London, an area that is totally out of your jurisdiction?

"Now, as I started to say. What moron planned this operation? I hope whoever it was wasn't stupid enough to allow you to have real bullets in those guns. If they knew you, they must have known that you are too dumb to be allowed to carry live ammunition."

Whitehead had backed into the wall. When he couldn't go any farther, he let his arm holding the gun drop to his side.

"That's what I thought," McCurry said. "Now I am going to tell you this just once and I want you to repeat it exactly to your superiors. Wacther and I are here for one reason only. We're here to see the sights and then move on as other normal tourists would do. When we leave here, we're going on to Hamburg. Then back to Berlin. We expect to be able to enjoy the rest of this trip or this whole thing could blow up in your face and the face of whatever moron planned it. Got it?

"Now, if you would be so kind," McCurry said as he turned to the cabbie, "would you let my buddy out of that room? Then the two of you can drive us back to our rooms and get the fuck out of our lives."

* * *

Wachter practically ran up the steps to their room.

"Hey man, what's the rush," asked McCurry when he got to the room.

"Gotta pack our bags and get the fuck out of here."

"Slow down, Horst. We're not going anywhere. Those guys aren't going to bother us anymore. They're on thin ice being over here, out of their jurisdiction. Frankly, I think it was a rogue operation."

"What d'ya mean?"

"The CID is a collection of wanna be cops. Not a bright bulb among 'em. Their main objective in Berlin is to uncover espionage operations. They probably thought they had a hot break with us. But no one in authority would have approved this kind of operation. So relax. Let's get some sleep and then tomorrow we can go see what Richard's got for us."

* * *

The Jag was in mint condition. Apparently the owner's late husband had bought it, reconditioned it and gave it lots of tender loving care right until his recent death. McCurry felt a little guilty after Wachter used his charm and wit to convince the woman she was getting a great deal by letting them take the automobile off her hands for all of 360 pounds. "It is a beautiful vehicle," he told her. "It must have been a labor of love for your husband. It shows. But you know, you're going to need to find someone who loves classic cars equally well to put up this kind of money for an *old* car."

They had been taken to her home by Richard. After Wachter counted out the 360 pounds in cash and had her sign the title over to them, McCurry and Wachter drove the Jaguar back to their room. "Did you really have to squeeze her for a lousy 40 pounds?" McCurry asked.

"Relax, Mike. Didn't you see how she was living? Her husband left her well off. I'm sure she was glad to get the thing off her hands for 360 pounds. If it makes you feel any better, I have no doubt I could have gotten her to shave another 20 or 30 pounds from the price if I wanted."

*   *   *

When Wachter and McCurry arrived at the Hippodrome, a local rock group was playing on stage. They found a seat and ordered a couple mugs of dark stout beer.

Before the waitress returned with their beers, a couple of young women in mini-skirts that barely covered their rears came up to the table and asked if they could join Wachter and McCurry. They introduced themselves as Sarah and Chloe. Sarah, who sat down next to Wachter, was about 5 feet, 10 inches tall with the longest legs McCurry had ever seen, although they may have been accentuated by the tiny skirt. She had blue eyes, a cute little nose and small breasts with erect nipples that pushed against the nearly transparent fabric of her blouse. Chloe, who became McCurry's seat mate, was somewhat shorter than her friend with petite features. She had flaming red hair and the greenest eyes McCurry had ever seen.

"We heard ya' talkin' and just knew you were Yanks," Chloe explained. "We really love Americans, don't we Sarah?"

"Ya' can say that again," said Sarah, who casually rubbed her leg up against Wachter to make her point.

"So how about you two?" Wachter asked, pleased that they thought he was an American. "You live here in London?"

"Nah, we're from a little burg just north a' London," Sarah replied.

"But we sure love the lights an' excitement a' the big city," Chloe bubbled. "We love ta drink an' dance an' then drink some more,"

Just then the waitress arrived with the beers. McCurry asked the women what they would like to drink, and both ordered martinis. American movies probably have given them the idea that this is a sophisticated drink, McCurry thought.

"So, aside from drinking and dancing, what do you do for a living?" McCurry asked, angling to get an idea about how old they were.

"We're both hair dressers," Chloe said, moving her foot up against McCurry's. "What about you two?"

"We're both in the law," McCurry said. "Had to defend a couple of GIs over in Germany. Thought we'd take a day or two to see London before going back to the States."

The waitress returned with the martinis for the girls. McCurry told the waitress that Wachter was paying, then turned to Chloe and asked, "Wanna dance? This group sounds pretty good."

"Sure," she said. She took a large sip of her martini, jumped up, grabbed his hand and led him to the dance floor. The band was playing a half-decent rendition of the Rolling Stones' "Satisfaction." As McCurry started moving with the rhythm, Chloe revved it up, showing what she meant when she said she loved to dance. She moved effortlessly and seductively. Her whole body kept time with the beat, particularly when she joined in with the band when it belted out, "I can't get no satisfaction."." At one point, she moved in real close, started rubbing up against McCurry while whispering in his ear, "'Cause I try and I try and I try and I try." Laughing, she backed away and continued in time with the band's "I can't get no, I can't get no."

When the song was over, they walked back to the table hand in hand. McCurry didn't see Wachter or Sarah. Chloe picked up her martini, took a sip and laughed. "Just like Sarah. She's probably outside makin' out with yer buddy, Horst. What kind a name is Horst anyway?" She asked.

"German," McCurry said, taking a long swig of his beer and pausing to think about his answer. "His father moved the whole family to America when Wachter was just a toddler."

Just then the band started playing Jefferson Airplane's "Somebody to Love." "Ooh, I love this song," Chloe said, taking another sip of her drink and pulling McCurry back out on the dance floor. The psychedelic sounds of the Airplane were perfect for Chloe to show off her moves. As she writhed in front of him, all McCurry could think about was her writhing under him. The green eyes were captivating and soon he found himself reaching out and pulling her in to him.

"Take it easy there big boy," she said, pulling away and giggling. "Let's at least finish our dance."

Afterwards, they went back to finish their drinks, just in time to see Wachter and Sarah returning from wherever they had been. Not bothering to sit down, Wachter picked up his glass of beer, drained it and said, "Well, Mike and I have to get up early tomorrow, but you girls are welcome to come back to the pension with us for a little bit. We've got a bottle of American whiskey hidden in our bags just waiting to be opened and shared with beautiful young women like you."

"Sounds good to me," Chloe said, grabbing McCurry's arm and pulling him close.

* * *

When he awoke the next morning, McCurry was still trying to wrap his mind around the fact that he had made love to Chloe while Horst and Sarah were doing the same in the other bed in their small room. He never thought he could really do something like that, but Chloe quickly made him forget there was anyone else around.

Horst told him to get packing so they would have some time to tour the countryside a bit before catching the late-afternoon ferry back to Ostend. They left the Jaguar at the bed and breakfast while exploring the beautiful green suburbs of London. Wachter particularly wanted to visit Dover. As with most things Wachter did, they were running late when they started out for Dover. After arriving, they had time only to take a few minutes to gaze in awe at the massive cliffs. Then they had to drive at breakneck speeds to get back to London to pick up the Jag and get to the ferry in time.

"As soon as we eat, we should try to find an open bunk below and get some sleep," Wachter said. "We'll get in to Belgium a little after midnight. Then we can drive straight through the rest of the night to get to Hamburg in the early morning. Unlike our stuffed-shirt British friends, Hamburg is wide open."

He said that not only were there no restrictions of any kind, there was lots of competition, so the entry fees to the different establishments were kept down as well. "You ain't goin' to be disappointed this time, boyo," he added, mimicking what he thought was an Irish accent.

There wasn't much traffic on the autobahn through Belgium. McCurry, driving the huge Jaguar touring car, found himself daydreaming and getting sleepy. Without much warning, the Volkswagen in front of him signaled and turned off onto one of the Brussels exits. Where the hell is that crazy German going now? McCurry thought. There can't be anything open at this time in the morning. But, Wachter had all the money and the maps, so he had no choice but follow.

After traveling through a portion of the spookily quiet downtown section of Brussels, the Volkswagen traveled into an obvious suburban area and then abruptly pulled into a driveway of a private home. What the fuck? McCurry thought. There wasn't enough room for his vehicle to fit in the small driveway, so he pulled up at the curb and got out. Just as he was rounding a hedgerow that lined the driveway, he saw a stranger closing garage doors on the Volkswagen he had been following.

Jesus fucking Christ, I've been following the wrong VW, he realized. Without trying to figure out how that automobile got between him and Wachter on such a sparsely traveled roadway, he retraced his path back to the autobahn, pulled onto the roadway and then parked on the shoulder. Nothing for me to do now but wait until Horst realizes I'm not behind him and doubles back, McCurry thought. Might as well take a nap.

McCurry didn't know how long he had been sleeping when he heard what sounded like some madman pounding on the window and shouting obscenities. When he finally roused himself and opened the door, Wachter was all over him. "You crazy mother fucker, what were you doing? I had to go twenty kilometers down the road to get to an exit and then, after I saw you on the way back, it was another fifteen before I could get turned around again. Are you fuckin' crazy? Why couldn't you stay behind me?"

McCurry let Wachter continue to release his rage. Once he had gotten all his frustrations out, McCurry explained what happened and apologized.

"Well, do you think you can stick with me now?"

"Yeah, yeah, I can. Let's get going."

They arrived in Hamburg in late morning, tired and dirty, and agreed to sleep the rest of the day before beginning to explore. Feeling like they had pretty well banished the CID buffoons after the London fiasco, McCurry was feeling he and Wachter could really enjoy Hamburg without the uneasy feeling that someone was looking over their shoulders. He didn't know then that the CID wasn't finished with him.

Gator Tread Stymied at the Gate

Another mids shift, McCurry thought as he waited for his bus to fill up. Wonder what I can do to stay awake for eight more hours?

"Hey Mike," Evans said, interrupting McCurry's reverie. "Landry told me to give you a heads up. Gators are out in the Grune on maneuvers so, in his words, 'Drive slow and don't cause problems.'"

"Yeah, right. That sounds like us, don't you think?" McCurry said, grinning.

McCurry knew no treads would get on his bus. Hell, even Landry sent the message through Evans rather than come on board and give McCurry the news in person. When the bus was full, McCurry closed the doors and then turned to face his passengers, most of whom were already high or in the process of getting there.

"Listen up," he said. "We'll be heading through enemy gator territory when we get on the Grune road tonight. War games, so, if it becomes necessary, open the windows and return fire."

With that, he sat down, started the engine and took off.

"You are one crazy motherfucker, McCurry, you know that," Evans said, taking his customary seat behind the driver.

"Yeah, but ain't we got fun."

Soon after they started up the dirt road that cut through the Grunewald to the Hill, McCurry saw a gator sergeant with a flashlight standing in the middle of the road, waving them down. McCurry slowed the bus to a stop, waited for the gator to get around on the side and then took off. A couple of the guys put their arms out the windows and shouted, "Bang, bang, you're dead."

McCurry figured the gator called ahead to his squad members when he saw a sign on the side of the road that read: CLOSED GATE. HALT.

"Are you fucking kidding me," McCurry said to Evans as he blew through the "gate." With that, several gators jumped out from the wooded area along the road and started firing on the bus. The soldiers were only using blanks, of course, but if McCurry were playing by the rules, he would have had to assume the bus was incapacitated by "enemy fire" and bring it to a stop. About a mile farther up the road, he reached the point where he turned off and ascended to their site on the Hill.

After everyone on the bus had gotten off, entered the compound and headed for the work building, McCurry heard a screech of tires and saw this jeep coming to a stop in front of the bus. A gator captain hopped out of the jeep and started heading for the compound gate.

In an instant, the MP guard came out of his hut with an M-14 not loaded with blanks.

"Where do you think you're going, sir?" the guard asked.

"Get out of the way, Sergeant. I'm going after those soldiers right there," he said, pointing at McCurry and company, all of whom had turned to watch the confrontation. "I wanna find out who the fuck the driver of that bus is and what he thought he was doing when he ran my roadblock."

"I'm afraid I can't allow that, sir. Now, please get back in your jeep and leave this site before I call in reinforcements."

"What the fuck is this place?" the captain asked.

"I'm not at liberty to answer that question. Now please, sir, get in your jeep and leave before you find yourself detained and interrogated for real."

"Mother fuck, that guy's got more guts than I would have given him credit for," McCurry whispered to Evans. They both knew that even the guards had no idea what the mission was.

As the captain jumped in his jeep shouting obscenities at the guard, McCurry raised his arm, made as if he were cocking a pistol and then fired. "Bang, you're dead," he said as the gator captain took off, kicking up a hailstorm of stones in his wake.

"Well, I guess you can't talk about how boring the mids shifts are anymore," Evans said.

Feed Me, I'll Talk

When McCurry arrived at work following the Warsaw Pact invasion of Czechoslovakia in the summer of 1968, he discovered Army tanks surrounding the Hill.

"What the hell is that all about?" McCurry asked one of the guys coming out to catch the bus back to base.

"Some goofball figured that if Russia was willing to invade Czechoslovakia they might just seize the opportunity ta roll on into West Berlin at the same time. Fuckin' morons. So now we got armored body guards and extended shifts."

"So, if the East German and Russian armies come rolling across the border, these guys are gonna protect us? Give me a break. I'd rather take my chances with the Russians."

For the next 30 days, McCurry and the others on B-trick, as well as a handful of C-trick personnel, worked twelve hours a day, twelve on with twelve off.

"This is beyond ridiculous," McCurry said to Evans, as the two tried to stay awake during their twelve-hour overnight shift. "From what I can tell, there hasn't been any German chatter worth noting."

"C'mon, you know the drill," Evans said. "These guys are scared shitless and don't know what to do. They'd probably lose their stripes if they owned up to the fact that this was a worthless exercise."

"Well, not totally worthless," McCurry said, chuckling. "Sezov told me during the last break that the Russian marys picked up some chatter about one of the Ruskies being in hot water after he practically bit the ear off one of the local's dogs. Seems the dog bit him, so he decided to return the favor."

"Man bites dog. That's a classic."

"But true," McCurry said. "Sesov says they have it on tape. Gonna send it back to NSA marked 'priority'. Wonder if it will dawn on 'em that they're being played for the fools they are."

"Probably not. As long as they act like it's important, nobody's got the balls to argue."

"Well, I think I have an idea that might help them see the light."

A few days after that conversation, McCurry got out a bed sheet he had pilfered from Supply at one time or another and carefully spray-painted the words, in three-foot-high letters, FEED ME, I'LL TALK.

He had the sheet stuffed into a small duffel next to him on the bus. As Evans was getting off, McCurry grabbed his sleeve and asked him to wait with him until the others had descended and were on their way in.

"Come with me, I need you for some special ops," McCurry said. As they entered the compound, McCurry diverted away from the others with Evans following closely. After reaching a section of fence that was pretty much hidden from sight from the front gate, McCurry dropped the duffel to the ground and pulled out the sheet, stretching it out on the ground so Evans could see the message.

"Mother fuck," Evans said, "what're you gonna do with that?"

"With your help, I'm gonna climb to the top of the fence, flip it over on the other side, and then hook it to the metal barbs at the top of the fence."

"You are totally out of your fucking mind, McCurry."

"Hey, c'mon man, someone's gotta make a statement about how ridiculous this whole exercise is. It's dumb-shit ideas like this that get wars started."

"All right, give me an end, but if we get shot I'm really gonna be pissed."

Each held an end of the sheet and started to ascend the fence. When they reached the top, they put one arm over to keep their balance and then carefully bunched the sheet up, lifted it over and dropped it into place.

As he was pushing his end through the barbs to hold the sheet up, McCurry looked over to Evans to ask how he was doing.

"Ow. Fuck. Shit. Goddammit."

"Jesus Christ, Dwight, what's the matter?"

"I tore my finger on one of these barbs. Fuckin' thing."

"Well for Christ's sake, keep it down. We really could end up getting shot by our own people with you making that kind of racket. How does it look?"

"Fine, let's get the fuck down from here before we're missed."

"All right, you two dildos, what the fuck're you up to now?" Landry called up to the pair as they were about to clamber down.

"Hey Sarge, d'ya think it's safe for you to be out here. You know, the Russians might show up at any minute. It would be bad news if ya got captured out here," McCurry said as he reached the ground.

"Cut the crap, McCurry. I'm not amused. What the hell's with the sheet?"

"Oh, that's right. I should've realized that you can't read it from in here. I just wanted to make sure we are treated right when the Russians show up, so I figured they'd get a kick out of a sign that said 'Feed me, I'll talk.'"

"What the fuck! Both of you, stay right here and don't move."

With that Landry headed for the front gate, walked out and around to where McCurry's sign was hanging. As Landry tried to pull it down, it kept getting caught on the barbed wire, turning the operation into a struggle that McCurry wasn't sure Landry would win. Ultimately, though, the old tread was victorious and marched back inside with the shredded sheet bunched up under his arm.

"What the fuck's the matter with you two."

"I don't know, Sarge. I guess we're just not the hero you are."

"Get back to your post, you morons. Make sure you meet me in the captain's office when we get back to the post."

After McCurry returned the trick bus to the motor pool, he and Evans walked back to Capt. Hanover's office. When McCurry knocked on the door, it sounded as if Landry and Hanover were engaged in a heated conversation. Hanover turned to the door and told the two to come in.

"Are you both completely out of your mind?" Hanover asked.

Before either could respond, the captain said, "Don't answer that 'cause no matter what you say I know you will piss me off more than I already am, and you don't want that. Landry here wants me to send you both right to the brig and charge you with treason, or some such nonsense. What he doesn't understand is how valuable you two are to the mission. Besides that, it would be hard to convince anyone that this was anything more than a dumb prank."

It sounded as if Hanover was trying to convince Landry through his lecture to McCurry and Evans.

"But I do have to punish you," Hanover continued. "So I am going to issue an Article 15 that will reduce you both one rank, and fine you sixty dollars a month for five months."

"As far as I am concerned, and I suspect Dwight feels the same way, I don't think so, Captain," McCurry responded. "I plan to exercise my right to demand a general court martial."

"Are you out of your mind?" Hanover roared. "You could get kicked out of the Army with a bad conduct discharge. An Article 15 won't even go on your permanent record."

"We'll take our chances," Evans said, surprising McCurry by stepping up to the plate. "We have every right to demand a general court martial and, as you said yourself, it would be hard to convince anyone that that this was anything more than a dumb prank. Not to mention how you would look bringing us up on charges."

"You two had better think about this," Hanover shot back. "You get me mad enough and I just might find a way to hang your asses. Now get the fuck out of my office."

When they got back to the barracks, McCurry told Evans that he knew the officers and gentlemen of the Army Security Agency worried more about adverse publicity than they did about this little escapade.

"They would look like a bunch of buffoons if they tried to subject us to a court martial for some dumb prank," McCurry said. "I just wish the sign had stayed up a little longer."

McCurry had taken some pictures of his masterpiece before taking it up to the Hill and looked forward to having the film developed. Landry knew about the photographs and must have passed the information on to Hanover. In the end, after some "friendly counseling" from Hanover, he and Evans were informed that no charges would be lodged over the incident ... as long as McCurry turned over the undeveloped film.

CID Revenge

McCurry left his VW microbus on a side street off the Ku'damm and started walking to Wachter's kiosk when a man he had come to know well approached him.

"Well, if it isn't Mr. Whitehead?"

"It's Jennings. Agent Jennings to you," he said, showing McCurry his CID badge and ID.

"Hmm, how refreshing. Using your real name and showing ID this time. You must've gotten a good ass kicking for that fiasco in London."

"Fuck you, McCurry. Follow me. You're comin' in for questioning."

"Oh yeah, asshole. On what pretext this time."

"On the 'pretext' that those two guys behind you will beat the livin' shit outa ya if you don't do what I say."

McCurry glanced over his shoulder to see two huge thugs following close behind. They looked as if they were more at home in a boxer's ring than a unit of the Army. Yeah, he thought, they could beat the living shit out of me.

Jennings led the way to a non-descript van, opened the door and shoved McCurry in. One of the goons followed while the other climbed into the passenger seat up front. Jennings walked around and got in behind the wheel. After about a half hour driving, Jennings pulled over to the side of the road. From the little McCurry could see through the front window, he guessed they were somewhere out near the Grunewald. He discovered his guess was pretty accurate when Jennings opened the door and the goon beside him shoved him out and onto the ground. As he got up, he saw they were next to a building nestled into a grove of trees. There was nothing else around except woodland.

"Move it, McCurry. You and I are gonna have a serious discussion when we get inside."

When Jennings opened the door, one of the goons shoved McCurry through. Catching his balance against a wall, he said, "Hey King Kong, you don't need to keep shovin' me around like that. I'm cooperating."

"Lay off him, Rankin," Jennings said. "If I need you to step in, I'll let you know." Turning to McCurry, he said, "Right through the door on the left, McCurry. Take the chair at the table and make yourself comfortable."

Jennings took a seat across from McCurry at the table. Rankin and the other goon stood next to the door. As if I'm going to try to escape, McCurry thought.

"All right," Jennings said, "Let's talk about what you 'n that Kraut were doin' in London."

"Let me ask you something Jennings. You don't by any chance have a top secret security clearance, do you?"

"What the fuck does that have to do with anything?"

"It has a lot to do with everything. Because of my clearance and our work with sensitive information, you don't have the authority to question me about anything without an officer from our unit sitting in."

Since he felt intimidated, McCurry pulled out a card he was required to carry but rarely used. It said, in essence, that the holder of the card, whether in civilian clothes or uniform, could not be stopped, questioned or harassed. It was signed by McCurry's company commander with his contact telephone number.

As he started to hand it over to Jennings, the CID operative just swatted it out of his hand.

"I'm fuckin' CID, you asshole. If I say ya gotta talk to me, ya gotta talk. Now, what the fuck were you and that Kraut up to in London."

"You don't get it moron. I'm not gonna say a fuckin' word to you until you get hold of my commanding officer and I'm given his approval to answer your questions."

"Hey Rankin," Jennings said, "throw him in that spare room and give him some time to think about the benefits of cooperation. And Rankin," he said, turning to face the goon, "you're welcome to throw him in."

When McCurry once again picked himself up off the floor, he sat down on the edge of a cot that had been set up in the room. There was a toilet and sink in the corner. Other than that, the room was empty. High up on one wall was a small window, which provided the only light.

Well, McCurry thought, I guess all I can do is lie down and wait to see what their next move is. He was concerned about Wachter, but didn't think Jennings was dumb enough to mess with a German national here in Berlin. Then again, Jennings should have known better than to have kidnapped someone with a top secret clearance. This was probably his way of paying McCurry off over his humiliation in London. He was sure Jennings' actions weren't sanctioned, which made him dangerous.

McCurry had just nodded off when he felt himself being yanked up off the cot and shoved through the door to the main room once again. The goon with no name turned McCurry around and slammed him down in the chair next to the table. Jennings came out from another room and once again sat down in the chair across from McCurry.

"Did you have a nice nap?" Jennings asked. "I know I did."

"Yeah. Great. 'Cept I didn't appreciate being manhandled by your goons again," McCurry replied. "By the way, Jennings, do they speak? Or did you just drag them out of the gorilla cage at the Berlin Zoo?"

"Fuck the bullshit, McCurry. Are you ready to talk or not?"

"I don't have to say a fuckin' thing to you, Jennings. You obviously don't realize the load of shit that's gonna come down on you for this."

"Listen asshole, I know you an' that Kraut've been up to no good for some time. I know you were meetin' someone in London and I wanna know what it was about. Long as I uncover what you were up to, I don't got nothin' to worry about. An' you're not leaving here until ya tell me everything. So, you wanna do it the easy way or the hard way?"

"Go fuck yourself Jennings."

"All right Rankin, throw him back in his room."

Rankin herded McCurry back to the room, followed him in and closed the door. Grabbing him by the neck of his shirt, Rankin slammed him face first into the wall. Pinning him there, he leaned over and whispered in McCurry's ear: "Guess what, numb nuts, I c'n talk jus' fine. I hope you don't, 'cause that'll jus' give me more chances ta beat the shit outa ya."

Throwing McCurry to the floor, Rankin said, "Whatsa' matter, McCurry? Where's your smart mouth now?" He turned and left the room.

Light-headed and dizzy, McCurry wasn't sure he could make it up to his cot. He turned over on his back and stretched out on the floor. Closing his eyes, he decided to wait until the room stopped spinning before trying anything else. These guys are totally nuts, he thought. I am really in some deep shit this time. Better start being a little more careful about taunting them.

* * *

McCurry didn't know when he had fallen asleep, but he opened his eyes to a room that was almost totally black. He was afraid to move because his body hurt all over. The taste of blood was making him nauseous and he was having difficulty breathing through his nose.

Being careful not to move too quickly, he reached up to feel his face, and found there was an abundance of stickiness around his nose and mouth. He figured this was the result of an accumulation of blood that hadn't completely dried. Slowly, he pulled himself up to a sitting position with his back against the cot, and waited for the room to stop spinning. After about a quarter of an hour, he felt he was stable enough to stand up and get to the sink, which was only a few feet away. When he got to his feet, he leaned over the cot to find the wall and then slowly followed the wall until his knees bumped up against the toilet. He knew the sink was just to the left of the toilet, so he took the chance that he could maintain his balance, let go of the wall and stood upright. He then carefully sidestepped around the toilet until his hands found the sink basin. Leaning over the sink, he turned the cold water tap full on and, with cupped hands, started ladling the water onto his face. The cold brought some relief to his battered nose and he thought he was managing to get most of the dried blood off. He would have to wait until the sun came up to get a better idea, although without a mirror he still wouldn't know how bad he looked.

After making his way back to the cot, he lay down and waited for sleep to bring relief to the aching pain he felt throughout his body.

*   *   *

"Wakey, wakey, wakey."

Oh fuck, McCurry thought, that must be Jennings himself come to torture me this time. He was a little afraid of opening his eyes, sure his head would explode if he did.

"Jesus Christ, McCurry, you look like shit. What did you do to yourself? Trip and hit the toilet or sink or something?"

McCurry took a chance, opened his eyes, pivoted so his legs were off the cot and sat up.

"Yeah right, Jennings. Who the fuck ya think's dumb enough to believe that story."

"Well, I can't imagine what else it coulda been. Think you can make it out to the table? I'll get you some aspirin and something to eat for breakfast."

When he got to the table, McCurry asked if there were a bathroom with a mirror. Jennings directed him to a door on the opposite side of the room and McCurry went in to inspect the damage. His left eye was blackened, but not swollen too badly, all things considered. His nose, on the other hand, was bent slightly to the right and was swollen nearly shut. Blood was still caked all around his nose, mouth and down his chin, He washed away the blood the best he could and used the wash cloth as a cold compress for his nose. After a few minutes' relief, Jennings shouted, "All right McCurry, get on out here. Trust me, shithead, you're not gonna die or nuthin'."

As McCurry gingerly lowered himself into the chair next to the table, holding the wash cloth on his nose, Jennings put a glass of water and two aspirin in front of him. "Take these, they'll help dull the pain."

McCurry decided he was going to say as little as possible. These guys were crazier than he thought and he didn't want to get beat up again. He took the aspirin and quickly drank down the full glass of water.

"Hungry, are ya?" Jennings asked.

McCurry shook his head in the affirmative. Jennings told Rankin to see if he would find a couple of bananas, then turned to McCurry and asked if he felt any better.

"That must've been a hell of a fall you took in there. You gotta be more careful, McCurry. Who knows what might've happened."

McCurry maintained his silence. When Rankin returned, he threw two overripe bananas down in front of him. McCurry quickly peeled one and wolfed it down in three bites. As he was beginning to peel the second, Jennings asked, "Feel more like openin' up and fillin' us in on what you and that Kraut were up to now?"

McCurry finished the second banana before responding. Slowly and calmly he said, "Listen Jennings, what Wachter and I were doing was perfectly legal and none of your business. Now, if you could just get me back to my unit, I will be happy to back up your explanation of my self-inflicted injuries."

"Oh, you ain't gonna get off that easy motherfucker. You're not leavin' here until ya lay it all out for us. Now, I'm sure you're hurtin' pretty bad right now, so why don't ya go back to bed and give that aspirin some time ta work. Ya might also want ta think about all the bad things that could happen when it gets dark again tonight."

McCurry got up and stumbled back to the bedroom, relieved when he was allowed to go in on his own without being shoved to the floor again by one of the goons. Had that happened, he wasn't sure he would be able to get up. He lay down on the bunk and was asleep again before Jennings had closed and locked the door.

* * *

McCurry wasn't sure how long he had slept when he was awakened by what sounded like pounding on the building's front door. He tried to sit up, but fell back down when the room started spinning again. The pounding started once more and then he heard someone shout, "Jennings, you stupid motherfucker, open this goddamned door." He heard the door open and the same voice shout, "All right Jennings, you psycho, what the fuck's going on in here."

"I don't know what ya mean, Captain. What d'ya think is going on?"

"Listen, Jennings, you see these MPs? They're gonna cuff you in a couple minutes and take you in for further questioning. So you're already in deep shit. Don't start covering yourself up with it. Is there anyone else here with you?"

"Well ya know, Captain ..."

"Just answer the question, asshole. Is there anyone else here with you."

"Over there in the bedroom."

McCurry heard someone fumbling at the door and then what sounded like his company commander's voice say, "Give me the key to this deadbolt." When the door opened, Capt. Hanover burst through and stopped short when he saw McCurry.

"Jesus Christ, McCurry, are you all right?"

"That kind of depends on your definition of all right, Captain. I'll live. Man, I never thought I would be glad to see you."

"Can you walk?"

"Probably, but some help would sure be appreciated."

Hanover called Evans in and told him to help McCurry to the car. "Wow, you even brought the cavalry along," McCurry said as his good buddy Evans came through the door.

"Not really the cavalry, just me," Evans responded. "Here, let me give you a hand up."

When Evans got McCurry situated in the back seat of the car, he finally let himself drift off into a deep sleep. He only came around when some emergency personnel were trying to get him out of the car and onto a stretcher.

*   *   *

McCurry awoke in a hospital room and saw Evans standing beside his bed.

"Man, I was beginning to think you'd never wake up," Evans said. "You really look like shit, buddy."

"I really feel like shit. How'd you guys find me?"

Evans explained that when Wachter left his kiosk to get some lunch, he noticed McCurry's VW microbus parked on a side street. "I guess it's good you painted all those flowers on it after all," Evans said. "At least it stands out."

Evans said Wachter came to him and said he was sure McCurry was in trouble. "Knowing you, I just said you had probably hooked up with some girl before getting to the kiosk and went off with her. 'You watch, Horst, he'll show up when we go to work on mids tonight.'

"Wachter told me about your encounter with the CID in London and how you had ridiculed the head of that operation. He said he was concerned the guy would seek revenge. I said I doubted it, but that in any case we had to wait to see if you showed up at work.

"When you didn't show up, I went to Lieutenant Vincent and told him the story Wachter told me. Vincent said it sounded hokey to him, but that if you weren't back by morning, he and I could go to Hanover to let him decide what to do.

"Long story short, in the morning Hanover called the CID commanding officer, Captain Jones, and, when he explained his concern, the CID officer suspected what was going on. Apparently this Jennings character is a loose cannon who has set up rogue operations before. Jones checked to see if anyone knew where Jennings was. When it was pretty well determined that he was missing, Jones told us of the safe house they maintained in the Grune. And you know the rest of the story.

"Hanover said they are going to try to find a way to prosecute Jennings and the two goons with him without bringing you into it."

A Really Hot Sauna

After McCurry had rested for a few days, Evans asked if he felt like joining him and his girlfriend, Sonja, on a trip to the sauna.

"I don't know, Dwight. I'm still a little sore. Think I'll just keep resting here for a while."

"C'mon Mike. It'll be good for you. It's co-ed, and a place where everyone goes au naturel. Should be good for your body and soul."

McCurry had learned from Evans that saunas in Germany were a manifestation of the relaxed attitude toward nudity. While there were some nude beaches and other beaches where women would shed their tops without complaints from those around them, the best place for a day of relaxation in the nude was at one of the numerous saunas.

How Evans met his new girlfriend, Sonja, was a prime example of the German's casual attitude toward sex. Evans told McCurry he had met Sonja at one of the popular clubs along the Ku'damm. After a few drinks and some dancing, she asked if he would like to come home with her.

"Wow, what a night," Evans had told McCurry at the time. "She was absolutely insatiable, but I wasn't complaining."

After they had finished their love-making, Evans said, he had fallen asleep. In the morning, however, he had just about jumped out of his skin when he was awakened by Sonja's mother coming in with a tray of coffee and lebkuchen, a richly-spiced gingerbread German specialty.

"She wanted me to feel welcome," Evans said. "Problem is, I couldn't exactly get out of bed and greet her properly."

Since that morning, Evans had been virtually living with – and had basically become a part of – Sonja's family.

"Well, a guess a little fresh air wouldn't hurt me any," McCurry said, getting up and putting on his shoes.

"Yeah, right. I'm sure fresh air is what you are looking forward to."

When they arrived at the sauna, they paid their entry fee in a clean, nicely appointed lobby. Each was given a towel and a locker key on a wristband. Since Evans knew the way to the locker room, they didn't need directions.

"Holy shit, Dwight," McCurry whispered. "We even share lockers with the women? I think I had better take a cold shower first."

It took a great deal of self-control for McCurry to keep from staring at Sonja as she was undressing. The three disrobed and stowed their clothes and valuables in the lockers. Sonja carried a small bag with essentials and offered to put McCurry's wallet in with her things. They then headed out into the main compound.

Beautifully kept grass ran down a slight incline to three pools. To their right was the sauna and down behind the pools were a small bar and restaurant. Lying around and sunning themselves on lounge chairs or towels were perhaps 30 or 40 men and women. What struck McCurry was that the women were among the most beautiful he had seen so far in Germany – and it wasn't because they were all nude.

McCurry had spent some time on beaches along the Wannsee, a large body of water near the Hill that was a popular recreation area among Germans. What he noticed there was that a great deal of the women were clad in bikinis – and the vast majority of those should not have been.

"You know the big, Brunhilda-type of bar maids you'd find at the beer halls in South Germany," McCurry once told a friend.

"Picture them in bikinis and that is what you will find in most places along the Wannsee."

I guess the beautiful women would rather have nothing on at all to wearing a bikini, he thought.

"C'mon Mike, we'll go and sit in the sauna for about ten or fifteen minutes," Evans said, bringing McCurry back to the present.

"Lead the way, McDuff."

As McCurry entered the sauna he noticed it wasn't large, maybe about twenty feet by twenty feet, with wooden benches all around and the heating element in the middle.

"This is really hot," said McCurry, thinking that he was thankful it was also very dark as he accidentally rubbed up against Sonja.

"Sit down over there," said Sonja. "You'll get used to it."

The temperature in the sauna was maintained at about 180 to 190 degrees Fahrenheit. Sonja explained that sweating was good for the body. "The sweat helps you get rid of harmful toxins and even some fat," she said.

"Why the three pools?" McCurry asked to keep his mind off toxins and fat pouring out of his body.

"One of the pools is very cold," Evans explained. "The one in the middle is warm and the third is hot. It's supposed to be good for your body to jump into the cold pool after you come out of the sauna, but if it's too cold you can jump into the warm one. The hot one is for relaxing later on."

This hot-to-cold temperature contrast, the new sauna expert Evans explained, seals the pores so the toxins excreted while in the sauna can't be reabsorbed. It also enhances circulation, he said.

These explanations by Evans reminded McCurry of the guys who insisted they bought Playboy magazines for the articles. But, oh well, who am I to complain.

McCurry thought he would need the cold pool rather often as the day wore on.

Taking what looked somewhat like a hard sponge from her bag, Sonja said, "What you need to do after you have been in here a little bit, Mike, is to take this and scrub your body with it. It helps draw out the toxins and remove dead layers of skin."

"What the hell is it?" McCurry asked.

"It's called a loofah," she said. "It's actually produced from a plant but is very good for exfoliating the skin. Here, let me show you."

Stepping over him so she could get some room on the other side, McCurry was once again thankful for how dark the sauna was. She got up on her knees next to him on the bench and told him to lean forward. She then began to vigorously rub his back.

McCurry let out an involuntary moan as the throbbing grew between his legs.

"See, it feels good, doesn't it?" Sonja asked.

"You could say that," he managed to get out.

She then leaned back and handed the loofah to him. "Here, now you can do the rest of your body." Thank god she didn't ask me to do her back, he thought.

A short while later, Evans said, "Okay, time to get up and hit the cold pool. You won't believe how good it'll feel."

Oh yes I will, McCurry thought. "I'll be right out. I just need a few minutes more," he said. He was still waiting for his erection to subside.

*   *   *

"Jesus fucking Christ is that cold!" McCurry exclaimed as he rocketed out of the pool. Evans and Sonja, who had been sitting on the side of the pool with their legs dangling in the water, laughed so hard they nearly fell in again.

"I told you it was really cold," Evans said.

"You didn't tell me there would practically be ice cubes floating on the surface," said McCurry, who had wrapped himself in a towel and was trying to keep his teeth from chattering.

"Don't worry, you'll feel great in a few minutes," Evans said. "When you collect yourself, we'll go over to the snack bar."

*   *   *

After Evans fished his wallet out of Sonja's satchel, she went off to find a table for them. When he joined McCurry at the bar, McCurry said he ordered three beers for them. "I'll pay for this round," Evans said, laying a ten mark note on the counter.

"Good thing, 'cause I don't seem to have my wallet with me," McCurry countered.

When the brews were drawn and placed on the counter, McCurry and Evans carried them over to join Sonja at the table. She was just finishing touching up her makeup. Jesus Christ, McCurry thought, she sure doesn't need any makeup to stand out in here. With that thought, he felt a stirring in his groin once again and quickly sat down and pulled his chair up to the table.

"So, how're ya feeling now, Mike?" Evans asked.

"I'm still a little sore, but getting better. This place is a big help. Thanks for asking me along."

"Oh goodness" Sonja remarked. "I forgot all about your bruises when I scrubbed your back in the sauna. I hope I didn't hurt you."

"Nah, most of the damage is to my face. Which reminds me Dwight, you haven't commented on how great I look with a crooked nose."

"I'll let you know when the swelling goes down, moron."

"Hey Dwight, all kidding aside, I don't know what would've happened to me if you hadn't acted after Horst contacted you. That was one fuckin' scary situation."

"Yeah, no problem," he said. Pausing a moment to take a sip of his beer, Evans asked, "What the fuck do ya think it was all about?"

"Bottom line, Jennings is just a psych job. Somehow he got it in his head that I was conspiring with Wachter to sell secret information. He actually followed us to London and tried to pull a similar trick there. I called his bluff there and sent him runnin' off with his tail between his legs. I think beating the shit out of me in the Grune was more a form of revenge than really trying to get information."

"Well, at least he's done for now," Evans said. "Captain said he would probably be bounced out on a bad conduct discharge."

"Better to send him to Vietnam."

"I'll drink to that," Evans said. "Speaking of drinking, let's finish our beers and go back for another round in the sauna."

A Cure for the "Walled-in Blues"

McCurry could feel himself falling prey to the Berlin "walled-in blues." For night life, there probably wasn't a city more exciting in the world than Berlin. In his early days here, he was pretty much consumed by the nearly constant parties that seemed integral to the lives of Army Security Agency personnel. More than a year into his tour now, he recognized that parties weren't enough of a distraction. If he felt he were stagnating in the States, he would just jump in his car and go for a two- or three-hour drive to clear out the cobwebs. Often he would take off for New York City, find a place to park near Battery Park and just go for a walk among the crowds. Here, a person couldn't drive much more than an hour in any direction without hitting a wall or fence.

Arriving at the hill for another eight-hour session listening to conversations of East German Central Committee operatives, McCurry felt the day already closing in on him. He wanted to make a right-hand turn at the gate and saunter on back down the hill and leave what he often felt was a fenced-in insane asylum behind him. Instead he went in and started setting up his tapes.

Around mid-morning, McCurry and Evans were able to get away and take a break from their listening posts. Instead of heading for the snack bar for something to eat, they had gone outside the fence for a smoke. Sitting on a slope on the northeast side of the hill, McCurry realized he still hadn't lost his fascination with the incredible views of Berlin's skyline. The most notable landmark seen from where he and Evans sat today was the world famous Olympic Stadium. Even here, though, the blues seemed to creep in and dampen the enthusiasm he once had for this city.

"Tell me Dwight. Have you ever felt this city was closing in on you? Can you imagine what it's like to live your whole life on this walled-in island, surrounded by hostile neighbors? Sometimes I feel like jumping in my car, blasting through the gates and not stopping until I reach West Germany."

"Whoa, buddy, take it easy. I been here longer than you, so I know how ya feel. Ya need to find some kind of distraction other than clubbing and parties."

"If you were back in the States right now, in the winter time, what kinds of things would you be doing?"

"Hey Mike, I'm from Newark, remember. Distractions there could get ya killed."

"If I were home, I'd be waiting for the first snow of winter so I could head out, find a good hill and spend an afternoon sledding."

"Well, man, you're sittin' on a pretty good hill right here. All we need is some snow and a sled and you'll be in business. 'Course, if ya break an arm or a leg, you're liable to be court martialed for damaging government property."

"Yeah, right," McCurry said, dropping his cigarette on the ground and crushing it out with the heel of his boot. "Better get back to our positions before Landry comes lookin' for us."

*   *   *

When their shift ended, Evans told McCurry to meet him at the Stork Club for a few beers after he turned in the bus. When McCurry arrived, Rich Sezov and Dave Alexander were sitting at a table with Evans.

McCurry grabbed a beer at the bar and went over to join his friends. "We've got a problem," Evans said after McCurry had settled into his chair and started sipping his beer. "Mike's suffering from a classic case of the 'walled-in blues.' It's our job to snap him out of it before he does something he'll regret."

"Yeah, ya mean like that asshole gator who drove his tank through the fenced-in zone," Sezov said. "What the fuck ever happened to him? Did we ever get the tank back?"

"Focus, Rich. This isn't funny," Evans said. "We gotta find him a distraction, something to plan for and take his mind off how confining life here can be."

"Yeah, like hot parties and easy women aren't enough of a distraction," said Alexander.

"Get serious, you two. You haven't been around as long as I have. Gators aren't the only people who lose their marbles and go on a rampage."

"Easy Dwight, I'm going to be okay," said McCurry. He felt more than a little uneasy about this discussion of his mental state. Even the hint of depression was enough of an excuse for those in charge to yank someone off the Hill and strip him of his security clearance.

"You're okay now, and here's what we're gonna do to make sure you stay okay," Evans responded.

Evans related McCurry's remarks about how an afternoon of sledding was something that could help him shake off his depression. He told Sezov and Alexander their job would be to find a sled they could use. In the meantime, he and McCurry would scout out an area that would be good for sledding once the snows came.

Evans had heard there was a small skiing center that operated on the back side of the Hill in the late '50s. The NSA had forced it to shut down after taking over the Hill, Evans said, adding that this could prove to be a perfect spot for their sledding activities. The next day the two had off, Evans asked McCurry if they could drive out to the Hill to see if they could find the old ski slope. Instead of turning off at the entrance to their work site, they continued around the Hill on an old dirt access road. After about a half mile, they came to an overgrown lot. Driving into and around the lot, they saw an old tractor set up on cement blocks that was obviously used for a rope pull for skiers.

"Well, I think we've found the spot," Evans said. "Now, let's follow the access road to see how far it is to the top. Think this fuckin' flower mobile can make it up the hill?"

"That's what flower power is for."

"Yeah, right."

Rather than going straight up the hill, the road veered off to the left on a gradual incline for about a half mile and then looped back towards the slope, continuing its upward climb until, after about another half mile, it came out to a clearing.

"This must be the top," Evans said, opening his door and jumping out of the microbus.

After a short walk, they came to the top of the run and looked over. The hill was a lot steeper than they expected and was broken up by several areas that leveled out a bit to allow skiers to cut over and slow their descent before dropping off again.

"I don't know, Dwight, that is one hell of a drop."

"Holy shit, is this the fearless McCurry talkin'? We're big boys now and we need a big hill to go sledding on. This is perfect."

"If you say so, Newark boy, expert on sledding."

"Hey man, the only place where we could find hills was next to the Turnpike. You had to be pretty good to stop before sliding out into the path of Turnpike traffic."

"Okay, fine. But how d'ya expect someone to get from the bottom back up here after making their run, assuming anyone *will* want to risk life and limb a second time?"

"That's just a matter of logistics, McCurry. What's the Army taught you anyway?"

"Besides German? Nothing."

"Well, I figure we'll just get someone like Stu Mason to be a shuttle driver for your microbus. He can drop people off at the top and then take them back up when they reach the bottom."

"Other than how cavalierly you offer up my VW, it really does sound like a great plan. Now I'm getting excited."

"Enough to run the blues off."

"Well, look at it this way, Dwight. If I can live through a day of sledding on *that* hill, I guess I can survive another year or so in Berlin."

"Okay, let's head back. Sezov and Alexander are expectin' us to meet 'em at the Stork Club tonight."

When asked if he and Sezov had found any sleds, Alexander said, "Even better. Lee Grimes said he's got a toboggan he bought right after coming here. It's in storage right now, but he'll get it out and we can use it as long as he can come along."

"Holy fuck. How cool is that," Evans exclaimed. "What d'ya think, McCurry. Can you imagine a toboggan on that hill?"

"I can imagine dying on a toboggan on that hill."

The four of them and Grimes were starting swings the next day. They would be on the four to midnight shift for seven days before their next break began. The third day into their rotation, Berlin was hit with one of its regular winter snow storms, guaranteeing there would be plenty of snow on the hill when the B-trick shift ended.

*　*　*

Evans, Alexander, Sezov, Grimes and Mason waited for McCurry to pick them up outside Andrews barracks. Mason had agreed to be the shuttle driver as long as he was able to get in one run down the hill. The heavy snow of four days earlier had been mostly cleared from the roadways. Since getting personnel to the Hill was viewed by NSA as a national security issue, clearing the dirt road through the Grunewald was a priority. None of the men knew how bad the old access road would be, but it wound its way through large evergreens which gave it some protection, so they thought it should be passable.

The day was cold and overcast, threatening the possibility of more snow. Evans, however, had already declared they would have enough time to get out to the hill and get in a few runs before any snow started. Since most of the route they would be traveling over was the same one used by the trick buses, they were sure help would soon arrive if they got bogged down in any snow.

"Where the fuck is McCurry?" Alexander asked, stomping up and down in an attempt to keep his feet warm.

"Don't worry, he'll be here soon," Evans said. "As a matter of fact, speak of the devil, there he is right now."

They all walked over to where McCurry had parked the VW. "A little late, aren't ya buddy," Evans said when they reached the microbus.

"I had to clean a lot of shit out to make sure there would be room" McCurry said. "As it is, it's goin' to be a little tight."

Grimes, Alexander, Sezov and Mason squeezed into the back. When they were situated, McCurry opened the rear door of the VW, and slid the toboggan in over their heads for as far as it would go, letting the door rest on the portion that wouldn't fit. Then he and Evans got in and started off.

"Sorry guys. Guess it will be a little cold back there with the door open, but at least it will acclimate you for the weather on the hill."

The access road proved tricky, but was passable. When they arrived at the clearing at the top of the run, the four passengers in the rear piled out and walked over to where they would be starting. McCurry and Evans got out and followed.

"Holy shit, are you two nuts?" said Grimes. "You know there isn't any steering device on a toboggan, right?"

"So what d'ya gotta steer for?" Evans asked. "It's a straight run down with no trees or anything in the way."

"You guys don't know shit about toboggans, do you?"

"What's to know? You sit down on it, grab the ropes along the side and hope you're still on when ya get to the bottom."

"Yeah, right," said Grimes.

"Well, all I know is I'm just glad you guys asked me to be the shuttle driver," Mason said. "Gimme the keys, McCurry and I'll meet you guys at the bottom. If ya make it that is."

McCurry and Evans walked back to the microbus with Mason. After they pulled the toboggan out and slammed the back door shut, Mason started up and headed back down the hill.

"All right, listen up," Grimes said. He had set the toboggan up on the far side of the launch site angled slightly toward the near side. "We're gonna try to start this thing on a slant so it doesn't pick up as much speed as it would going straight down. I'll be up front. If I lean left, you all lean left. If I lean right, you lean right. Got it."

"Yes sir," said McCurry, saluting smartly.

"Knock it off, McCurry. This takes teamwork, or otherwise we'll all be flying down the hill without a toboggan under us. Speaking of which, if you do feel we are going over or you're falling off, just go with it. The only way you'll get hurt is if you tighten up and fight it. Okay?"

Grimes got on first, bringing his knees up and sliding as far forward as possible. McCurry followed, sliding up against Grimes and stretching his legs out on each side. Evans and Alexander followed McCurry. As Sezov started to get on behind Alexander, Grimes told him to slowly push the toboggan forward and, when it started moving on its own, to jump on.

The toboggan picked up speed at an incredible rate, plowing across the snow and hurling it up into the faces of the riders. McCurry was virtually blinded by the storm and wondered how Grimes was going to be able to see well enough to steer. Nearly as soon as that thought entered his mind, he felt Grimes lean hard to the left. He followed suit and felt Evans, Alexander and Sezov do the same. The toboggan seemed to tip, but remained on its edge as it started to turn, decreasing in speed significantly the further it came around. They hit the first shelf area and slowed even more before reaching the lip and hurling back down once again. Grimes leaned hard to the right, turning the toboggan into another angling slide in an attempt to keep some control over the increasing speed.

Before McCurry even realized it, the toboggan under Grimes' guidance had made it down to the last shelf and turned into the final downhill run. Grimes had apparently gained confidence and let the sled run nearly straight down on this last leg. Just as they were nearly at the end, the toboggan hit something buried in the snow and went airborne, with its riders hurling off in several directions.

Grimes was the first up and on his feet. "You all okay," he called out.

"I'm fine," said McCurry, who had just managed to pull himself up and out of a snow drift. Evans, who was right behind McCurry said he was okay. "Me too," yelled Alexander, who was at least fifteen feet off to their left.

"Hey Sezov, where're you?" Grimes called. It was then that McCurry heard the low groans coming from a point some twenty feet to their rear. Simultaneously, he, Evans and Grimes started scrambling up the hill. Sezov was laying on his stomach. There was blood coming from a wound about mid-calf of his left leg. The portion of his leg below the wound angled away from the remainder of the leg.

McCurry pulled off his jacket and started unbuttoning his shirt. "What the fuck are you doing?" asked Alexander, who had just reached them.

"We gotta wrap the wound and immobilize his leg as best we can and then we gotta get him the fuck out of here."

When he had gotten his shirt off and was down next to Sezov, McCurry said, "Listen to me Rich. Your leg is fucked up and bleeding. I have to wrap it to stop the bleeding before we can turn you over. I'm sorry, buddy, but it's probably gonna hurt like a bitch."

Sezov just continued to moan until McCurry started to lift the leg so he could get the shirt under the bleeding portion. The moans turned to screams and, impossibly, he tried to move away from McCurry. "Hold on to 'em," McCurry shouted. By the time McCurry got the shirt wrapped around the leg and knotted over the wound, he was covered with blood. Oh shit, he said to himself, this is really bad.

Pulling his jacket back on, McCurry said, "All right, we've gotta get him rolled over on his back and we need the toboggan to get him down to the van."

"Is it safe to move him?" asked Alexander.

"Do we have any choice?" Grimes asked.

When Grimes looked down the hill to see if he could determine where the toboggan had landed, he saw Mason at the bottom, probably drawn to the scene by Sezov's screams. "Hey Stu," he called, "Find the toboggan and bring it up here."

Mercifully, Sezov's screams had ceased once they had him on the toboggan. McCurry surmised he passed out from the pain. Using a knife he always carried with him, Evans cut the rope away from the toboggan, which they used to secure Sezov for the trip down the hill and to the van. Once they had slid the toboggan on top of the seats, Mason, Alexander and Grimes got in the back to hold it in place. Jumping in behind the wheel with Evans sliding in on the other side, McCurry said they needed to get Sezov up to their work site where an ambulance could be summoned.

"Oh fuck," said Evans, "this ain't gonna be good"

"We don't have any choice, Dwight. Right now, I'm only worried about Rich."

*   *   *

McCurry, Evans, Grimes, Alexander and Mason stood in Capt. Hanover's office waiting for their commanding officer to finish studying papers on his desk. All five had been confined to the barracks after returning from the hospital the day before. At six this morning they had been roused from their sleep by Jim Gleason, the company clerk, who told them to report to Hanover's office at zero eight hundred. "And McCurry," Gleason said, "if I wuz you, I'd wear clean fatigues."

When they arrived at the hospital the night before, escorted by the military police who had met them at the top of the Hill, they were told Sezov had been rushed into surgery as soon as the ambulance arrived. Each of the four had told the emergency room doctor that they were okay, after which the MPs had escorted them back to the barracks.

Looking up from his papers, Hanover said, "You'll be happy to know that Sezov made it through his surgery okay. He is in serious condition, but the docs say he will have a complete recovery.

"Now, what the fuck do I do with you five? That was a foolhardy stunt, even for you McCurry. What would've happened if you had all been injured? You could have lay in the snow and died before anyone found you."

McCurry wanted to correct him, letting him know that Mason was their driver and not on the toboggan with them, but thought it more prudent to keep his mouth shut for a change.

"You guys are lucky in two ways. First, McCurry, the doctors said Sezov might not have made it if you hadn't acted quickly to bind his wound. Second, I am not about to gut the mission by taking all five of you out of action. Do you think that scare was enough to knock some sense into your heads?"

All five said "yessir" in unison.

"All right. Get the fuck out of here. You're dismissed."

Heading back to the barracks feeling relieved over how events had unfolded, Evans asked McCurry, "Think this helped cure you of the walled-in blues?"

"Yeah, at least it did that."

McCurry Vs. the Russian MiGs

The next break he got, McCurry headed out to meet Wachter at the kiosk. After closing it up and making sure it was secure, the two went to a nearby pub, ordered a couple of beers and went to a table in the back. Wachter said a new friend of his, an Australian named Daniel Harris, was planning to meet him here. While in Australia, Harris had married a German national who had emigrated there from her home in Berlin. Harris was a master wood worker, Wachter said, who created magnificent cabinets and other furniture. After Harris and his wife, Andrea, had been married nearly 10 years, the economy turned sour and Harris was having difficulty finding work.

Andrea's family suggested things might be better in Berlin, so Harris, his wife and two children had moved back here nearly two years ago.

Before Wachter and McCurry had finished their first beer, Harris arrived. Wachter waved to him. Harris picked up three beers and joined them. "This is Mike McCurry, Dan. I was just telling him about you."

"Nice to meet ya, Dan," McCurry said.

"Nice to meet you as well, mate. Horst has told me a lot about you."

"Uh oh. I'm fucked."

"No, no man. All good."

"So, how has your move back here worked out."

"I'll tell ya, man, things aren't a hell of a lot better here than they were in Australia," Harris said. "If Andrea weren't getting some help from her family, we'd be lucky if I made enough to feed us."

McCurry thought Harris would have people lining up to buy the furniture he created. The problem though, Harris explained to McCurry, was that the cost to produce his pieces was steep. To make a profit, he had to charge what were extraordinarily high prices, compared to store-brand furniture. In the current economy, there just weren't that many people who could afford it.

Harris had gotten some work in a shop that created furniture for stores that was essentially an assembly line. The low wages he earned there weren't enough to house, clothe and feed a family of four.

"Ya know, Dan," McCurry said, "we have a storage room where I work filled with cartons of C-rations. I think they were used before a mess hall was built there and I heard they're planning to throw a lot of them out to make room for regular food."

McCurry said the main courses don't taste that bad – "at least they are meat and potatoes" – and there are always things that even the Army can't spoil like peanut butter, crackers and some of the desserts.

"Want me to see if I can pick up some of 'em for ya?" McCurry asked.

"That'd be great," Harris said. "It's gotta be a lot better than some of the stuff we eat."

Because the cost of meat in Germany was so high, many families subsisted on a variety of different meals made from potatoes during the week, saving any meat they could get for the Sunday meal. While many hausfraus got pretty creative with their potato recipes, it still left a lot to be desired in the daily menus.

The meals in storage on the Hill were officially labeled MEAL, COMBAT, INDIVIDUAL, or MCIs. Soldiers still referred to them as C-rations. They had several different meat "meals" such as meat chunks with beans in tomato sauce, ham and lima beans, beef slices with potatoes in gravy, among others. While they didn't sound very palatable, a good cook could create meals that weren't too bad.

But then these meal packages also contained peanut butter and cheese spread, good sources of protein that couldn't be screwed up, along with crackers.

The next day at work, McCurry went to the mess sergeant and asked if it was true they were getting rid of a lot of the C-rations in the storage room.

"We've got to dump at least thirty cases," the sergeant said. "Frankly, I don't know why we have to keep any, but then I just follow orders."

"I have this friend who has a family of four and is having trouble finding work who could sure use them," McCurry said. "Mind if I just cart them out of here to get them off your hands?"

"Are you fuckin' kidding me? I could get busted for a trick like that. Regs require them to be trashed and destroyed."

"You mean to tell me, you're going to destroy them but you can't give them to somebody who's having difficulty feeding his kids?"

"What can I tell you, McCurry? It's the Army. But then, if they just happened to disappear without going out the front gate, I doubt anyone would miss 'em. 'Course I don't know how somethin' like that could happen," he said, turning to go back to work.

McCurry realized that the top of their infamous toboggan run wasn't far from the fence that circled their work site. He contacted a buddy of his who was working mids, a time the mess hall was all but deserted. He told him about his dilemma, and asked if he could get a couple friends to help him carry thirty cases of the C-rations around back and pass them over to McCurry, who would be there with Wachter and Harris to load up his VW microbus.

"Fuck yeah," his friend said. "I can't believe this fuckin' Army and its ridiculous regulations."

Two days later, Harris had enough C-rations to help feed his family for the next six months. McCurry never learned if anyone ever discovered the missing C-rations. He seriously doubted it.

*   *   *

One afternoon at work, McCurry was daydreaming while leaning back in his chair with his feet up on the console as usual. He nearly did a backflip out his chair when a roar that sounded as if it emanated from hell itself consumed the facility, shaking equipment and splitting ear drums.

"Jesus Christ, what was that?" he screamed, hearing himself as if under water.

"Just a periodic visit from our Soviet brethren," said Maynard Johnson, a German linguist who had been at the Hill more than six months longer than McCurry. He explained that the Soviets used a variety of means to harass the residents of West Berlin. One was to play a surprise visit by sending in several MiG fighters to buzz the city, rattling nerves as well as buildings with each pass.

One of the unsettling aspects of living in West Berlin during these times of high tension with the Soviets was the fact the city was virtually defenseless. Surrounded by East Germany and its garrisons of Soviet troops, it would be very difficult if not impossible to stop Russians from marching into West Berlin and taking it over. This fact was never far from the minds of West Berliners.

The British and American soldiers atop Teufelsberg often got advance warnings of these runs and got a close-up view. Since Teufelsberg was near the western border of the city with the downtown section spread out to the east, the MiG pilots used the nearly four-hundred-foot-high hill as a sighting point for their approach. In succession, two, three or four of the Soviet fighters would roar by less than a hundred feet to the north and slightly above the installation on the Hill.

Before the day ended, the Soviet fighters made three more passes, their pilots bringing them in at nearly roof-top level over downtown Berlin.

When McCurry got back to base at the end of the trick, he went straight to Sezov.

"Do you guys pick up any chatter to let you know when those Russian fighter jockeys are going to buzz the city?" McCurry asked him.

"Of course we do," Sezov said. "We usually just get a window on when they will be coming, depending on the weather."

He said this day's passes were the first of several planned. According to his division's intercepts, Sezov said, a few more runs were expected in the next couple days.

That night, McCurry checked out a sporting goods store in the area and found what he wanted – a slingshot used for hunting. He bought the slingshot and a box of steel shot for less than five bucks.

"What the fuck did you buy something like that for?" Evans asked when McCurry showed him his purchase.

"Those MiGs are supposed to be coming back this week and I wanna be prepared."

"What do you mean prepared?"

"Shit man, I'm a red-blooded, flag-waving, apple-pie eatin' American soldier," McCurry said. "I'm not gonna let those jets buzz my Hill without a fight. When they arrive next time, I'll be ready with my trusty slingshot."

"You are a moron McCurry. For the life of me I don't know why I hang out with you."

"Maybe so, Dwight, but I know you love me."

The next day McCurry smuggled his slingshot and ammunition onto the compound. It wasn't difficult to surreptitiously bring anything in or out of the work site. All the guards cared about was seeing a person's badge as he went through the gate.

About halfway through the shift, Sezov came over to McCurry's wing to let him know that the jets were on their way.

"Hey Dave, can you cover for Evans and me while we go out to take a look?" McCurry asked Alexander.

"Sure 'nough. I feel safer in here anyway."

The two told the guard they were going outside for a short break and then walked slowly around to the side of the Hill. When the first jet came screaming in, the roar of its engines and immense size caught them both off guard and they froze in their tracks.

"Shit, fuck," McCurry said. "I didn't even have my slingshot out. I'll be ready for the next one," he vowed as he pulled it out from under his shirt and loaded it with shot.

Off in the distance, they heard the muffled roar of another MiG. McCurry could just make it out well north of the Hill as it started to bank to the south and set up its approach from the west. He knew from Sezov that it was a MiG-21 with its distinctive pencil shape. As it headed toward its western approach point, McCurry was impressed at how sleek the aircraft appeared. Before he knew it, it had made the turn and was starting its approach. It may be a hundred feet to the north, he thought, but it feels like it is coming right down on top of me.

McCurry decided he wasn't going to let it spook him this time. He drew back the sling and took aim. He was facing head on to the jet when it surprised him by taking what was obviously an evasive maneuver.

"Oh fuck, d'ya think he did that because he saw me and didn't know what I was doing?" McCurry asked Evans.

"Can't think of what else it might be," Evans said, laughing almost hysterically.

McCurry shoved the slingshot under a bush and the two high-tailed it back up the Hill, slowing to a walk and lighting cigarettes when they got near the fence.

When they reached the gate, Landry came running out.

"What the fuck're you two doin' now?" their trick sergeant demanded.

"Just takin' a break and watching the jets fly by," McCurry said.

"Is that all you were doin'?"

"Yeah. Why? What the fuck else would we be doing?" McCurry shot back.

"I don't know, but the Russian marys said the Ruskies are going nuts out there. Something spooked their pilots. When I heard you two were outside the compound, I figured ya had to be up to somethin'."

"Can't imagine what we could do to spook 'em," McCurry said, crushing his cigarette butt under his boot. "If you don't mind, Sarge, we'd better be getting back to our positions."

When they were back inside, Alexander met them at the entrance to their wing.

"What happened?" he asked. "All hell broke out here and Sezov came over to find you guys and tell you to keep your heads down."

"Well it appears these Ruskie fighter jocks thought McCurry was going to take them out with a slingshot," Evans said, trying to keep a straight face.

"We didn't do nothing," McCurry said. "That's our story and we're sticking to it."

Not hearing any more about it, they figured those higher up the food chain came to the conclusion that the jets were just practicing evasive maneuvers, using the chatter about being spooked as a cover for their real intent.

When McCurry heard this, all he could say was, "They take convoluted thinking to new heights. It's a good thing there aren't any real hostilities to worry about."

The Sensitive Work of Espionage

One bright spring morning in 1969, Evans and McCurry learned they had been assigned to courier detail for the upcoming shift. Unlike other special duties, the assignment as a courier was sought after. Couriers carried material between the Hill and Rudow, another ASA base in Berlin. Courier duty meant a release from tedium of sitting in front of a bank of tape recorders for eight hours at a time. Much to his delight, Evans was issued a sidearm to carry while on duty.

Evans was a highly intelligent young man, which he would tell you was in spite of his upbringing in a Newark, New Jersey, ghetto. To help shield him from the violence, his parents sent him to Catholic schools. Odd jobs and a number of small, specialized scholarships helped him make it through Rutgers University. He graduated with honors in June 1966. He quickly realized that if he didn't join a branch of the Armed Forces, he would soon be drafted and probably sent to Vietnam. A disproportionate number of young black men were being shipped off to Vietnam and returned to their parents in body bags. Evans decided he didn't want to become one of them. He realized it was unlikely the U.S. would need German interpreters in 'Nam, so he joined the Army Security Agency to obtain the guarantee of training at the Defense Language Institute.

Evans often talked with McCurry of the stereotypes he and other black men had to endure in the racist culture that was one of America's insidious and seemingly incurable diseases. As much as he liked watermelon and fried chicken, Evans refused to eat them in public. He spent years training himself to enunciate properly when speaking and always dressed well, but conservatively.

Evans' cocoon unraveled, however, when the riots erupted in Newark in the summer of 1967. Nearly a week went by before Evans was able to confirm that his parents came through it unharmed. The ugliness of the riots transformed Evans. When he congregated with other blacks, he reverted almost immediately to the street slang that marked him as a product of the urban American ghetto. He started associating with the loosely formed Black Panther organizations in Berlin and adopted their rhetoric against the white American establishment. He began smoking marijuana and hashish almost daily, although that was true of many of the Americans overseas, including McCurry. And, he became fascinated with guns, which is why he enjoyed having the sidearm when they were on courier duty. McCurry still hated weapons of any kind, so he did the driving and Evans carried the courier bag.

Rudow was a small outpost in southeast Berlin, known as Alpha. Here different kinds of espionage activities were carried out. Drivers from this facility, for example, would take their vehicles into East Berlin and see how close they could get to East German military sites before they were fired on. McCurry thought this was a rather low-tech way of testing the East German security measures.

The operations were housed in an old Nazi garrison, shaped like a box. Two sides of the box comprised the buildings in which the various activities were planned. In front of them creating the other two sides of the box was a large, stone courtyard. The sides of the courtyard were defined by the fenced-in no-man's land that created the separation between West Berlin and, in this corner of the city, East Germany. East German soldiers manned twenty-foot-high wooden towers that were erected at regular intervals along the perimeter to keep an eye out for anyone trying to flee to the West.

One of these towers was just outside the far end of the courtyard. Soldiers in this tower were more interested in any activities taking place in or around the courtyard than they were in any potential refugees. McCurry had heard that the guys working at Alpha – no doubt as bored as those on the Hill – regularly devised pranks to keep the tower guards on their toes.

There was a canteen on the second floor of one of the buildings with a window that overlooked the courtyard. From this vantage point, one could see the wide, neatly raked no-man's land on the other side of the first line of fences. Running down the middle of this heavily mined strip were two rows of cement devices that resembled children's jacks meant to stop tanks should an East German citizen manage to get one for an escape attempt. The fencing on the far side was lined with street lamps.

When Evans and McCurry went up to the canteen for a cup of coffee, they found a group of guys gathered around the window overlooking the courtyard. There was a lot of raucous laughter. Walking over, Evans asked, "What the fuck's so funny?"

"Jenkins created this thingamajig that's had those guys in the guard tower going nuts for more than an hour now," one of the guys said.

Jim Jenkins had a reputation as the master of practical jokes at this facility. When Evans and McCurry managed to push their way to the front of the window, they discovered his latest prank. Using what appeared to be parts from an Erector Set, Jenkins had created a small, electric-motor-powered device that had several spinning and whirling parts on its sides and top. He had apparently set it up so it kept going in a wide circle.

"Those fruitcakes in the tower have had binoculars trained on it for more than an hour now," another of the guys told Evans. "Twice superior officers have come up to the tower, talked with one or the other a little and then left. There's probably an entire intelligence unit working right now trying to figure out what it's for."

"Sort of mimics the kind of work we're doing," McCurry said.

A few minutes later, Jenkins appeared in the courtyard. He was carrying a sledge hammer. Shading his eyes and taking a moment to look up at the tower, he picked up the sledge and smashed the device into a flat piece of scrap metal. Immediately one of the guys in the guard tower was on the phone to his superiors again.

On the way back to the Hill, Evans remarked, "We can do better than that."

"Yeah?" McCurry asked. "What d'ya have in mind?"

When they got back, the two rooted through a supply shed in the Hill compound until they found what they were looking for – a four-foot-long piece of pipe that had once been used with a wood-burning stove for heating. "I knew I had seen this at one time," Evans said. "What d'ya think they'd have had a wood-burning stove up here for?"

"Probably during wintertime construction on the Hill," McCurry conjectured.

When McCurry and Evans arrived at Rudow the next day, they proceeded directly to the courtyard. Evans carried the stove pipe under his arm and McCurry held a Coke bottle. They stopped in the middle. Evans kneeled and planted an edge of the pipe between two cobblestones with the top part angled toward the guard tower. "Down a little," said McCurry, shielding his eyes from the sun with a hand and peering up at the guardhouse. He looked at the pipe and back up. "Right a little," he commanded.

The two repeated the procedure a few more times to insure they had the attention of the guard in the tower as well as an audience in the canteen. Then McCurry knelt, dropped the Coke bottle into the stove pipe, covered his head and ducked. Within a fraction of a second, the guards leaped from the tower, apparently thinking a mortar round was about to turn the tower into splinters. Later McCurry heard that one of the guards had broken his leg in two places while the other landed unscathed.

*   *   *

That ended Evans and McCurry's stint as couriers and nearly caused an international incident. This time both might have been court-martialed except that the powers that be just wanted it to all go away.

A Deuce-and-a-Half
and the Bike Race

"I can't believe they expect me to take the guys to work in a deuce-and-a-half," McCurry said to Evans as he pulled up in front of the barracks with one of the 2 1/2-ton all-purpose Army vehicles used to carry everything from supplies to soldiers in the field.

The vehicle's cargo bed had wooden-slat sides with a canvas canopy over the bed. Wooden benches were attached to each side of the bed. It was meant for heavy-duty work, so anyone riding in the back felt every minor bump in the road.

ASA members were accustomed to the comfort of the 37-passenger Mercedes buses. There were times, however, when the motor pool didn't have enough of the buses in service for a trick change and issued a deuce-and-a-half instead.

"Can you imagine the shit I am going to get from the guys," McCurry said. "They're going to blame me every time we hit a bump and one of them gets thrown off the bench."

"Yeah, you'll have a mutiny when we go through the Grune," Evans said. "Better make sure they've got a lot of weed on hand."

"No worry about that," McCurry quipped.

The last three miles of the trip to the Hill through the Grunewald was a dirt road that was consistently filled with ruts. Anyone riding in the back of a deuce-and-a-half would feel every one of them.

"I'll ride up front with you," Evans added. "I'll be damned if I'm going to be bounced out of the back of this piece of shit."

As the guys started showing up and seeing these behemoths waiting for them, the griping began immediately.

"What the fuck, McCurry? You expect us to ride in these things?" asked Charlie Anderson, the chronic B-trick complainer.

"Nah, Charlie, you can walk for all I care. Better get started now if you want to get there in time for the NAAFI truck."

The NAAFI is somewhat akin to the American PX system for British soldiers – only better. Each evening on the Hill – shortly after the start of the swing shift – a NAAFI truck showed up to sell food and drink. For practically pennies, one could get what McCurry believed to be the greatest gift of his UK colleagues – fish and chips loaded with salt and vinegar and wrapped in a newspaper.

"How ya supposed to get up into this fucker?" Barry Berkowitz griped.

"Hey Dwight, why don't you go back there and goose 'em," McCurry said to Evans. "That'll get 'em up and on in a hurry."

When McCurry had a full load, he put the truck in gear and headed off for the Hill. As usual, all treads waited for any vehicle but McCurry's, so his load included just the guys he worked closely with every day. Because of this, he tried to avoid rough areas, but knew it would get brutal when they hit the Grunewald.

"Doesn't it figure, Dwight," McCurry mused as they left the center of town and hit the smooth surface of the autobahn, "that the fuckin' Herms would put a paved bicycle trail right next to that piece of shit they call a road in the Grune."

The paved bicycle path running parallel to the dirt road leading to the Hill was up a small rise and separated from the road by a lightly wooded area. It probably wouldn't even be noticed if someone didn't already know it was there. Army personnel – and especially ASA members – weren't known as avid cyclists.

"You're not thinking what I think you're thinking," Evans exclaimed.

"C'mon Dwight. It's a beautiful day. We're way ahead of the other two trucks. I think it's a great time to forge a new path to the Hill, as it were."

"How do you expect to get up there?" Evans asked as they exited the autobahn and headed into the Grunewald.

"Give me a break, man. These things were designed to get through anything. You don't think a few trees and a little hill will stop it, do you?"

When he got to an opening, McCurry shifted down into first, swung a hard right, and gave it the gas to power his 2 ½-ton missile up the hill. Saplings were crushed to the ground and kicked out the rear with the dirt and other debris. The guys in the back, who had been passing tokes around while on the autobahn, realized that something was different with this ride but didn't really care. It was a miracle none tried to stand up to see what was going on.

When he hit the pavement, McCurry swung a hard left and Evans screamed "Oh shit!"

A couple dozen cyclists, apparently engaged in a race of some sort, were coming right at them at a high rate of speed. There was no room for the deuce-and-a-half to pull off the path and the cyclists were forced to veer off into the woods to keep from being run over.

McCurry shifted up and sped away as quickly as he could. "Hey Mike, what're you doing?" Evans asked.

"Getting as far away from that cluster fuck as I can.

"I looked back and as far as I could see no one was seriously hurt in the melee. Can't say the same for the bikes. I just don't want to hang around to confront an angry German mob. Let the trucks behind us handle that."

When McCurry had put some distance between his truck and the cyclists, he slowed down and started looking for an opening to exit the path and get back to the road again. When he found one, he plowed his way back down and then pulled over to the side of the dirt road. He got out and walked around back.

"You guys enjoying the ride," he asked.

"Fuck yeah," they echoed nearly as one.

"Sorry for that rough patch. The last rainstorm really made a mess. None of you saw anything interesting along the way, did you?"

"We're cool, McCurry," Sezov said. "Let's just get the fuck out of here before the rest of the trick catches up to us."

It seemed to take a while before the other trucks arrived. When they did, McCurry's trick sergeant, Buck Landry, came storming up to him. "Hey McCurry, when we got into the Grune we were hailed over by a bunch of really angry German nationals. They said something about a crazy man driving a big Army truck forced them off their bike path and could have killed them if they hadn't reacted quickly enough."

"Shit, that sounds bad, Sarge. What d'ya think, one of those crazy gators got lost on maneuvers."

"There ain't any maneuvers scheduled for this month, McCurry."

"Well maybe one of the gators went off the reservation for a joy ride. Only explanation that makes any sense, don't ya think."

"Get to work, you crazy son of a bitch. You're probably lucky the Army'll want ta smooth this over without a lot of publicity. One of these days, though, they're really gonna nail you. I just hope I'm around to see it."

"Don't worry, Sarge. If you're not here, I'll send you an invitation."

As Landry stormed off, McCurry turned to Evans and whispered, "Fuck 'em if they can't take a joke."

Taking on the Commanding General

The first time McCurry saw Carl Rosen, he was walking from the off-base apartment he shared with his wife to Andrews to pick up the bus for work. His head was down and he looked kind of lost. McCurry offered him a ride and over the intervening weeks the two had become friends who worked together on the Hill, but not much more.

"Hey Mike, what's the story with this Rosen?" Evans asked one afternoon while the two were sitting on the bus waiting for it to fill up before heading up to the Hill for the swing shift.

"I mean, I see you bringing him into work a lot, he says 'thanks' and then shuffles off to the snack bar. He acts like he doesn't have a friend in the world."

"He's sort of a sad case," McCurry said. "He keeps to himself pretty much because I don't think he knows how to make friends. Besides that, his wife keeps him on a very tight leash. From the little I've gotten out of him, I guess she outweighs him by some 30 or 40 pounds and it's not unusual for her to take a whack at him if he pisses her off."

"Are you shitting me? Why would somebody stay married in a situation like that?"

"I don't know. I guess it's just a case that he can't see far ahead enough to know it's got to end someday. If he could, I think he would move into the barracks tomorrow."

"Why don't we grab him and drag him into the Stork Club after work tonight?" Evans asked.

"All right by me, but I don't really think he'll go."

That night, Evans took on the task of convincing Rosen to join them in the club while McCurry returned his bus to the motor pool. When McCurry got back to the club he was more than a little surprised that Evans and Rosen were inside sharing a beer.

"Well, I don't see mine," McCurry said.

"You'll have to get your own," Evans retorted. "And while you're at it, pick up two more for Carl and me."

When McCurry returned to the table with three bottles of Lowenbrau, Evans and Rosen were involved in an animated conversation.

"So what's got you two so excited?" McCurry asked.

"Hey Mike, this guy really knows his music. He not only knows 'In-A-Gadda-Da-Vida,' he's actually found the album."

Some seventeen minutes long, "In-A-Gadda-Da-Vida" by Iron Butterfly was the music of choice when friends got together to share a bowl of hash or pass a joint around.

"So, you're a pothead after all," McCurry said as he sat down and started sipping his beer.

"No, no I could never get away with that. My wife, Eva, would kill me. But I love music and as long as I'm not bothering her, I can listen to all I want," Rosen said.

McCurry looked at Rosen. At nearly six feet tall and about 240 pounds, he was built like a fire plug. When he walked, he shuffled, looking down at the ground most of the time. For the few months McCurry was giving Rosen a ride on and off, he had never met the guy's wife nor learned much about him.

But Evans had managed to light him up over a beer and a discussion of music.

"The music scene's changing so fast, it's hard to keep up with, isolated as we are here in Berlin," McCurry said. "After all the years that Motown ruled, this new psychedelic stuff is a radical shift.

"I think the Beatles opened people's eyes to all the possibilities music offers and other artists expanded it even more. Look what Jefferson Airplane is doing with their new album, *Surrealistic Pillow*. Grace Slick's 'White Rabbit' will just blow you away."

"For my money, Pink Floyd is going to set the bar high for the next 10 years," Evans said. "Their album *A Saucerfull of Secrets* is light years ahead of everything else."

For the next couple hours, the trio talked about all the new groups coming on the scene, each lamenting at some point how much they were missing being stuck here in Berlin.

"Wow, I had better get home," Rosen said when he realized how late it was.

"Hey man, it's two in the morning. Your old lady should be sound asleep and won't know what time you got in."

"You don't know her. She wakes up at the drop of a pin. Who knows though," he said through the haze of his sixth bottle of Lowenbrau, "maybe I'll get lucky tonight."

He wasn't lucky. When McCurry saw him walking to work the next day, he stopped to pick him up. As he was getting into the VW microbus, McCurry saw that the whole left side of his face was swollen and black and blue.

"Eva was waiting for me and when I came in she let me have it with a cast iron frying pan."

* * *

"We've gotta do something to help Carl out," McCurry said to Evans later that evening when they were taking a break.

"We really oughta stay out of it, Mike. That's his problem and he needs to take care of it."

"That's bullshit. He's a good guy and he deserves better. Here's what I think we oughta do."

In the early afternoon on their next break from work, McCurry and Evans, dressed in their Class As for the first time since their arrival in Germany, went to Rosen's. They were pretty sure Carl wouldn't be home since he said would be taking the loop bus to the commissary for groceries on the first day of the break.

When Eva answered their knock, McCurry asked if Carl was in. When she said he was out doing errands for her, McCurry asked to come in and speak with her on a subject of great importance.

"You know Eva … it's all right if I call you Eva?"

"Yes."

"You know Eva, Carl is prohibited from speaking with you about anything that goes on in our work on the Hill. I am sure that can be frustrating at times."

"I don't know. I really don't care what he's doing up there."

"Well, as his superior, I think you should know that his competence and ability are very important to me and our mission. Your husband's job requires intense concentration and, believe it or not, the fate of the free world rests on him and the rest of us on the Hill doing our jobs well. Do you understand that?"

"Uh huh," said Eva, who was beginning to look very small despite her 260 pounds.

"I am sure you are treating him with the respect he deserves, even if you don't know what work he is doing," McCurry said. "Because if you treat him in a way that imperils our mission, there will be consequences. Do you understand?"

"Yes, yes I do," she said.

"Good. Now there is one other thing you need to understand. You know Carl has to keep the secrets he learns on the Hill. Well, as his wife and partner, you need to keep some secrets as well. Carl doesn't need to know we were here today. That might upset him and, as I said, I don't want anything upsetting him. He is a very important man, Eva, very important to our mission and the nation. Got it?"

"Yes, yes. My lips are sealed."

"And one other thing, sometimes the pressure of our work is so unbearable that he needs to take some time and have a few beers with his trick mates to unwind. When those circumstances arise,

I am sure you will be understanding when he comes home a little late. Right?"

"Oh yes, yes."

"Good. It was very nice meeting you, Eva, and I'm so happy to see you recognize how important it is to support Carl in his service to our mission."

As they were walking back to McCurry's VW microbus, Evans said, "Laid it on a little thick, didn't ya?"

"Maybe so, but she seemed to be eating it up, don't ya think?"

"Well, only time will tell."

"C'mon, let's get back to Andrews and get the hell out of these Class As. If anyone sees us it will ruin our reputations."

A few days later when they returned to work on mids, Rosen seemed almost ecstatic.

"You wouldn't believe," he told McCurry after getting into McCurry's VW on the way to work. "All of a sudden, Eva is being really nice to me. She even said she is proud of how important my work is, although I can't imagine where she got that impression. She actually said if I need to stay after work from time to time to unwind, it's all right with her."

"Well, I guess people really can change," said McCurry, although not really believing it.

* * *

Over the next few months, Eva's transformation continued to evolve and surprise even the cynical McCurry. He actually saw the two of them having beers with other members of the trick in the Stork Club. Recently she went so far as to host a cookout at her home, supplying the beer and bratwurst.

So Evans was worried when he picked up Rosen and saw that he was visibly upset.

"What's the matter Carl? Eva isn't giving you any problems, is she?"

"No, she's still great all the time. But now our landlord's throwing us out."

"What d'ya mean, throwing you out?"

"He knocked on our door yesterday and told us we had thirty days to get out."

"Did he give you any reason?"

"He said he didn't have to. He said it was his apartment and if he said to get out, we had to get out. I really don't know what we're going to do. It's going to be difficult to find another place that quick."

"I'll tell you what you're going to do. Fuck him, you're going to stay there. When I get finished with that fuckin' Herm, you may even get a reduction in rent."

After getting the name and address of the landlord from Rosen, McCurry brought up the problem with Wachter, who was always looking for a good fight.

"What's he pay in rent?" Wachter asked.

"I think he's paying four hundred marks a month."

Wachter said that four hundred marks a month was low when compared to how much rents had gone up in the past year. The influx of more GIs with their wives along with the prohibition against living anywhere but in the American sector had heated up the market.

"This guy thinks he can take advantage and kick Carl out and jack up the price for the next renter. I think we need to make a call on Herr Müller."

Gerhard Müller, Rosen's landlord, lived in a much better neighborhood than that in which his rental properties were located, although it was still in the American sector of Berlin. Wachter and McCurry climbed his stoop, knocked on his door and got ready for the games to begin.

When a wizened up old man smelling of greasy food and foul body odor answered the door, Wachter asked, "Herr Müller?"

"Yes, what can I do for you?"

"My name is Wachter and this is my American friend, Herr McCurry. Would you mind if we come in?" Wachter wanted to give this wretched man the impression that he was showing the deference to Müller's age as Germans were expected to do, regardless of a person's character.

"Certainly," Müller said, showing them the way to his formal sitting room, a place German's usually reserved for special guests.

"Can I offer you some tea?" Müller asked as Wachter and McCurry settled themselves in the overstuffed chairs in the room.

"That's very kind of you, but we're fine," Wachter said.

"Well then, what can I do for you?" Müller asked, sitting down in a chair facing the pair.

"For starters, sir," Wachter said, now with a noticeably hard edge to his voice, "you can tell your tenants, Herr and Frau Rosen, that they are welcome to stay as long as they like and that you won't raise their rent at any time during their occupancy of that hovel you call an apartment."

"How dare you," Müller said, standing up and turning a fiery red.

"Sit down mister and listen to me," Wachter said with such force that Müller literally dropped into his chair.

"You will either do as I say, or Herr McCurry here will take whatever action is needed to insure you are blackballed by the American military. You'll be lucky to get fifty marks a month for any of your properties. Do I make myself clear?"

Müller managed to pull himself together and stood up. Pointing to the door, he said, "Get out of my home, right now. We'll see who's giving orders around here."

"Very well," Wachter said as he and McCurry rose from their chairs, "but I would think very carefully before taking any precipitous action. Do you really want to take on the American military establishment in Berlin?"

With that, Wachter turned and he and McCurry left.

"What d'ya think?" McCurry asked as they walked back to his VW.

"I think he is a lot of hot air. In the end he'll give in while trying to find a way to save face doing so."

*   *   *

Three days after his confrontation with Müller, McCurry was called into his commanding officer's office.

McCurry had found Capt. Hanover easy to get along with, although sometimes his antics gave Hanover huge headaches in dealing with the treads McCurry angered. Hanover was obviously not a tread and just biding his time until he could return to civilian life. But, as McCurry entered his office, he sensed immediately that Hanover was ready to explode.

"Tell me, McCurry, did you by any chance visit a Gerhard Müller two or three days ago?" Hanover asked.

"Yes sir, I did."

"And what was the purpose of your visit?"

"This guy is Carl Rosen's landlord. He notified Rosen that he was evicting him and he had thirty days to get out. I thought I could maybe find out why and convince him to change his mind."

"And was it just you or did someone accompany you?" Hanover asked, still seeming uncharacteristically angry.

"A German buddy of mine came along. I wanted to make sure there weren't any language difficulties."

"And did you or your buddy threaten Herr Müller?"

"What the hell, Captain? What's going on here? What would we threaten him with?"

"What's going on here is that you may have really screwed the pooch on this one, McCurry. This Herr Müller has filed a complaint with the commanding general's office. I was personally called on the carpet by General Sullivan. He basically told me that I would either make this go away or heads would roll."

"So, the fucking Germans are going to dictate policy in the American sector? You know this is bullshit, Captain. He would've been thrown out on his ass in the British or French sectors."

"I'm not going to argue with you on this one, McCurry. You will visit Herr Müller immediately and apologize for anything you or your friend may have said to him that offended him. You will make sure he is totally mollified by the time you leave. If you need to, you'll bring him a fifth of whiskey as a good will token. Whatever it takes, you will do. Understand?"

"Like hell, I will. This guy is just trying to fuck over American soldiers and there is no way in hell I'm going to apologize to him for anything."

"This is really serious this time, McCurry. I can give you a week to change your mind and make this guy happy. After that, you may finally get the court martial you keep demanding. Now get out of here."

"Yes sir," McCurry said, turning and leaving the office.

* * *

"So, any ideas over what's next?" Wachter asked as he, McCurry and Harris shared a beer together.

"You can apologize and chalk it up to being overwhelmed by a superior force," Harris joked.

"Yeah, like that's gonna happen ... when hell freezes over," McCurry said. "I guess for a while I could play chicken with 'em 'cause I know they just want it go away. But I think ultimately they would court martial me for 'disobeying a lawful order' if they felt they had no other choice.

"Which means," McCurry continued, "that I should go on the offensive. I don't know whether this is a Hail Mary or could work, but I'm gonna contact *Stars & Stripes.* Wonder if they would be interested in a story about American soldiers in Berlin being taken advantage of by unscrupulous German landlords?

"Let's see if they live up to their claim of being editorially independent of the Department of Defense."

McCurry called a telephone number listed in an edition of the paper circulated at Andrews. When he told the person who answered he had a story about a problem American soldiers were encountering in Berlin, he was asked for his name, rank and a telephone number at which he could be reached.

The next day, Jim Fortunato, who identified himself as a reporter for *Stars & Stripes,* contacted McCurry and asked if they could meet. McCurry told the reporter of a local pub he and Wachter frequented and they made arrangements to meet up there that afternoon at four.

McCurry greeted Fortunato at the bar when he arrived and ordered a couple of beers. He told him that one of his work mates and his wife lived on the economy in off-base housing. As with all other American military personnel whose wives had joined them in Berlin, McCurry explained, regulations required they live in apartments located in the American Sector.

"Germans know about this requirement and regularly jack up the price over what it would be if the market weren't so restricted," McCurry explained.

He pointed out that British and French troops can live in any sector in Berlin and in addition to this their commanders have issued regulations capping rents at reasonable rates in their sectors.

Fortunato said he had heard of this problem and had even been investigating it on his own.

"You're right, Mike, rents are significantly higher in the American sector for comparable units. Problem is, to do a story, I need a way to put a human face on it."

"Well, I may have the answer to your problem" McCurry said after ordering another round of beers.

He then related how Rosen and his wife were being kicked out of their four-hundred-mark-a-month apartment, not because the landlord had had any problems with them but because he could get considerably more if he put it back on the market now.

"Do you think Rosen will talk with me?" Fortunato asked.

"I am pretty sure he will, since he is at his wits end about where he will go if he loses this apartment," McCurry said. "I'll find out and get back to you."

When McCurry picked Rosen up on his way to the barracks for the swing shift the next day, he told him of his discussion with Fortunato and the reporter's interest in doing a story on the disparity of rents in the American sector when compared to the other two zones.

He explained that to write a story, the reporter needed a human interest angle, something that gives it a face and makes it worthwhile writing about.

"He thinks your situation is the perfect hook," McCurry said. "He's standing by to meet with you tomorrow morning if you think that'd be okay."

"I'll have to see what Eva says, but I don't think she will have any objections."

"I'll get back to Fortunato. As long as it's okay with Eva, we'll pick up some pastries and meet at your place at ten tomorrow morning for coffee. I think this is going to work, Carl. You may get to keep your apartment and I may avoid a court martial. Something if the good guys win, huh?"

After his discussion with the Rosens the next morning, Fortunato walked back to McCurry's VW with him.

"What d'ya think, Jim? Think you have the 'hook' ya need?" McCurry asked.

"I'll say. That really sucks."

"Ya wanna get the ball rolling in a real hurry? This is what you need to do."

McCurry told him the story of the meeting he and Wachter had with the landlord, how arrogant Müller was and the fact that McCurry was being ordered to apologize to him.

"Here he is, ripping off American soldiers and all he has to do is complain to the sector commander to keep his scam going," McCurry said.

McCurry suggested Fortunato contact General Sullivan to ask outright why he hasn't implemented regulations to cap rent rates in the American sector as they have done in the British and French.

"You may not be allowed to speak with him directly, but you can relay your message through whatever aide they give you and then wait for the firestorm to begin."

"That's a good idea, Mike. What should I call this, the battle between the commanding general and the spec 5?" Fortunato said, laughing as he referred to McCurry's rank.

"Whatever. As long as we get some results. This is a situation that has needed to be addressed for some time."

* * *

"Guess you've heard what's happened since our meeting last week," Capt. Hanover said to McCurry after calling him into his office before trick change.

"Not quite sure what you mean, sir," McCurry said.

"General Sullivan is issuing orders limiting how much Germans can charge servicemen in the American sector and requiring landlords to show just cause before they can evict an American tenant. This decision was made, apparently, during an interview with a reporter from *Stars & Stripes*. From what I understand, this will be the gist of a story that will soon appear in the newspaper.

"You wouldn't know anything about this, would you McCurry?"

"About the general's decision? No sir, I hadn't heard?"

"No McCurry. I mean about how the reporter decided to do a story about this situation."

"Well sir, I may have chatted him up after buying him a couple beers."

"Well McCurry, you win this time. I'll deny this if you repeat it, but, for what it's worth, I am glad the general made the decision he did. As usual, though, I am not sure I approve of your tactics. While you may have won this battle, you'd better watch your back. The general knows who you are now and I am sure he'll be looking for a way to make you pay."

The Big Splash

"Well we'll just have to go out and have a real celebration," Wachter said after hearing of the general's decision.

"A celebration sounds like a good idea, Horst. Might as well eat, drink and be merry while waiting to see what the general's next move will be."

"First we've gotta eat and I think I know just the place."

Wachter drove McCurry in his Austin Healey since he didn't enjoy riding in McCurry's VW microbus with the bright flowers painted all over it. After making his way uptown to the Ku'damm, Wachter pulled in behind a discreet little restaurant.

"This is the Heising, a new place I just heard about," he said, getting out of the Austin. "The food is supposed to be great, the prices aren't too bad and it's not the kind of place any of your treads would go to."

After being seated in a quiet corner of the room, they ordered large mugs of Paulaner Weissbier, a wheat beer that McCurry had grown particularly fond of during his days of pub crawling in Berlin.

"Ein Prosit," Wachter said, lifting his glass.

"Ein Prosit to what?" McCurry asked, going through a little routine they developed to get under the skins of the Herms with no sense of humor.

"Der Gemütlichkeit, of course."

"Okay, to the Gemütlichkeit, wherever you may find it."

When the waiter arrived, they placed their orders. Wachter asked for erbsensuppe, or pea soup, to start with, herring in a creamy dill sauce for his main course. McCurry ordered a cucumber salad and then his favorite main course, zigeunerschnitzel, a pork schnitzel with a spicy sauce of bell peppers, tomatoes and onions.

"You should be pretty happy with your achievement," Wachter said. "Not only does Carl get to stay in his apartment but no one else can be bullied by a German landlord like he was."

"Maybe so, Horst, but it may have come at a price this time. As Captain Hanover pointed out, I have the attention of the commanding general now and there's no telling what his next move will be."

"C'mon Mike, it can't be anything you wouldn't be able to handle."

"General Sullivan is the quintessential gator hard ass. It's common knowledge that he hates the fact that Army Security Agency personnel are, in his view, coddled."

"He would relish the opportunity to fry the ass of an ASA soldier."

McCurry was interrupted by the waiter who arrived with their erbsensuppe and cucumber salad. "Guten Appetit," he said. McCurry ordered more Weissbier and the waiter retreated.

"Wow Mike, maybe Fortunato had it right when he asked whether he should call the story 'the battle between the commanding general and the spec 5'."

"Ah, fuck it, Horst. It's not worth thinking about. But I'll have to admit, the constant battle with these morons is getting tiresome. There are times when I just wish I didn't care. And then something else pops up to make my head explode."

"Well drink up. Tonight we are celebrating a victory in your little war and I don't foresee you falling to any defeats."

The waiter arrived to take away their dirty dishes and serve the herring and zigeunerschnitzel. Wachter ordered more beer for both of them.

As the pair worked on their main course, McCurry explained that in six months, he will have been in Berlin two years. A normal tour of duty is three years. Since his enlistment will end before his three years is up, McCurry explained, the Army has the option of either allowing him to finish here or sending him back after two years.

Most soldiers whose enlistment will end before the three-year tour is up are given the option to stay in Germany until it is time for them to go back to the States and muster out. Some even take a European discharge so they can travel afterwards. "But I suspect that Sullivan is going to make sure that I am at the very least sent back to the States after two years as a punishment," McCurry said.

"Well, it's not like you to worry about these things, Mike. Tonight's a time to celebrate, so have another drink and eat your schnitzel. The night's young and we've got a lot to do."

After a period of silence as they continued to work on their meals, McCurry said, "You know what. Horst, you're right. I've only got a little more than a year to put up with this shit. Tonight's a celebration of the sanity that's finally within sight."

"Ein Prosit to sanity," Wachter said.

"I'll absolutely drink to that," McCurry agreed, clicking his glass against Wachter's and then draining it.

When their desserts arrived, Wachter said, "Eat up. We're going to the Back Stage next and you know how much you love that place."

* * *

After leaving the Heising, Wachter headed south on Bundesallee to Hohenzollerndamm, where, after turning right, he pulled up in front of the Back Stage Club, billed as one of West Berlin's hottest dance clubs and live music venues. Wachter and McCurry had lost several nights at this club during the past year. Women went there to dance, drink and basically go wild. Guys were only too happy to oblige.

As McCurry and Wachter entered the club, they were greeted by ear-splitting music and a packed dance floor. The band was bathed in a psychedelic liquid light show emanating from an overhead projector. The impression of many who experienced the Back Stage Club for the first time was that they had entered an altered universe. And in many ways they had, considering how many mind-altering drugs were in circulation.

McCurry and Wachter pushed their way through the crowd to the bar and looked for a spot where they could squeeze in when McCurry spotted Evans.

"Hey man, make room for us," McCurry shouted as he pushed his way in and tried to get the attention of the bar tender. "Where's Sonja? Out on the dance floor without you?"

"Her mother isn't feeling well, so she stayed home to take care of her. I'm just playing voyeur tonight."

When McCurry got the attention of the bartender, he ordered three Beck's and turned his attention back to the dance floor.

When the beers arrived, Wachter put a few bills on the bar and handed a bottle to McCurry and Evans. "Ein prosit to voyeurism."

"A toast I can appreciate," McCurry said and clicked his bottle with that of Evans and Wachter.

After he had drained his Beck's, McCurry said, "Well, I think I'll wade in and see what I can find." He had discovered on previous trips that once on the floor it was easy to hook up with a girl eager to dance and, more often than not, much more. He quickly found a redhead willing to dance with him and lost himself in the music and movement.

He was brought back to reality when she turned her back to him and began rubbing up against him in time with the music. He figured she could easily feel the effect she was having on him, but he didn't much care as he pushed up harder against her.

He grasped her shoulders and leaned in towards her ear, saying "If we are going to get this familiar, I should at least know your name."

"It's Heidi," she giggled, rubbing a little harder to let him know she enjoyed the familiarity.

"Well, Heidi, all I can say is you're one hell of a dancer. But, let's take a short break and I'll buy you a drink."

When they got back to the bar, McCurry introduced Heidi to Wachter and Evans. She asked for a vodka, neat, and he ordered another Beck's for himself. Excusing themselves, Wachter and Evans headed off to wade into the mass of humanity on the dance floor.

"Do you live here in Berlin?" McCurry asked.

"Yes, and very nearby," she said coyly.

"What d'ya do?"

"I'm a student at the Freie Universität majoring in political science."

She told him she and small group of other students were studying ways to rebuild Germany after reunification, ways to build a new pacifist Germany. McCurry, who wasn't entirely sure he ever really wanted the two Germanys to reunify, was intrigued by her point of view and asked if she really felt the citizens of these two countries could overcome their differences and find a common ground for reunification.

Heidi said she felt reunification was inevitable because of the close ties West Germans have with old friends and family in the East. Ultimately, she said, family will triumph over politics.

"Honestly, Mike, I believe it's only a matter of time before that damned wall and all the fences fall and Germany becomes one once again," Heidi asserted.

"Well, here's to a reunified Germany," McCurry said.

She clicked her glass against his bottle and downed the vodka. Giggling once more, she said, "That's enough serious talk. Let's dance."

After about an hour of grinding it out on the dance floor with Heidi, McCurry felt Wachter tug on his arm and start to pull him back over to the bar.

Holding on for a moment, Heidi leaned into his ear and said, "Don't get lost. As soon as you ditch your friend, we can go back to my apartment."

"Oh god, I hate this, Heidi, but I promised Horst I'd tag along with him tonight. Do you come here often? Maybe we'll be able to meet up again."

"Yeah, maybe," she said disappointedly, and then made her way back onto the dance floor alone.

"Listen, before you get too drunk or try to ditch me – you don't think I missed that do you? – I've got one other place I want to hit tonight and timing at this place is important, so we'd better get going."

"You're right this time. You are really lucky I didn't ditch you, so you owe me one. Let me say goodbye to Dwight if I can find him and we'll hat up."

"He already took off," Horst said. "He said to tell you good night and good luck."

*　　*　　*

Wachter headed back toward the Ku'damm and, after crossing over it, pulled into a small side alley. He parked and the two got out and headed toward a brightly lit storefront with a sign, in English, reading THE WET AND WILD CLUB.

As they approached the club, Wachter explained that it was owned by an American expatriate. Even though the sign was in English, the club catered mainly to Germans.

"What makes it so special?" McCurry asked.

"Just be patient," Wachter responded, "you'll see soon enough."

When they entered the building, McCurry saw there was a small, above-ground pool in the middle of the room, deep enough that it needed a ladder to get into it. Around the pool on tiers were various sized tables designed to seat from two to six. Music was playing, but most of those in the room were engaged in conversations with one another.

Wachter and McCurry made their way to a table for two near the back. A waiter arrived shortly and took their beer orders.

"The guy who owns this place is somewhat of an eccentric, but he has become well known in the German community," Wachter explained while they waited for their drinks. "He put the pool in planning to have private sex parties, but ended up being shut down after neighbors complained. So, he opened as a drinking establishment, but kept the pool. He started a nightly contest that, when word about it spread, helped fill his business nearly every evening."

"And this contest is ...?"

"You'll see," Wachter said. "As a matter of fact, it is about to begin now."

The music stopped, the lights went down and a spotlight was turned on and focused on a man with a microphone near the pool.

"Meine Damen und Herren, willkommen," he said. Continuing in German, the master of ceremonies explained that it was time for their nightly contest to determine if there were any truly courageous women in the audience. The object of the contest was to determine how much money it would take to convince some woman to strip and take a dip in the pool.

"We'll start the bidding out at twenty marks," he said. When a hand went up, he went on. "We've got twenty, do I hear forty," and another hand went up. "Ladies, when the price is right, just put up your hand. But, if you want the cash, don't wait too long because someone might beat you to it."

As he continued the bidding, with no response from the women, McCurry noticed that the couple at the table next to them was engaged in an argument. "Hey Horst," McCurry whispered, "listen to this. I think she wants to go up and he's saying absolutely not. She's obviously pretty sloshed too."

McCurry saw that each time a bid was made, she tried to put her hand up and her date fought to keep it down. Finally, when the bidding hit 200 DM, she just stood up and said, "I accept."

Her announcement drew cheers and applause, giving her the courage to start down to the pool. A spotlight was focused on her, following her progress. To get there, she had to go around the table McCurry and Wachter were sitting at and then walk down the aisle and series of platforms right next to them. When she got to the top of the first level, she stopped, pulled her sweater off over her head, dramatically swinging it around in a circle and dropping it. The audience showed their appreciation with raucous cheers and whistles.

At the next platform, she unsnapped her bra, swung it around and dropped it. She turned to the audience and swung her breasts back and forth, bringing on a new crescendo of appreciation. The last platform brought her nearly to the pool level. She kicked her shoes off and then slowly lowered her slacks and underpants, leaning way over to get them over her feet. Climbing the ladder at the pool, she stopped at the top, carefully turned around and blew kisses to members of the audience, bringing a round of loud applause.

Turning back to the pool, she jumped and went completely under. When she came up, it wasn't difficult to see that the cold water in the pool had sobered her up almost immediately. Totally mortified was how McCurry described her look to Evans when he told him the story the next day in the snack bar at Andrews.

"Trying desperately to cover herself with her arms," McCurry said, "she quickly got out of the pool and ran up the aisle, collecting her clothing along the way, and headed to a dark corner at the rear of the building to dress. She had tears running down her face when she got back to the table next to us and discovered her boyfriend had left.

"All in all, it was pretty sad. I mean, here was this woman out on a date. She clearly drank too much and who knows whose fault that was, hers, or the dickhead who was with her? He was clearly encouraging her to drink more the whole evening. And maybe if he had treated her better, she wouldn't have decided to 'show him.'

"In the end, she was totally humiliated and to top it all off, her date left her there alone. It's possible she'll never get over that experience. That's not my idea of entertainment. I felt almost sick about it. I should have abandoned Horst at the Back Stage Club and gone home with Heidi."

"Who are you kidding," Evans said. "You would never abandon Wachter. You guys are like the Cisco Kid and Poncho. Two caballeros riding off each day to make the world a better place."

"Shutting that place down would definitely make the world a better place, that's for sure."

The Return of Heidi

McCurry was, in his mind, taking a day off from the world. He had escaped to the Wannsee early that morning to spend the day on the beach, alone. He was tired. The battle with the general had, he hated to admit, shaken him. It left him wondering where he would be headed from here. It also reinforced the realization that, more often than not, he was alone when taking on the treads. Granted, members of the Army Security Agency pushed the envelope more than those in the regular Army. But, when it came to drawing a line in the sand, he knew without turning around that there was no one behind him.

I've only got less than a year to go, he thought. Less than six months until a determination about whether he could remain in Berlin until his enlistment was up. When McCurry was engaged in a battle with one of the tread morons, he was in control. There was no way he could influence whether or not his request to remain in Berlin would be granted. He hated the feeling that someone else had control over his destiny. Ever since the incident with the coffee cup at the beginning of his enlistment, he had pushed back against regulations that had nothing to do with his performance on the job. Now he faced what could be the end of his time in Berlin and an uncertain fate after returning to the States.

McCurry's father would say, relax, this too shall pass. Maybe that was true, he thought as he drifted off to sleep in the warm, early summer sun.

When he awoke, a woman was sitting cross-legged in the sand staring at him. The sun was behind her, blinding him for a moment, so he couldn't make out who it was. Before he came fully to his senses, she said, "Guten morgen, Herr Mike. Schläfst Du gut?"

"Heidi?"

"Ah, at least you remember my name. That's a good sign."

"What are you doing here," he asked as he drew himself up into a sitting position.

"I just came for a swim, but as I was heading for the water I saw you here sleeping so soundly, like you didn't have a care in the world."

"Yeah, don't I wish. Sleeping does help me clear the cobwebs but, unfortunately, it doesn't make my cares go away. So, did ya get your swim in?"

"Before I answer any more questions, Mr. Mike, we need to be properly introduced. My name is Boehm, Heidi Boehm. And you are?'

"McCurry, Mike McCurry at your service, madam."

She giggled at that. It made him remember how much he enjoyed her giggle when he met her at the Back Stage Club.

"I need to wake up. Let's go for that swim you were planning." He got up and raced for the water's edge. When he got about waist deep, he dove in, gliding out to deeper water before coming up for air. When he did, she was right beside him.

They treaded water beside each other, and she said, "You didn't think you were going to be able to get away from me again, did you?"

"I wasn't trying to get away from you before, Heidi, I just didn't feel right about ditching Horst."

"I didn't think I would ever see you again. I think I realized that night that you were different than the other Americans I meet over here. I wanted to get to know you better. That's why I asked you back to my place. I didn't mean to scare you off."

"Trust me. You didn't scare me off. And I am *very* glad you found me ... and waited for me to wake up," he said, laughing. They had drifted out some, so he starting swimming back to where they could stand comfortably. She was right behind him. When he turned to her, she put her arms around his neck, wrapped her legs around his waist and began kissing him.

When she came up for air, she said, giggling once again, "That's what you missed by running off with your friend. You won't get a third chance."

"Don't worry, I won't let you go," he said, and returned her kiss, this time not stopping to exchange small talk.

* * *

After their swim, they returned to the blanket McCurry had brought with him and lay down next to one another.

Lying on his side and facing her, McCurry asked why she thought he was different from the other Americans she met.

"Well, first of all, you weren't patronizing. When you asked a question, you actually listened to the answer. Most of the Americans I have met aren't very intelligent and just want to make small talk until they can get into my pants."

"You just described most of the men in the world, not just Americans," McCurry said. "Women want to talk. Men want to skip the talk and head straight for the bed."

"Go ahead and kid all you want, but I don't think you're like that."

"No, maybe not. I do prefer a woman who can keep up her end of a conversation, even if I don't agree with her. If a woman is boring, it doesn't take long before the sex becomes boring as well."

"Now that our formal introductions are over," he said, deciding to move the conversation away from sex, "tell me a little more about yourself."

Heidi said she was twenty-three years old and had lived in Berlin all her life. Having been born shortly after the war had ended, her early life was hard. Even though the economy was beginning to improve during her childhood years, food was still scarce. She had to scavenge for wood to burn in order to heat their home. Her parents were proud people, she said, but the bombing and near total destruction of Berlin had broken their spirit and left them with little hope for a better future.

"That's why I feel so strong about doing whatever my friends at the university and I can do to build a better and, most importantly, unified Germany."

"I guess it's pretty hard for me or anyone who grew up in the post-war America to identify with what you went through," McCurry mused.

McCurry said he had pretty much of an idyllic childhood, growing up in a small town where a number of relatives were within walking distance. Fortunately, he said, his parents had moved the family to Philadelphia for his teenage years.

"Why do you say fortunately?" she asked.

"Because small towns breed small minds."

"Well, I wouldn't know since I have lived my whole life here," Heidi said. "But, you like Philadelphia, yes?"

McCurry said Philadelphia has its faults like any big city in America. But, he said, there are a number of great colleges and universities that contribute to a wide-ranging discourse on any number of current events. It has a host of museums, a great orchestra and superb theaters.

"And, from my point of view," McCurry added, "it's got great sports teams. I'll have to show you sometime how I bleed green."

"Bleed green?"

"An expression for someone who is a die-hard Eagles fan."

"Eagles?"

"The Eagles are a football team," he said, "an American football team."

"Well, you can teach me all about American football later. All I want to do now is to go back to my apartment and make love."

"I'm not going to argue with that," said McCurry.

Heidi and McCurry spent the good part of the next forty-eight hours in her bedroom, mostly making love but taking time out to get to know one another better as well. When he left to return to the post for the beginning of his days shift, he recognized that he was totally under her spell.

* * *

When Evans climbed aboard his bus, McCurry couldn't wait to tell him about his time with Heidi.

"You know last week at the Back Stage Club, that girl I met on the dance floor and brought over for a drink with you and Horst?"

"You mean the one you ditched to go off with Poncho? Of course I remember her. She was a stunner."

"Stop calling Horst Poncho, or I'll have to throw you off my bus."

"Sorry. Is he Cisco?"

"Fuckin' smart ass. At any rate, during shift break, I went down to the Wannsee for a day alone for rest and relaxation. And who d'ya think I met there? Heidi. I had fallen asleep and when I woke up, she was sitting there. I thought I was dreaming at first."

"What, is she stalking you or something?"

"Yeah, she thinks I'm Peter Fonda. Of course she wasn't stalking me. She had gone there to take a swim and saw me sleeping on the beach."

McCurry told Evans how they decided to take a swim together and the next thing he knew, she was in his arms kissing him. He said he was especially taken by her quick wit. He summarized one of the discussions they had about Germany's reunification. Evans knew how McCurry felt about this and said it sounded as if she was turning him around.

"What can I say, Dwight. She was able to counter each of the stumbling blocks I raised with good arguments about why they would be overcome. Sure, she's young, a student and an optimist. But if her friends in school are as enthusiastic as she is, maybe this country has a chance after all. It's sure going to take a monumental cultural shift to happen. But she even convinced me that may be possible."

"And, is that all you did, talk?"

"No, we went back to her apartment. And man, Dwight, she is a tigress in bed. She wore me out."

"Well, that's not saying much."

"Yeah, right. Seriously though, Dwight, she is the total package. Granted I don't know her very well yet, but I could find myself falling in love with this woman."

"Shit, Mike, how many women would you say you've bedded since you arrived in Berlin. A half dozen at least. And you've always kept the relationships casual, right? So why, after such a short time, have you decided Heidi is so special?"

"I don't know, Dwight. Maybe it's as simple as already I can't wait to get back to her. Whatever it is, I'm willing to go with it."

"Well, just be careful buddy. You know you're already under scrutiny because of your relationship with Horst. All you need to do now is add a German woman to the mix and you could end up in real hot water with the CID."

"Fuck, Dwight, I'm not worried about them. With the morons they have here in Berlin, they should be known as the comical idiots division."

* * *

After work, McCurry met up with Heidi at her apartment. At her urging, he agreed to go out with her to pick up some bratwurst at a corner vendor and then rendezvous with her friends at their favorite pub. She explained that she and her friends were all members of the Arbeitsgemeinschaft Auf Deutscher Wiedervereinigung. Heidi said that the Arbeitsgemeinschaft Auf Deutscher Wiedervereinigung, or Study Group on German Reunification, managed to gain recognition as a legitimate line of study at the Freie Universität. Those who participated got extra credits toward their degree.

"We spend a lot of time in discussions, which can become very heated. So you don't have to worry about offending anyone. They can either defend their position or not," she said. "They've had to capitulate to me on more than one occasion," she added, giggling.

As they ate their bratwurst, which McCurry slathered with his favorite hot German mustard, Heidi said she didn't think he would have any problem getting along with her friends. As was true with McCurry, her friends were uniformly against all wars, Heidi said. They wanted to insure that a newly unified Germany would be one dedicated to pacifism. "Gerhard Holtzmann, for example, believes that there should be a constitutional convention following reunification. He believes a new constitution should be crafted to include a neutrality clause, requiring the country to remain neutral in any and all wars," she said. "Come on, let's go to the pub. I'll introduce you to Gerhard and the others."

The Brauhaus am Ku'damm was a small, cozy pub situated in an alley off the Kurfürstendamm. Its patrons were mostly students of the Freie Universität, meaning that beer flowed nearly as freely as dissertations on topics of the day.

When Heidi and McCurry entered, they found Gerhard at a table in the corner with three other members of the study group, all engrossed in an animated discussion. As Heidi approached, they stopped talking and turned to greet her. Holtzmann was a short man on a very sparse frame. His faded vest covered a shirt with a frayed collar. He peered out through thick glasses that made his eyes appear larger than they actually were. He had a grin that was infectious and immediately made McCurry feel welcome to the group.

In addition to Holtzmann, there were Erica Fenstermacher, Hans Metzger and Heinrich Schmitt. Heidi said that while other people attended the study group from time to time, she and these four friends made up the hard core. "And you had better believe that she is hard core," said Erica, a rotund young woman who had a twinkle in her eye that McCurry immediately recognized had a mischievous spark to it.

As the group made room for Heidi and Mike to sit down, McCurry went to the bar to pick up a pitcher of beer. "I'm told the new guy buys the first round," he said on his return.

"Sounds like my kind of rule since I will never be new again," said Holtzmann.

"You were old the day you were born, Gerhard," Fenstermacher remarked.

"Well, all I can say is danke and prosit," Schmitt added.

"Prosit," said the others in unison.

The group returned to its discussion, which centered on President Kennedy's "Ich bin ein Berliner" speech of June 26, 1963. While each of them was merely a teenager at the time, it had a profound impact on everyone living in Berlin. It didn't cause a ripple in McCurry's life and he only barely remembered it being mentioned in one of his school classes. For Heidi and her four friends, it was one of the highlights of their lives. Six years later it was still a topic of conversation.

"You have to realize, Mike, that this was a scary time for anyone who lived in Berlin," Holtzmann explained. "The wall had gone up less than two years earlier and many people felt it was only a matter of time before the Soviets and their East German puppets took over West Berlin by force."

Heidi explained that from the time the wall went up until Kennedy's visit, Berliners felt alone and cut off from the West. Kennedy's "Ich bin ein Berliner" speech boosted morale and put the Soviets on notice that the West would defend West Berlin.

Hans Metzger added that many in Berlin felt that American support evaporated with Kenedy's assassination. Johnson became bogged down with Vietnam and American influence suffered in other parts of the world.

"God only knows what will happen now that Nixon is in office," he said.

McCurry was struck at how well Europeans followed and understood politics in America. He was lucky if he could even name the leaders of the European nations, let alone understand the nuances of their foreign policies.

The group continued to discuss and argue over the importance of Kennedy's speech to the reunification effort for another hour or so before Heidi said, "I think this is enough for Mike for one day. Don't want to scare him off too soon."

"Nice meeting you, Mike." Holtzmann said. "Hope to see you around again."

"Thanks Gerhard. I look forward to seeing you all again as well."

*   *   *

After he and Heidi had been seeing each other steadily for a couple of weeks, McCurry took a week's leave so they could have an uninterrupted period to get to know each other better. Heidi had borrowed a bike for McCurry and the two of them set off the first day to tour the city's famous Tiergarten, a magnificent park crisscrossed with paths leading to tranquil lakes and gardens.

As they made their way toward the Victory Column in the center of the park with Heidi explaining some of the most significant landmarks, McCurry was distracted by the feeling that someone was following them. Don't be ridiculous, he told himself. We are in the middle of a major tourist area on bikes. Who the fuck would be able to follow us? Still, the feeling lingered.

"Mike. Mike are you listening to me?"

"Sorry, Heidi. Just caught up in some strange thoughts. A hazard of my job, I guess. What were you saying?"

"Just that if you feel like stopping, I could show you something of interest in the Victory Column."

"Fine with me," he said, pulling over and parking his bike next to the granite base.

The two-hundred twenty-six-foot high column had a spiral staircase inside, accessed by a tunnel on each of the four sides of the base.

"Wait until we get inside," Heidi said. "You'll be amazed at how the walls surrounding the stairway are 'decorated'."

As soon as they got through the tunnel, McCurry discovered what Heidi had meant by decorations. The walls surrounding the circular stairway were covered with what to him looked like graffiti.

"Believe it or not, it has become over the years a canvas depicting the history of the structure and its visitors," Heidi said. "As we go up, you can read people's names along with some facts about them or their visits to Berlin."

About halfway up, she pulled a felt pen from her back pocket and wrote: "Heidi and Mike were learning about each other during a visit here in 1969."

"There, now we are part of the history too," she said.

After looking at some of the other sights, they descended the column, retrieved their bikes and started west again along one of the avenues. About halfway to the park's exit, Heidi pulled over to the side of the road and suggested they walk with their bikes to the Neuer See, a meandering lake just west of the roadway. When they arrived at the side of a narrow portion of the lake, McCurry was awestruck by the striking beauty of the setting. Trees along the banks were reflected in the glassy, calm waters. Sun shining through the branches created puzzle-like patterns in the grass. The only sounds were the whispering of a light wind through the trees.

When they found a secluded spot under a canopy of trees, Heidi took a picnic basket she had strapped to the carrier on the back of her bike. She surprised McCurry once again when she opened it to reveal a neatly folded blanket, a bottle of Liebfraumilch, a loaf of French bread, some cheese and utensils. "This is a beautiful day for a picnic lunch, don't you think," she said.

"You continue to amaze me," was all he could think to say.

*   *   *

After lunch, McCurry lay down to rest with his head in Heidi's lap. His eyes were closed and he was thinking about where this relationship was going. He recognized that he was falling in love with Heidi. He felt she had the same strong feelings for him. But, he thought, was he setting them both up for a painful parting if he allowed this to continue? He had put in his request to remain in Berlin, but there was a better than even chance it would be denied. Even if it weren't, his full enlistment would be up in a little less than a year. Then what? He planned to make his life back in the U.S. Heidi was still in school and seemed to be dedicated to the reunification movement, which could take years before success was achieved. He didn't have any right to ask her to abandon her dream and come to America with him.

"Hey Mike, are you there?"

"Sorry Heidi, just lost in thought again. I was thinking I want to close my eyes and remain right here forever."

"You'd miss an awful lot if you did that," she said, giggling a little at the thought.

"Yeah, you're right. Come on," he said while getting up, "let's go back to your apartment and see if there is a way we can stay there forever."

*   *   *

McCurry managed to push his concerns aside for the remainder of their week together. He enjoyed playing the role of a tourist with Heidi as his guide. They had dinner at a popular tourist spot, Funkturm Restaurant, and visited the makeshift memorial for Peter Fechter, the first victim to be mortally shot by East German border guards while trying to escape over the wall.

Their last excursion of the week took them to Potsdamer Platz, which before World War II was one of the busiest squares in all of Europe. As with much of the rest of Berlin, it was laid waste during the late war bombing raids. It remained a desolate, isolated area during the post-war years and was completely leveled and divided in two when the wall went up in August 1961.

According to Heidi, Potsdamer Platz was a potent symbol for the distress Berliners felt over the division of their country. It also became a highly frequented tourist attraction. As a result, a number of shops along Potsdamer Strasse sold a wide variety of souvenir goods.

After visiting several of the shops, Heidi took McCurry up to the top of an observation platform that had been erected to allow visitors to view the area on the other side of the wall and looked over at the heavily armed Volkspolizei.

The Volkspolizei, or more commonly known as vopos, were hated by West Berliners as a symbol of the heavy handed repression in the East.

"C'mon," she said, leading him down from the platform, "I want to show you something else."

McCurry stopped suddenly and turned around. He had the distinct feeling once again that someone was following him, but couldn't imagine who it might be among the crowd of tourists behind him.

"Mike, what's the problem?"

"Oh nothing, really. Just wanted another look back."

"Well come on. I want to show you one of the real-life ramifications of living in a divided city."

She took him a few blocks away to a U-Bahn, or subway, station. After paying their fares, they boarded a line that took them into and through a portion of East Berlin. Stations located in the eastern sector, including the Potsdamer Platz stop, were sealed and patrolled by the armed vopos. These stations became known as Geisterbahnhof, or ghost stations.

"Now watch," Heidi said to McCurry as the train began to slow. "The Potsdamer Platz stop is coming up."

The train slowed significantly as the station came into view. Although the lighting was muted, McCurry could clearly see the armed guards leaning against a wall and smoking cigarettes as the train passed by.

As they passed by Potsdamer Platz, Mike remembered that ASA members were prohibited from riding the U-Bahn lines that ran through East Germany. If a train broke down in the portion running through the East, passengers were required to wait for the arrival of East Berlin border guards to escort them off. Unless he was wearing a big sign saying ASA, he figured these guards could care less who or what he was. He just hoped that if he were really being followed, his tail hadn't boarded the train with him.

They got off at the next stop, walked back to where they had parked their bikes and then returned to her apartment to spend the last day of his leave there, mostly in bed.

* * *

"Hey Dwight, what're you and Sonja going to do when your enlistment is up?" McCurry asked as the two were waiting for the trick bus to fill up.

"To tell you the truth, I haven't really thought about it that much. I'm having too much fun to worry about what will happen next week, let alone next month or next year."

"But man, you're practically a part of her family now. Don't you think it'll be devastating if you just hat up and head back to the States?"

"Neither of us has made any commitments about the future, Mike. We haven't even talked about it. Ya gotta lighten up, man. Tomorrow is tomorrow. Enjoy what you have today."

"I don't know. Is it right to come over here, allow a relationship to develop and then just say, 'Bye, it's been nice,' when our tour ends? One-night stands or casual relationships are one thing. But what you have with Sonja seems like the real thing. How can you *not* think about what will happen tomorrow?"

"Hey Mike, are you talking about me or is this a question you're struggling with? Sonja and I are content to let the question about the future resolve itself when the time comes. If you're talking about you and Heidi, only you can decide what's best."

"Hey McCurry," Dave Alexander shouted from the back of the bus, "we're full. Are we going to get the fuck out of here or are you and Evans going to shoot the shit for the rest of the night?"

"Put a cork in it, Alexander, I'm going," McCurry said as he turned back to the front and pulled the door closed.

During the shift, Sergeant Landry told McCurry that Capt. Hanover wanted to see him when he got back to base that evening.

Oh fuck, now what, McCurry thought. Since he had been away for the past week, he couldn't have pissed anybody off. And he was discovering that he was enjoying his time with Heidi so much that he was pretty much able to ignore the treads.

At least there's enough traffic to make the day go by quickly, he thought as he put on his headset and started monitoring a couple channels that had clicked on while Landry was talking to him.

* * *

He went to see Hanover as soon as he had turned in his bus after returning to Andrews.

"Listen McCurry, you're a good voice intercept operator and with some of the people we are getting now, we need all the help we can get," Hanover said. "I supported your request to stay here until the end of your enlistment, indicating I need you for the mission."

Hanover told him the request had been approved. He said he was told by staff members in the commanding general's office that since the *Stars & Stripes* affair had brought such good publicity concerning the general's concern for enlisted personnel under his command, he had forgotten how it all got started.

"You dodged a bullet on this one, McCurry. All I can say is just do your job and try to keep your head down for the next eleven or so months and maybe you can leave here on good terms."

"Yes, sir, I'll try to do just that."

As McCurry started to turn and leave, Hanover said, "Not so fast McCurry. You still need to clear up one problem before you are really in the clear."

* * *

"So what's the word?" Evans asked when McCurry arrived at the Stork Club.

"Well there's good news and there's bad news."

"Give me the good news first."

"My request for a European out has been approved."

"So, what's the bad news?"

"Remember Captain Jones and the intrepid CID affair? I gotta go see him tomorrow and talk with him before I'm totally in the clear."

McCurry told Evans he didn't really know what Jones could possibly want to talk about, but he was expected to report to the CID office the next morning at ten.

*   *   *

"Here's the problem, McCurry," Jones said. "Jennings and Rankin clearly had a few screws loose. I sent them back to the States and they may even be on their way to Vietnam by now. But the problem is, they did file official reports that required me to follow up."

Jones said he assigned a couple of his agents he knew he could trust to follow McCurry for a while to make sure there was nothing to Jennings' allegations.

"Are you fucking kidding me, Captain? What are you guys, trying to emulate the Stasi?"

"Cut the dramatics, McCurry. If we were anything like the Stasi, you'd be in a prison by now. Fact is, your behavior *could* raise some questions."

Jones said he had the report filed by Jennings and Rankin detailing McCurry's travels with Wachter while they were handling the surveillance. He said, even given their bias, McCurry seemed to spend a lot more time with Wachter than with his American friends.

"Let's face reality, McCurry. You've got a top secret clearance and even I'm not allowed to know what your job entails. Mix that with the fact that there are probably more intelligence operatives here than any other place in the world, and it's not hard to get suspicious when someone like you spends too much time with a German national."

"And ..."

"And Jennings and Rankin couldn't really uncover anything damning about your relationship with Wachter."

"No kidding. So you just called me in here to tell me that."

"Not exactly. I was ready to put the report to bed when I got word that you were now spending an inordinate amount of time with a German woman who is a part of some group of students that meet regularly in a small pub off campus."

"Oh man, you've gotta be kidding me. You guys may not be as brutal as the Stasi, but other than that you're pretty close."

"Just shut up for a minute, will you McCurry. I had no choice but to put you under close surveillance for a while. You have your job and that's mine."

"So, it was your guys following me around while I was on leave with Heidi, huh?"

"You picked them up?"

"No, I just had a feeling, but thanks for confirming the feeling wasn't just Berlin paranoia."

"Well, you'll be happy to learn that she's just who she purports to be. Born and raised here and no connections to any Communist organization."

"I didn't need you to tell me that."

"Our guys told me they didn't find anything to be concerned about while they had you under surveillance," Jones continued, ignoring McCurry's remarks. "So, as far as I am concerned, the case is closed."

"So then, why the meeting? Just wanted me to know you wouldn't be shadowing me anymore so I can go back to meeting with my East German handler."

"Wow, I don't know how your commanding officer can stand you. No, it's just that I am required to meet with you before I can close a case and mark it without merit. That's done. I'll send a report to Hanover telling him you're off the hook. You might like to know that he had complete faith in you."

"No shit," McCurry said. He turned and walked out of the office without saluting Jones.

A Time for Decisions

The next several months went by pretty quickly for McCurry. Surprisingly, he was discovering through Heidi and her friends that perhaps the younger generation of Germans could indeed have a positive effect on the culture. He continued to attend Heidi's Study Group on a regular basis and got into some pretty spirited debates.

"I don't know, Mike, but you seem as if you don't believe that as Germans, we can't create a culture that opposes the use of war as a tool of foreign policy," Gerhard Holtzmann said to McCurry during one of their drinking sessions at the Brauhaus.

"I'm just saying, Gerhard, that the roots of militarism run pretty deep in Germany's history and culture. And Hitler proved that German citizens could almost universally embrace the concept of creating a world ruled by an Aryan master race."

"Are you saying that because our fathers and grandfathers helped bring Hitler and his thugs to power, we are condemned to repeating those mistakes?"

"You, Heidi and everyone else here give me hope. But you know, Gerhard, a large segment of German society would jump at the chance to return to the glory days under Hitler."

"Mike, I really believe that sentiment is dying," interjected Heidi. "The devastation we suffered as a result of the last World War shook our country to the core. People of my generation want no part of that past ... and, we will be the people who will be running the country in the years to come."

"I wonder," said Holtzmann, "if you're not looking at Germany through the prism of what is going on back in the States."

McCurry had admitted in earlier discussions that things were looking pretty dismal in the U.S. The growth and popularity of the hippie subculture in America and its message of peace had frightened the country's established leaders who had marshaled their forces by whipping the flames of the radical right. Vice President Spiro Agnew had been crisscrossing the nation since the '68 Republican Convention and his subsequent election as President Nixon's "hatchet man," creating an atmosphere of hatred for anti-war protestors and selected journalists.

As friends who had returned from leaves in the U.S. told McCurry, the mood of the country was scary. Everywhere they went, they said, they saw signs proclaiming "America, love it or leave It." Surprisingly, McCurry had admitted, the country he loved had become so polarized by the tactics of Nixon and Agnew that it couldn't embrace intelligent debate and disagreement. The cry of the right was, if you don't agree with us, get out. Unfortunately, many of the country's most intelligent citizens were doing just that.

"Okay, Gerhard. I'll admit that what is going on in the U.S. has dimmed my optimism that any nation can create a culture that embraces peace over war. You've seen the news. People calling for peace are drowned out by the war mongers. They are actually being physically beaten in the streets. What chances do they have to actually change policy."

"It may seem like that now, Mike, but they're not quitting, are they? We won't either. Changing these kinds of entrenched attitudes may take years, but ultimately we will prevail."

"I wish I had your faith, Gerhard. If nothing else, I promise to keep an open mind. In the meantime, who wants another beer?"

That particular discussion had shaken McCurry and had a profound effect on his changing view of the German people.

*   *   *

Later that night, after he and Heidi had made love, McCurry was smoking a cigarette while thinking of the afternoon's discussion with Holtzmann. "What d'ya think, Heidi? Do you think your group and others like it really have a chance in changing attitudes? I mean real change that affects a broad spectrum of society?"

"Whenever anyone asks me a question like this, I usually quote your Bobby Kennedy, a quote Teddy used at Bobby's funeral last year: 'Some people see things as they are and ask why. I see things as they never were and ask, why not?' So, my question to you, my love, is, why not?"

"Yeah, and look what they did to Bobby."

"Don't be cynical, Mike. It's not like you. It's up to us, you and me and others in our generation, to really believe that cultural biases can be changed. To really 'see things as they never were and ask, why not?'"

"Well, I guess I'll have to look to you for my inspiration. Meanwhile, I think I'd like some more of what you do so well," he said, putting out his cigarette and pulling her back down to the bed on top of him.

*   *   *

The next day after work, McCurry and Evans changed clothes and headed into town. Heidi was still in class and Sonja wouldn't finish work for at least another hour. Before leaving that morning, McCurry and Evans had suggested the four of them meet at the pub near Wachter's kiosk on the Ku'damm before heading out for a night on the town.

"So, how are things going with Heidi's study group?" Evans asked after they had both grabbed a beer at the bar and found a table where they could sit and wait for the two women to arrive.

"Interesting, to say the least," McCurry replied. "Frankly, Dwight, they're a courageous group. They love Germany the way I guess you and I love America. But they're willing to pull back the curtains covering darker parts of their history in order to find a better way to move forward."

"Ya mean they don't subscribe to the mantra, 'love it or leave it'?"

"Not even. And they're forcing me to take a closer look at America at the same time."

"And how's that?"

"Well, for example, look at the history of America's treatment of the black man, Dwight. Something you obviously can relate to. I mean, you can't read anything on race relations in the U.S. and the treatment of black men and women from the days of slave trading right up until today without getting sick to your stomach."

"True, but it is getting better."

"Fast enough for you? For the kids you and Sonja might one day have?"

"If I didn't believe that someday, as our generation takes up leadership roles in the institutions of government, we wouldn't be able to make racism unacceptable, I'm not sure I would want to go back to the States."

McCurry said he couldn't understand how Americans could continue to criticize German society for the persecution of the Jews and the unspeakable atrocities during the Hitler years when America's early expansion was built on seeking the virtual genocide of the American Indian. "Even today, the living conditions of those American Indians who are still on reservations," McCurry said, "are no better than those one finds in developing countries."

"And then there's the way Americans were so easily persuaded to accept rounding up Japanese Americans living on the West Coast after the attack on Pearl Harbor and putting them into concentration camps," Evans said. "That's a little scary no matter how you look at it."

"Speaking of being easily led," McCurry added, "What about the 'red' scare and the rise of McCarthyism?"

Having grown up during that era, McCurry had been dumbfounded that American sat by as McCarthy, without any evidence, accused a wide swath of Americans with being communist sympathizers. As a result, thousands of American citizens lost their jobs, had their careers ruined and, in some cases, were actually jailed.

"Yeah, good ole America," McCurry said. "Scare people enough and they'll even let you kill people without having a shred of evidence of wrongdoing."

Even though he was only a child, McCurry could remember how Julius and Ethel Rosenberg were actually convicted of spying and put to death in the electric chair, in spite of the lack of credible evidence.

"As far as I'm concerned, the McCarthy era demonstrated how easily residents of America could be swayed by irrational fears into persecuting fellow citizens, not at all unlike how Germans turned on its Jewish population due to the agitation of Hitler," McCurry said.

"Sorry to burst your balloon, Mike, but fear has always proved to be a potent tool in politics. Make people afraid and they'll follow without thinking."

"You're right, Dwight, and I'm worried that until Americans recognize how hatred and fear are used for political purposes, it will go on unabated. It's kind of like a cancer that is destroying the very attributes that made the country great."

"Hey, what the heck's got you two looking so serious?" said Heidi. McCurry and Evans were so engrossed in their conversation they hadn't noticed when Heidi and Sonja had arrived at the pub.

McCurry stood up and gave Heidi a kiss before answering. "You know," he said as he pulled a chair out for her. "Just a typical GI bitch session."

"Well," said Sonja after sitting down next to Evans, "do you think you guys could buy a couple of working girls a drink?"

*   *   *

Later in the week, at another meeting of Heidi's study group, McCurry brought up his concerns over how fear and hatred were being used as political tools in the U.S.

"I realize this strays a bit from your stated purpose to focus on Germany's reunification," McCurry said, "but if you don't mind, I'd like to get your views on the subject."

"I'm not sure a discussion like this shouldn't be an important part of our overall purpose," said Hans Metzger, who often held back in the group's discussions. "Examining mistakes America has made in addressing its social issues may ultimately help us to come up with new and better solutions to issues like race relations, tolerance in political discourse, and facing irrational fears."

"Perhaps we should start by examining the methods a government can use to instill tolerance in its citizenry," said Holtzmann, who usually framed the topics for discussion at the beginning of each session.

"Good luck with that one since Germans are such a tolerant race," said Erica Fenstermacher.

"Which is why it may be one of the most important issues we examine," Holtzmann shot back.

Heinrich Schmitt suggested that some kind of human relations commission should be established as a cabinet level body and play a prominent role in unified Germany's constitution. Its mission, he said, should be to create educational programs to promote mutual respect for the views of others as well as understanding and tolerance.

"That's an interesting idea, Heinrich," Fenstermacher responded. "A human relations commission could be given the task of creating educational material for all ages in our school system."

"In order for something like this to work," said McCurry, "it would have to be an ongoing part of the educational process from the earliest grade through university."

Holtzmann argued that rather than being created as a cabinet level agency, which could be dominated by the executive branch, a human relations agency should, perhaps, become a fourth separate but equal branch of government.

"This would be a potent expression of the new Germany's dedication to mutual respect and tolerance for the views, religions and race of others."

The group agreed that it would take some of the best minds available in the country to create an effective program for the development of real mutual respect and tolerance. Even then, it would probably take years to bring about a change in attitudes.

McCurry pointed out that the U.S. has been struggling with ways to integrate its public schools for the past 12 years, ever since the Supreme Court ruled that laws requiring segregated educational systems were unconstitutional. Those children being brought up in integrated schools were proving to be far more tolerant than their parents.

"Children spend more waking hours in school than they do in the home," McCurry explained. "They may hear biased statements from their parents at the supper table, but they can learn it doesn't jibe with their experience with other races in the school yard."

McCurry lamented, though, that in the current political climate in the States, progress on the human relations front would probably be stymied. "Martin Luther King was appearing to make some progress, and they killed him. I think his death last year ended any hope I had for a reconciliation of the races in the U.S."

Startled by this statement, Heidi asked, "What are you saying, Mike?"

"I'm saying I am not so sure I want to go back to the States at all. I haven't been proud of being an American in quite some time."

* * *

Several days later, Heidi packed up a picnic lunch and the two set off for another bike ride in the Tiergarten. They stopped once again at McCurry's favorite spot next to the Neuer See. After they had eaten and were enjoying a new wine Heidi had found, McCurry said they should probably talk about what they would do when his tour of duty came to an end.

"When we first started dating, I realized I was falling in love with you and it scared the hell out of me," McCurry told her. "I knew you were committed to being part of a new Germany and I felt my life would be back in the States. It seemed as if our relationship was doomed from the start."

He said the last several weeks had convinced him that he could now envision a life together in Germany. If he took a European discharge, he said, he could continue his college studies at the University of Maryland extension center in Berlin and expand his business enterprises with Wachter.

"I can't guarantee the Army will authorize a European out for me, but they did at least authorize my request for an extension. Even if I have to go back to the States to muster out, I can come back here afterwards. What do you think?"

"I was afraid to bring it up," Heidi said. "I have been so thoroughly happy since I met you and I didn't want it to end. Do you really think you would be happy here?"

"I think I could be happy anywhere with you. But yeah, to tell the truth, America has been looking more and more like a foreign country to me."

The Final Battle

On January 23, 1968, the USS Pueblo, on an intelligence mission off the coast of North Korea, was attacked by North Korean naval vessels and MiG jets. The ship was ordered to stand down to be boarded. Although the captain, Cmdr. Lloyd M. Bucher, tried to evade the North Korean forces for nearly two hours, he ultimately signaled compliance after a crew member was killed by North Korean artillery fire.

Meanwhile, down below, naval personnel were furiously working to destroy their trove of top secret, sensitive documents. Although they had more than an hour before being boarded, there was far too much to be destroyed. Ultimately, cartons of documents as well as the ship and its spying equipment were captured by the North Koreans. This development had repercussions at U.S. intelligence installations around the world.

As with the Army Security Agency and its Teufelsberg listening post, the Pueblo was under the jurisdiction of the National Security Agency. Cmdr. Bucher was subjected to extreme criticism from the NSA for not scuttling his ship to keep it from falling into the hands of the North Koreans. Bucher maintained that the ship and its equipment could be replaced; the lives of the eighty-two remaining crew members could not. Top officials at NSA believed otherwise.

Teuflesberg, situated as it is on a virtual island in the middle of the Soviet-dominated East German "sea," caught the attention of the NSA after the Pueblo incident. For well over a year now, discussions among top NSA and ASA brass centered on how documents and equipment could be quickly destroyed if Berlin were to be overrun by the Soviets. This fear was magnified when Warsaw Pact troops invaded Czechoslovakia just seven months after the Pueblo Incident. There were those who speculated that the tanks that were deployed to "protect" the Hill, should the Soviets decide to roll on to take over West Berlin at the same time, had a more sinister purpose. McCurry was right about the absurdity of thinking that a dozen or so tanks could hold off a Warsaw Pact army. They could, however, turn their cannon around and quickly destroy the compound. The more than eighty personnel on the Hill would just have to be considered acceptable collateral damage.

As 1970 opened cold and blustery as usual, most of those working on the Hill had pretty much forgotten about the Pueblo incident and the subsequent invasion of Czechoslovakia. McCurry was about to learn that the incidents were far from forgotten by those men and women working back at Ft. Meade's NSA headquarters.

* * *

Returning to work after three days off, McCurry was in high spirits and actually enjoying the crisp winter morning. Sitting and thinking while everyone was getting off his bus, he realized the last several months with Heidi had been the happiest of his life. She had a mind that challenged him, a sense of humor that cheered him, and a sexual energy that left him completely spent every time they made love. He had glided through this period without any incidents at work. Heidi had a way of insulating him from the lunacy that threatened to set him off every time he went to work. Ignore them and keep a low profile, she advised. They are just sad little men whose only way to feel good about themselves is to put others down.

Of course, she had no idea of what went on in his workplace. But she certainly understood the mentality of the treads he had to work with. Growing up in Berlin, she told him, she had come in contact with them her whole life. As a beautiful young woman, she often saw the worst of them when she went out with friends in the evening. He had seen how she remained calm and serene when whistled at on the street or approached by a drunken GI in a bar. They're just insecure people, she would say to McCurry, who cover their insecurities with bravado and moronic behavior. They aren't worth a second thought.

"All right, up and at 'em," Evans said as the last man exited the bus. "We've got guys waiting for us to relieve 'em and a free world that needs protecting."

"Yeah, right on. I feel in a very protective mood this morning," McCurry said as he grabbed his hat and followed Evans off the bus.

As soon as he and Evans entered their building, McCurry recognized that something was wrong. There were a number of men milling around who weren't members of his trick or the one he was relieving. They must have the clearance, he thought, but what the hell are they doing here. Things looked even more ominous as he entered the wing where he worked and saw that the racks of recorders had been moved farther away from the walls than usual, far enough to allow a person to get behind to be able to work on them.

"What in hell is going on?" he asked Kurt Samuels whose position he was taking over.

"I don't know, man. A bunch of guys I never saw before were working all night moving the racks out from the walls and generally just being a pain in the ass. They're pretty tight-lipped about what they're doing."

"You really don't have any idea?"

"None at all. Don't care, either. I'm bushed and all I want to do is get back to the barracks and hit the sack."

After Evans relieved the guy in the position next to McCurry, McCurry turned to him and asked him what he thought.

"I don't know, man. Makes no sense to me."

As they settled in and started setting up their tapes for the day's traffic, two guys came into the room carrying boxes that were clearly marked DANGER. EXPLOSIVES.

"Whoa, what the fuck are you planning to do with them?" McCurry asked.

"It's none your business," the biggest of the pair shot back.

"Like fuck it's none of my business. Nobody's going to bring boxes marked 'explosives' into the room where I work and not tell me what's going on."

For once, McCurry was joined in his challenge by not only Evans but the other seven operators in the room as well. "If we don't get some kind of explanation, you're not getting behind any of our machines," said Dave Blake, who usually shied away from confrontations.

"Fuckin' A. You can take that shit and shove it up your ass before you'll get behind my position," said Hank Andrews. At six-foot four and 250 pounds, Andrews was always intimidating. McCurry was glad to see him join in the fray.

Before things really got out of hand, their trick sergeant, Buck Landry, came in the room to see what was going on. Sensing the tension and wanting to diffuse it quickly, Landry ordered everyone back to their positions. Andrews, however, refused to budge.

"If you want any of us to do our job today, Sarge, you'll tell us what is going on," Andrews said. "Ain't that right, guys?"

No one was about to go against Andrews, so they all held their ground waiting to see how Landry would react.

"All right, settle down and move to the back of this room so these guys can get to work," Landry said. Apparently in an effort to save face he added, "You would've heard more before the end of the shift today anyway."

Landry went on to explain that headquarters had gotten orders from Ft. Meade to plant explosive charges behind every operator position on the Hill. These would all be wired to a central location where, if there were ever an invasion, they could quickly destroy everything on the Hill.

"It's all going to be perfectly safe," Landry said. "Now you know, so get back to work."

"Perfectly safe my ass," said Andrews, but he moved back to his position and everyone else followed suit.

McCurry sat in front of his console for about ten minutes, not talking nor setting things up for work. Then he got up, walked out of the room, out of the building and out of the compound before sitting down outside, his back against the fence and his knees pulled up to his chest. He wasn't about to work in a facility where some simple-minded asshole could blow them all up with the flip of a switch.

*   *   *

McCurry thought Landry's head was going to explode as the trick sergeant stood over him ordering him to return to his position. All McCurry could think was that Landry and the other treads like him would probably love to go up in a blaze of glory. After all, it is those kinds of images that attract his kind to the military. McCurry, on the other hand, had joined the Army Security Agency as a way to survive.

"Get off your fuckin' ass and get back in there right now," Landry shouted as spittle dribbled down his chin. "I don't know what you're trying to prove, McCurry, but this trick could land your ass in the brig."

McCurry refused to say anything. He continued to sit there with his knees drawn up to his chin, the bill of his hat pulled down over his eyes.

"I give up," Landry said. "Maybe one of your friends can convince ya ta get back to your post. If not, I'm calling the MPs to haul your ass off this Hill."

A few minutes later, Evans came out and squatted down next to McCurry.

"Hey man, do you know what you're doing?" Evans asked.

"Not really, Dwight. I just know what I'm not doing – going back there while those morons work to turn the compound into one big bomb that can be set off with a flip of the switch."

"C'mon Mike, you've only got what, less than four months to go. The Soviets aren't going to roll into Berlin before then."

"That isn't the point, Dwight. It just pisses me off that they can come up with a plan like this. And it pisses me off even more that I can't say anything about it. I might not be able to go to a reporter and say, 'Hey man, you wouldn't fucking believe what they are doing up there on Teufelsberg,' but I can let the treads know that, from my point of view, the only sane thing to do is to refuse to go back in there."

"Are you prepared to let them call the MPs to come up and haul your ass off to the brig?"

"Guess I'll just have to play it out and see where it goes, Dwight. It's all right, buddy. You can go back in and tell 'em I've refused to return."

About 45 minutes later, two burly MPs drove up to the gate where they were met by Landry. Minutes after that, the two MPs marched over to where McCurry was squatting against the fence." Get on your feet soldier," said the one with the crooked nose and a forehead that sloped back to short-cropped blonde hair.

Not wanting to be man handled, McCurry slowly rose and casually leaned back against the fence. "Your sergeant over there says ya refuse to go in and man your post. Is that correct?" said his partner, a Neanderthal with tattoos of a dagger on one forearm and a cobra coiled and ready to strike on the other.

As he did with Landry, McCurry remained mute. These guys, in his estimation, didn't deserve a response. Of course, the MPs didn't know why he refused to go in. I wonder what their reaction would be if they knew what was going on in there, he thought.

"We're not fucking with ya dickhead. Are ya goin' back in there and report for duty or not?"

McCurry just stared at him and said nothing. "All right prick, turn around and put your hands behind your back," said slope head, who was quickly losing his cool.

Leading McCurry over to the car, slope head shoved him into the back seat, smacking his head against the door jamb in the process. Landry told them that because McCurry had a top secret security clearance, they were to transport him to the company commander back at Andrews rather than the military prison.

When they arrived at Capt. Hanover's office, Hanover told the MPs that they could leave and he would take care of McCurry.

"What the fuck is wrong with you, McCurry?" Hanover said after the MPs left the office. "You've done really well during the last several months and now, with less than four months to go before your discharge, you pull this trick."

"Would you trust those NSA morons if they were wiring up a bomb under your desk, Captain?"

"I'm not the one that has to answer any questions here, McCurry. Are you going to go back to work or not?"

"No sir, I'm not. "

"All right, McCurry, for now you're confined to the barracks until I figure out what to do with you. With only four months to go, you'd better think long and hard about whether you are ready to face a court martial that could put you in a prison for a lot longer than four months."

*   *   *

"How ya doin' Mike?" Evans asked when he went to see McCurry after trick change. "At least you didn't end up in the brig."

"For now I'm confined to the barracks. Actually, this is looking more and more like I thought it might go."

"What d'ya mean?"

"When I saw those two goons coming to get me, I thought, of all the MPs that might have responded, was it just a coincidence they dispatched two of the ugliest, meanest looking available? And then it hit me, they were just trying to scare the shit out of me."

McCurry said if the NSA plan were ever made public, members of Congress would immediately start looking for scapegoats to take the fall for such a hair-brained measure.

"Mothers would go berserk to think their sons were being sent to work on what, in essence, is a ticking bomb. Landry and the trick commander were hoping the intimidation of seeing the MPs would convince me to go back in."

When he let them put the handcuffs on, McCurry said, he essentially called their bluff, which is why he was sent to Hanover's office instead of prison."

"So, what d'ya think'll happen now?" Evans asked.

"They're probably shitting their pants back in Meade right now trying to figure that out."

McCurry suggested that the career Army types at Ft. Meade probably assumed when they developed the plan, everyone would go along and no one outside the Army Security Agency would ever know anything about it. If they decided to court martial him, McCurry said, he would be entitled to a lawyer and to put on a defense that he disobeyed a direct order to return to his post because of the unnecessary danger the dynamite presented.

"They've got to know that, even if there is some way to hold the court martial behind closed doors, word about what was going on would inevitably get out," McCurry said. "My guess is they will realize they made a serious miscalculation and decide to scuttle the plan. They just have to decide right now what to do with me.

"Hey, Dwight, can you do me a favor? Go see Heidi and explain what is going on. Let her know that I'll be all right."

*　　*　　*

Several days passed with no word from anyone in command. With the passage of time, McCurry began to have doubts about his prediction for the outcome. Evans told McCurry that his action had caused a virtual chasm to develop between the treads on the Hill and the operators. "Sergeant Canty came over to our wing from the Russian posts, stuck his head in the door and asked, 'When is that moron McCurry going to come to his senses and get back to work?' That almost led to a fistfight between him and Andrews."

"Andrews' support really surprised me," McCurry admitted.

"Are you kidding me?" Evans said. "I think you have the support of every operator on every trick. The tension between the two factions is getting really bad and they're going to have to do something soon or there could be an explosion without the help of dynamite."

Evans said since McCurry's departure, no further work had been done to wire up the explosives. The boxes of dynamite were moved to a secure location, he said, and the racks of recorders had been left where they were, pulled out from the wall.

"Heidi is doing fine," Evans said, without being asked. "She's spending a lot of time with me and Sonja. She said to hang in there because she's sure everything will turn out fine."

"Ah, the optimism of youth," said McCurry.

Two days later, Evans came rushing into McCurry's room after getting off from his swing shift. Since it was nearly one in the morning, he had to shake McCurry repeatedly before he awoke.

"Hey, what the fuck, Dwight?"

"Just shut up and listen. You may be hearing something pretty soon. Those guys who were doing the installation finally came back tonight and started moving the racks back near the walls again. When Andrews asked where their dynamite was, they just told him to go fuck himself. I guess they don't like us very much."

"So, it looks like they blinked, huh?"

"No other answer I can come up with," Evans said.

"So now, I wonder what they have in mind for me?"

＊　　＊　　＊

In the morning Jim Gleason, the company clerk, stopped by McCurry's room after breakfast to say that the company commander wanted to see him at ten hundred hours.

"What's that, ten o'clock, or does he want to wait a thousand hours before he ever sees me again?" McCurry asked.

"Sorry about that, I just get caught up in the tread speak from working around them all day," Gleason said. "But he did say he expected to see you in clean fatigues and polished boots."

"You haven't seen them erecting a gallows anywhere on post, have you? No? Then I guess I'm good for another day."

"Just be there at ten, Mike. You've caused Captain Hanover a lot of problems, but he doesn't appear to be particularly angry about it."

* * *

"McCurry, I don't know whether to be furious with you or thank you," Hanover said after he let McCurry into his office and closed the door. "I'll deny it if you ever quote me, but that really was a bonehead move by Meade. I don't know how they thought no one would balk or that it wouldn't get out. But, as of now, it never happened."

Hanover told McCurry that at first, no one up the chain of command knew exactly how they should proceed. The hard liners wanted to court martial McCurry for abandoning his post in a time of war, but since there was no war here, that would have been a tough argument to make. Others said he should be offered another opportunity to return to work, but Hanover said he knew McCurry well enough to know that he wouldn't budge from his position.

"You've probably heard by now, McCurry, that the plan to wire up the Hill with explosives has been scuttled. But I was ordered to find a way to punish you. So here's what's going to happen."

Hanover said that McCurry would be reduced in grade from an E-5 to an E-4. Also, his top secret clearance was being pulled, effective immediately. This would make it difficult, if not impossible, to get a clearance should he ever seek employment in a company that required one. Hanover said he made the case that this was a pretty serious punishment in and of itself.

"I pointed out that since no one will be able to discuss anything going on at the Hill with you, you will be pretty well isolated during your remaining time here," Hanover said. "This seemed to satisfy the powers that be. It gets you out of their hair and still covers their asses because action was taken to punish you for your insubordination."

Until his discharge in the spring, Hanover said, McCurry would work as a straight-day bus driver. His duties would be to make a trip to the Hill and back in the morning and then again at the end of the day shift. All personnel, Hanover said, would be instructed that McCurry no longer carried a top secret clearance so that no sensitive information would be discussed with him. No sensitive information was supposed to be discussed outside of the Hill compound in any event, but that rule sometimes broke down on the bus ride back to Andrews.

"You've got less than four months left, McCurry. Do you think you can do this job without getting into any more trouble?"

"Yes sir."

"Okay, I went out on a limb for you … again," Hanover said. "So give me a break and keep your nose clean. Now, get the fuck out of here."

The punishment was incorporated into an Article 15, one which McCurry this time happily accepted. It would be expunged and he would leave the Army with an honorable discharge. He even got to keep his good conduct medal.

*   *   *

Since it was the beginning of the weekend, and he would only be working Mondays through Fridays now, McCurry left base right away to get over to Heidi's flat. He was so excited, he couldn't remember if she had any classes on Friday mornings. He had a key to her apartment, so if she wasn't in, he would just wait until she returned and surprise her.

Much to his delight, she was home. "Mike!" she exclaimed when he came through the door. She ran to him and threw her arms around him. "Are you finished with them? Are you all right?" she asked.

"Yes and yes," he said, grinning broadly.

"Good. You can tell me all about it right after we make love." With that, he went willingly as she pulled him toward the bedroom.

*   *   *

"So tell me all about it," Heidi said as McCurry rolled over to the side of the bed to get a cigarette. "Are you going to be able to stay here in Germany?"

McCurry said that as long as he doesn't get into any more trouble, he would be able to get his European out. "The way they've set things up, it's going to be pretty difficult to get into any more hot water," he said. "All I am doing is driving a bus. I think they just want to get rid of me as quickly and quietly as possible. According to Dwight, my little insurrection filtered through to the rest of the guys working on the Hill. They don't need that kind of unrest."

McCurry said he was busted a rank, but with the money he made from his businesses with Wachter, he wouldn't feel any financial pinch.

"But what was it all about?" Heidi asked. "Dwight was pretty skimpy on details. All he would say was that you walked off the job and refused to work."

"Dwight was exactly right and, unfortunately, that is all either he or I can say about it. We need to be careful about what we say. And, this close to the end, I don't want to give them any *real* reason to hang me out to dry."

"So, your only punishment is driving a bus?"

Mike explained to her that his company commander, understanding how the minds of treads worked, convinced his superiors that McCurry's real punishment was having his top secret clearance yanked. "You know how it is, there goes my chance for a career in the CIA after I get out," he said. "They just want me to disappear, and that is absolutely fine with me.

"Now, come on back here and I'll show you how glad I am to be out," he said as he pulled her on top of him.

*   *   *

As Evans came out of the barracks Monday morning on the second day of his day shift, McCurry was sitting in the driver's seat of the almost forgotten Chevrolet beast. "I thought they got rid of this after you rolled the tires off the rims," Evans said as he boarded the bus.

"You didn't expect the treads to make it easy on me, did you Dwight? They're not happy with my so-called punishment, so they're going to be looking for ways to trip me up. The motor pool sergeant was practically salivating with pleasure as he assigned this piece of shit to me. 'You'd better take real good care of this bus, soldier,' he said.

"I've got less than four months to go, so I can take a lot of shit knowing how soon it will end. Then I'll stand outside the gates here and laugh my ass off at them all."

"Sounds like a good attitude," Evans said. "Now, let's get this beast on the road and start the beginning of the end."

Epilogue

Heidi's prediction that the people of East Germany would eventually rise up and rebel against their communist leaders proved to be accurate, although it took almost two more decades to come to fruition. The Communist bloc began to falter in the late '80s after Soviet Communist Party General Secretary Mikhail Gorbachev consolidated power and began to enact a series of widespread reforms.

The reforms in the Soviet Union had filtered through to the other communist countries, especially Poland and Hungary. On August 23, 1989, Hungary opened its borders with Austria. East German tourists used their chance to escape to Austria from Hungary and in September 1989 more than 13,000 East Germans escaped via Hungary within three days. The East German government, facing what appeared to be the possibility of a full-scale revolt, suddenly announced on November 9, 1989, that all border checkpoints between East Germany into West Germany or West Berlin would be opened to East German residents.

Word of the announcement traveled quickly and thousands of East Berliners went to the border crossings. At the Bornholmer Strasse border crossing, people demanded the border be opened and at 10.30 p.m. it was. Soon other border crossing points opened the gates to the West. McCurry sat in front of his television in his Washington D.C. apartment and joined the world in watching as tens of thousands of East and West Berliners climbed atop the wall, linked arms and began a celebration that lasted throughout the night. Many came with sledge hammers and anything else they could grab and began to chip away at the hated structure.

After her graduation from the university, Heidi became an active participant in the Social Democratic Party along with Gerhard Holtzmann, her friend on the Study Group on German Reunification. Both soon realized that reunification was still a distant hope and, in any event, they would have little support for creating a new constitution for a reunified Germany, let alone for their hope to make war a constitutional impossibility. Both continued to work within the Party to strengthen civil rights and maintain their opposition to war as a tool of foreign policy. Following reunification, they were successful in the movement that mandated that German military forces not be deployed by the government outside of NATO territory without a specific resolution of parliament.

Heidi was at the wall, wielding her own sledge hammer on that fateful night in November 1989. It was a bittersweet moment for her. She was overjoyed that the wall had finally fallen just short of her 40th birthday. On the other hand, she wished that McCurry were there to celebrate with her. The two had spent eight blissful years together, Heidi rising within the ranks of the Party and McCurry finishing college and working with Wachter to build a legitimate car business, ultimately securing a BMW franchise. In the fall of 1978, Heidi recognized that Mike was becoming increasingly restless and pressed him to find out why.

"I'm beginning to feel it's time to return home and see what I can do to make things better there," he told her. "I just don't feel right sitting here in Germany criticizing the way things are in the U.S. without trying to be a part of the solution to the problems."

McCurry told her he had been thinking about it for quite a while, but particularly so after Jimmy Carter became President in January of the previous year. He saw Carter as an idealist, particularly in his efforts to bring peace to the Middle East. McCurry said he wanted to be a part of what he half-jokingly referred to as the reunification of America. "The wounds of the '60s and early '70s aren't healed. They've just been put under wraps and covered over with scabs because of the deep recession and inflationary problems the country is facing."

As soon as he was sworn in as President, Carter issued an unconditional amnesty for those Americans who had fled to Canada to avoid the draft for the Vietnam War. More than 100,000 Americans had flocked to Canada during the war. While thousands were returning, thousands more were making the decision to remain as expatriates.

McCurry left Germany to return home within a few months of his initial discussion with Heidi. Through a friend from college, he got a job on the staff of a Democratic congressman from New Jersey. Through the years, he continued working on the staffs of various Democratic members of Congress. He kept in touch with Heidi and even managed to get a call through to her after the November 9 celebration. But both recognized that the spark was gone. As they approached middle age, they realized that the only way any change could be achieved was to work within the system and working within the system required compromise.

As the 21st century approached, McCurry recognized that his war had finally come to an end. He looked at the coffee cup on his desk and smiled.

About the Author

Chuck Thompson served as a voice intercept operator with a top secret/crypto security clearance from 1967 to 1969 at a sensitive intelligence installation located in West Berlin on Teufelsberg, a hill built from the rubble of World War II bombings. Today, Thompson is a semi-retired marketing consultant living with his wife in Levittown, PA. For 13 years before starting his own marketing agency 10 years ago, he worked as a journalist, winning numerous awards for both general assignments and investigative pieces.